Risking HIS Heart

A BUENA HILLS ROMANCE

ALLISON GYGI

Published by Castlerod Press

Chicago, IL

Cover design by Raneé Clark of Sweetly Us Book Services

https://allisongygi.com

ISBN: 979-8-9860561-3-5

❀ Formatted with Vellum

For Spencer
You have taught me more about bravery and never giving up than anyone or anything else in my life. Thank you for being you. I love you!

Author's Note

Risking His Heart is a stand alone novel related to the Buena Hills series. The same characters you've fallen in love with from the rest of the series play an important role in the story, but the book doesn't neatly fit in the chronology of the rest of the books. It falls a little bit after Elise (Chasing Her Heart) returns from her study abroad in Ireland, but before the second half of the book picks back up.

Chapter One

Cassie Schalk was absolutely, one hundred percent certain the day couldn't get any worse. Standing outside her apartment building across from Central Park, she struggled to catch her breath as she watched the cab pull away from the curb. The cab that she'd called thirty minutes ago while gathering her damp curls into a hasty updo because she hadn't had time for her morning routine. That's what she got for hitting the snooze button on her alarm one too many times.

Once the driver, who sounded eerily like a young Sylvester Stallone, had called to tell her he was waiting outside, she hobbled out the door, clumsily putting on her heels as she went. It couldn't have been more than five minutes since he'd called, but just as she'd burst through the front doors of her building, a man with an unfortunate combover slid into the backseat and shut the door, stealing her ride to work.

Without an empty taxi in sight, thanks to the Friday morning commute, she set off to walk the ten blocks to the design studio, her grumbling drowned out by the angry honks and revving engines bouncing off the skyscrapers.

Didn't Mr. Combover realize how uncomfortable it was to walk in heels? She could break her neck, for crying out loud. Especially with all the puddles glistening on the cement from last night's rainstorm.

Shifting her Gucci handbag more securely over her shoulder to keep it out of the way of more people hurrying past, she picked up her pace. Her boss would be furious if Cassie wasn't at her beck and call by the time she was ready for her morning coffee run. Not to mention the never-ending task list she had for the day on top of ordering the fabric samples for next spring's product line.

Cassie puffed out a breath. Such was her life as a fashion designer's assistant.

Lifting her face to the threatening clouds above her, she let out a silent plea. *Something good has to come out of this day, right?*

"Right," she said out loud, unconcerned with the people around her. They were too consumed with their own lives and problems to care about a random woman talking to herself. Stranger things had happened in the Big Apple.

Cassie's heel dug into a crack on the pavement, and she stumbled before yanking her foot out of the cement. Her ankles already ached from the walk, and she couldn't wait to free them from their Prada-encased prisons. Only a few more blocks.

In her attempt to bypass a large puddle overflowing from the storm drain to her left, she bumped into a fellow pedestrian. "Excuse me." She held her hands up in apology and moved back into her original position, grimacing at the oil and mud glistening on the surface of the brackish lake. Soggy bits of newspaper floated in its midst. At least it hadn't crested the top of the curb. As long as she didn't step into the street, she'd be able to avoid getting her feet dirty.

But life in New York City was never that simple. And sometimes, like right now, it had a way of turning a person's day into a walking cliché. That's the only way she could describe the random taxi swerving out of the line of bumper-to-bumper traffic. It gunned its engine as it sped past her to jockey for a better position in line. The wheels hit the puddle, hydroplaning through the water.

Cassie held her hands up in front of her, but it was too late. A tidal wave shot in her direction, smearing her side with filth.

An angry gasp escaped her lungs, and she shook her fist at the offending cab. "Watch where you're going!" she hollered after it, but her words were drowned out by the sound of the traffic.

Around her, more people hurried past on their way to their destinations as though they hadn't seen her get thoroughly soaked only two seconds ago.

"Great," she muttered, opening her bag to search for something to clean off the mud now drenching her bare arm. As she dug around her wallet, keys, an extra comb, and several types of makeup, among other things, her eyes fell to the brand-new Versace pencil skirt she was wearing. She froze, then bent to get a closer look. "No. No, no, no. This can't be happening."

Mud and oil covered most of the left side of it. She gingerly peeled off a scrap of soggy newspaper and held it out by her fingernails before letting it go. It plopped to the ground.

With another angry gasp, she continued digging in her bag until her hand closed around her phone. Pulling it out, she jabbed at the screen until she found the number she wanted.

After initiating the call, she resumed walking, holding the phone up to her ear and praying her fiancé hadn't buried himself in his work already.

"Hey, sweetheart," Drew's deep voice came through the line. "What is it? I'm on my way to a meeting."

"Drew, you're never going to believe this." Cassie talked quickly. "Some idiot hydroplaned through this giant puddle right in front of me. I'm covered in mud, and I'm pretty sure my new skirt is ruined."

"I'm sorry, baby. That's awful," he said, his tone making it obvious he wasn't really listening. "Where are you? I'll call you a cab."

Cassie's step faltered, her foot squishing in the bottom of her soggy shoe. "I don't need you to call me a cab."

She heard the click-clacking of his laptop keyboard in the background. He was probably working in the cab on the way to his meeting. Typical. "Then why did you call me?"

Truthfully, she wasn't sure what she'd expected from him. An understanding voice? A little sympathy maybe? Certainly not the dismissal he gave her now.

"I don't know," she admitted in a shrinking voice. "I'm sorry. I know you're busy right now."

"Cassandra." He sighed, long and slow, which only made her feel smaller. "I'm sorry. Listen, I have to go, but how about dinner at Olivier's tonight? Then shopping? I'll buy you two new outfits to make up for the skirt."

Cassie's heart trickled down to her stomach. Lavishing her with fancy dinners and expensive gifts wasn't how he'd always operated. What had happened to the compassion he'd shown early in their relationship? The emotional connection? When they'd first started dating, he'd been so attentive, so in tune with her feelings, that she'd known from the day they met at that fateful Christmas party more than five years ago that she'd become Mrs. Andrew Covington.

Now that day was only three months away. Why wasn't she more excited?

She shook away the discouragement. She *was* excited. This was only her bad mood talking. Pasting on a smile, she said, "Sure. That sounds great. I'll see you then."

"Perfect. I'll make the reservation. And Cassandra?"

She stopped outside the entrance to Adriana's design studio. "Hmm?"

"I love you."

Her mouth turned up a little, despite the heavy feelings swirling in her gut. "I love you too. I'll see you tonight."

The line went dead, and she dropped her phone back into her bag before yanking the door open. Once inside, she slunk around the outside perimeter of the open room, hoping to avoid any weird looks she was sure to get if she walked to the elevator near the main hub of the bottom floor. What would the interns think if they spotted Adriana's assistant looking anything but perfect?

Sneaking into the stairwell, she tried to ignore her wet skirt rubbing uncomfortably against her thigh. And the water dripping into her heels, irritating her already aching feet even more. She pulled out her phone again and sent a frantic text to the one person she could trust in this situation.

> Cassie: Emergency! Second-floor bathroom. Please come now!

She pushed into the blessedly empty bathroom and rushed to the sink, yanking paper towels from the dispenser. After getting them wet, she set to work gently attacking the mud caked to the side of the skirt.

"Come on, come on," she whimpered, desperately pleading with whatever higher power would care to listen. She knew she could get the mud out. But the oil? That was another story.

This skirt had cost a small fortune. There had to be some way to salvage it. The thought of all that money going down the drain sent nausea rippling in her stomach. She prided herself on always wearing the latest fashions, but she also knew the value of her hard-earned paycheck.

The bathroom door burst open, and Cassie whirled to face the intruder. Her shoulders sagged in relief to see Sylvie, her work bestie, standing in front of her.

"What kind of emergency?" Sylvie asked, wielding scissors and a small box of pins in one hand. In the other, a tampon and travel detergent stick. "You didn't specify, so I came prepared." Her eyes scanned the length of Cassie's body, then widened when the situation registered. "Oh honey, what happened to you?"

A high-pitched laugh escaped Cassie's throat, the sort of laugh someone made when they were trying not to cry. And she was desperately trying not to cry. "Help me get some of the mud out. I'm not leaving this bathroom looking like this."

No more questions were asked as Sylvie jumped right in to help. Cassie appreciated that about her friend. In an industry that thrived on cutthroat competition, her coworker had proven to be a true confidante.

Sylvie dabbed at the stains with the detergent stick while Cassie turned in an almost unnatural angle to massage the soap into the fabric.

"Just take it off," Sylvie finally said, noticing her friend's precarious position. "It'll be much easier to work with on a flat surface."

Cassie glanced at the door, not thrilled with the possibility of someone walking in while she was stripped down to her underwear. Then again, was that really more embarrassing than her current state?

After sliding down the back zipper, she shimmied out of the skirt and handed it to her friend. They continued working while she filled the other woman in on her disastrous commute.

"You walked the whole way?" Sylvie stopped working to shoot an incredulous look at Cassie. "In those heels? You're lucky you didn't land in the ER with a broken ankle. Why didn't you take a cab?"

Cassie sighed. "Some idiot stole mine, and I didn't have time to wait for another one. I told you about the Covington's fundraising gala, right?" That was a rhetorical question. She'd been stressing about the event to raise money for Doctors Without Borders for weeks. Though the gala itself hadn't been the cause of her anxiety. It was Drew's mother. Theresa Covington had never shied away from letting Cassie know in her own subtle ways that she didn't belong in the family's social circle. All because she didn't have access to a large inheritance. "Anyway, it was last night. I didn't get home until late, so I overslept."

Sylvie grunted, the sound oozing with the distaste she already had for Drew. "Girl, if you don't tell that man no every once in a while, he's going to walk all over you for the rest of your life. His priss of a mother too."

Cassie didn't give her friend the satisfaction of seeing her frown as she fingered the six-thousand-dollar engagement ring on her left hand, admiring the diamonds glittering in the bathroom's overhead light. "He works really hard. The least I can do is be there for him when he needs me." Even if he rarely bothered reciprocating the gesture.

You're not being fair. Sure, their relationship had taken a few hits over the last couple years, even almost ending once, but she was positive they could find their footing again. He'd already promised to spend more time with her once he'd wrapped up the Abramson case. And they'd have seven whole days in California together when they flew out for her twin sister's wedding next week. Everything would be fine again once they had more time to reconnect.

Sylvie *tsked* but didn't continue arguing her point about Drew. She stepped back and placed her hands on her ample hips, surveying her work. "If you keep your back away from everyone, I don't think anyone will notice."

Cassie did her own assessment. A few small streaks of oil remained on the black wool but most of the mud had lightened enough to avoid notice unless someone looked really hard. "You're a miracle worker, Sylvie. How will I ever repay you?"

Sylvie swung her arm around Cassie's shoulders and pressed their cheeks together. "Well ... since you're feeling altruistic, I'd love some help at my niece's party on Sunday. If you're not too busy getting ready for your sister's wedding, of course."

"I should be able to squeeze that in. I'm not leaving until Tuesday."

Her friend clapped her hands together in an expression of pure relief. "Bless you. My sister is seriously stressing me out with all her *brilliant* last-minute ideas." She rolled her eyes. "She wants a pony. Come on, Adelaide's one. She won't even be able to stay on."

"That sounds intense." Cassie tossed a soiled paper towel in the garbage by the sink. "Now I understand the reason for the frazzled gleam in your eyes."

Someone who didn't know Sylvie would assume she had no affection for her sister or niece. But the number of pictures decorating her workspace told a different story. She loved that little baby, and she'd do anything to make her happy. Even if that meant being in charge of a pony at a one-year-old's birthday party.

"Don't worry about a thing," Cassie said. "I'll be there to help you manage the chaos."

"Thank you, thank you!" Sylvie squeezed her neck harder, her sleek, raven ponytail falling over them both. "I'll swing by your place around eleven."

When Cassie finally managed to free herself from her friend's tight embrace, she retrieved her skirt from the bathroom sink and slipped it on. The fabric hadn't dried completely, but it looked far better than it had a few minutes ago.

"I'll be ready," she said, taking one last look at herself in the mirror and tucking an errant curl behind her ear. She'd fretted so much about her hair this morning, but it was the least of her problems now. "I'll even have your favorite Frappuccino from that coffee shop down the street waiting for you."

"Toasted marshmallow?"

Cassie nodded, grabbing her purse from the blue-tiled floor and slinging it onto her shoulder.

"You're an angel, Cassandra Schalk. An absolute angel."

Cassie laughed as she headed for the door. "I should get to my desk. Adriana is probably wondering where I am. She won't be happy if I'm not there when she's ready for her next coffee." She made a face, then held her head high and yanked open the bathroom door, as if she hadn't just spent the last twenty minutes in a state of near panic. Subconsciously, she felt her damp skirt. *Everything is fine*, she told herself.

"I don't think Adriana has noticed yet," Sylvie said, leading Cassie past the long, white tables littered with fabric waiting to be cut. She bumped into someone draping an unfinished garment over a mannequin and touched the woman's arm in apology before addressing her friend again. "I saw her legal team heading for her office a few minutes ago."

"Her attorneys are here? I didn't see anything on her schedule for this morning." Why hadn't Drew mentioned he was meeting with Adriana today?

Sylvie made a quiet humming noise but didn't say anything. Good. Cassie didn't need any more comments about all the ways Drew didn't measure up. Her friend was wrong. Everyone who doubted their relationship was wrong. The gorgeous ring on Cassie's finger and the way they always came back together even after a hiccup should've proved the longevity of their commitment to each other.

"Did you ever get a chance to show Adriana your designs?" Sylvie asked as they arrived at her side of their shared workspace, a set of L-shaped desks connected at the long side. "What did she think?"

Cassie pressed her lips together in irritation. It had taken a long time to work up the courage to show her boss one of her designs in hopes of finally getting a chance to prove herself as more than an assistant. "She said I should stick to cutting fabric and leave the designing to those who know the industry."

As if Cassie didn't. She'd made it her business to know everything about fashion since she'd cracked open her first copy of *Vogue* at twelve-years-old. She hadn't expected Adriana to use her design in next year's product line, but she'd at least hoped for a little recognition of her talent.

Sylvie leaned in close, dropping her voice. "Honestly, Cass, I don't know how you've put up with her for as long as you have. I've only been working here for six months, and I'm already thinking it's time to start looking for something else."

"It's fine." Cassie shrugged. "Someday, I'll prove my worth."

She'd been telling everyone that for two years. Every time her sister asked if she was still happy in New York. Her parents when they wondered if she was living up to her fullest potential. Even herself when she desperately pleaded to be seen as more than an errand runner. Silently, of course. She'd never breathe a word of her doubts to anyone. Not even Sylvie. Offending the boss wouldn't help her reach her goals. No matter how much she hated her job, she could bide her time here until she got her big break.

The day was coming. She could feel it brewing.

Her friend gave her a look, half commiseration, half mutual frustration, then pulled out her chair and sat. "Lunch today?" she asked, an unspoken sign she was deliberately changing the subject. "Or will the dragon lady be sending you out for more errands?"

"I don't have anything until this afternoon. Lunch sounds great." Cassie reached her own chair, only then noticing the black portfolio laying neatly on the pristine white desktop. A quiet squeal escaped her mouth as she did a little clap of excitement. After her terrible morning, she'd all but forgotten that Adriana wanted her to order the sample fabrics for next year's spring line. Which meant Cassie got an early peek at the new designs.

She sat down and flipped the cover open, eager to see what masterpieces Adriana had come up with this time. For all the frustrations Cassie had about not being appreciated, she had to give credit where it was due. Her boss was a genius when it came to fashion.

Her eyes hungrily scanned the first design. Then she stopped.

Wait a minute. This had to be a mistake. The A-line skirt and heart-shaped neckline looked eerily similar to the dress she'd shown Adriana a few weeks ago. She leaned closer to the page for a better look, and her blood ran cold.

No, not similar. Even the accents at the waist were like a carbon copy of those on Cassie's design.

A sick feeling settled in her gut. This was *the* dress. The same one Adriana had looked at with disinterest, declaring that Cassie didn't know fashion.

Did Adriana even realize how much that comment still hurt? Cassie was proud of that design. She'd been planning to wear it to Gemma's and Tyler's rehearsal dinner until her boss turned up her nose at it. Why would she steal it after telling Cassie it was no good?

Maybe this was all an honest mistake that could be cleared up with a calm, rational conversation.

But deep in her heart she knew it wasn't.

It could be her terrible morning preventing her from thinking rationally. Or maybe attempting to gain her boss's favor and always falling short had finally gotten to her. Whatever the reason, Cassie was done being taken for granted.

She tore out the design and slammed the portfolio closed. Before she had time to talk herself out of it, she grabbed her sketchbook from her purse and pushed back her chair. The forceful movements alerted Sylvie.

"What's up?" she asked in alarm.

Cassie didn't answer as she stormed past. If she paused to vent, her friend would likely try to talk her out of what she was about to do.

She stalked the length of the design floor, attracting the attention of the people she passed, who all stopped to stare at her. Arriving at Adriana's office, she blew out a few breaths for good measure, then lifted her hand and knocked.

Chapter Two

"Come in!"

Even through the thick door, Cassie could hear the annoyance in those two words. She waited outside the office for a few more seconds, attempting to still her racing heart. Barging right in with a bunch of accusations wouldn't get her anywhere fast. This conversation required a level head. And diplomacy. Two skills she'd had to develop since coming to work for Adriana.

She blew out a breath, rolling her shoulders back as she lifted her head higher. Then she pushed the door open.

Sitting behind her long, glass-topped desk like a queen on her throne, Adriana stopped talking midsentence and directed a narrow-eyed glance at her. "What is it, Cassandra?"

The three other occupants in the room all turned to look at Cassie. A stone-faced woman with the pointy nose, her blouse buttoned up to her chin. Drew's father, his graying hair neat and dignified. And the final member of Adriana's legal team: Drew, his dark eyebrows raised in surprise.

Cassie shifted her weight from one foot to the other. In her haste to confront her boss, she'd forgotten all about the meeting Sylvie had told her about only moments ago. *It wasn't on the schedule,* she reminded herself to justify her actions. Adriana couldn't expect Cassie to remember something she hadn't bothered mentioning. Why did she even need to meet with her attorneys anyway?

"I'm sorry to interrupt, Adriana," she said, adding a respectful air to her words. Her eyes flicked to Drew. His head tipped to the side as he watched her warily. She ignored the flutter of nerves in her stomach and took another breath, not thrilled to have an audience for this conversation. "I need to speak to you about one of your designs for next spring's line."

Adriana leaned forward, resting her forearms on top of the desk, which doubled as her design table. "Can't it wait?"

For a second, Cassie considered coming back later. But she had to address this before she lost her nerve. "No, ma'am. It can't."

Adriana sighed, but it sounded more like a groan. "Fine. What is it?" Her words were fast and clipped.

Cassie realized she should've figured out her approach before barging in on Adriana's meeting. Should she give her boss the benefit of the doubt? Or rip the bandage off the predicted deception? If she went with the first option, she *might* be able to keep her job.

"This dress." She held up the design in her hand. "It looks similar to the one I showed you a few weeks ago."

Adriana's eyes narrowed. "That's impossible." She held her hand out for the design.

Cassie stepped to the desk and set the paper in front of Adriana, keeping her own design book closed to give her boss the opportunity to admit her mistake. The tension in the room thickened as the three attorneys looked on silently.

Adriana studied the paper, her body language giving nothing away. Then she placed her hands flat on the tabletop and fixed Cassie with a cool stare. "You are the mistaken one. This dress was the very first design I created for this line. It's been in the works for several weeks. Long before you showed me that silly drawing." She motioned at the book under Cassie's arm.

Several weeks? Her boss had always been strict and intimidating, but until now, Cassie hadn't realized she was also a liar. Either that or delusional. Nothing in Adriana's demeanor even hinted at the possibility that she knew she'd been found out. Cassie's blood began to boil, heat blazing up her chest. She'd been nothing but loyal to Adriana for two years, and this was the thanks she got?

"It's not a mistake," she said, her rising anger fueling her confidence. Her job hung in the balance with every word, but did she even want to work here anymore? "This is the dress you told me wasn't good. If you'd already been working on a similar one, why didn't you tell me then?"

"I'm not required to share my designs with you," Adriana said coldly, her jaw tensing.

Cassie scanned the room, her eyes landing on her fiancé shifting in his seat. Drew! He'd been the one who'd encouraged her to show the design in the first place. He had to help her.

Snatching the paper from Adriana's desk, she stormed over to him. "You've seen it. This is my dress. Tell them, Drew." She opened her book and thumbed through until she found the matching dress, then dropped it in his lap. "And here, this is the original design. See how they're the same?"

Drew's dark eyes widened before he hesitantly took the paper she handed him. She held her breath as he studied it.

After what seemed like an eternity, his eyes slid up to her again, a mixture of steely defiance and regret in their depths. "I can't help you."

Cassie's heart plummeted straight to her toes. She stared at him with her mouth open, but no words came out. Disbelief mingled with heartbreaking disappointment. This was her fiancé. Her partner. How could he do this to her?

"Drew?" His name emerged as a strangled whisper.

The weight of everyone's attention fell hard on her, thick and suffocating, and she wanted nothing more than to leave this office, this building, and run. Not too long ago, she'd been sure the day couldn't get any worse. But it had. So much worse.

The stolen dress was the least of her problems right now. Drew's betrayal cut so much deeper.

Finally, Adriana broke the silence.

"I don't appreciate the accusation you're throwing at me, Cassandra," she said, ice crystals dripping in her words.

Cassie turned slowly to face her, preparing for the final blow that was no doubt coming. She wouldn't allow her boss to end her employment without defending herself. "I've worked here for over two years. You know I have more integrity than to make false claims." She jabbed her finger at her design book in Drew's lap. "This is my design."

"I am not a thief," Adriana insisted. "And frankly, I'm surprised at this behavior from you. You've been a good assistant. But I expect absolute loyalty from my employees. If you're unable to give me that then I have no further use for you."

She stopped talking, and Cassie sensed she was expecting a response from her. An apology, or something. Or for Cassie to grovel at her feet, begging for mercy to keep her job.

Except Cassie refused to grovel anymore. Refused to bend over backwards trying to impress her. "I'll go pack my things," she said, resolutely. Giving Drew one last scalding look, she snatched her design book from his lap and stalked out of the office.

But her anger burned too hot to stick around long enough to throw her belongings into the cardboard cage of shame. She stopped at her desk only to grab her purse. She'd ask Sylvie to drop everything in a box later. Willing herself not to cry, Cassie made her escape, hardly registering her friend calling after her. Eventually, she'd tell Sylvie what happened, but today was not the day.

For the second time that morning, she found herself bypassing the elevator. After shoving her design book into her bag, she stormed down the stairs, her heels clapping against the concrete, hoping to escape the building before anyone witnessed her completely fall apart. Moisture stung her eyes by the time she pushed out into the mid-summer humidity.

It was a strange feeling to walk along the streets of New York filled with people going about their business as if her entire world wasn't crumbling into pieces at her feet. But that was life in the Big Apple. The anonymity could be empowering at times. Now, Cassie only felt crushing isolation.

"Cassandra!"

She ignored Drew's voice behind her and increased her speed, bursts of pain shooting up her Achilles'. Why hadn't she chosen to wear flats this morning? She wouldn't be surprised if her ankles were swollen balls by the time she got home. If it weren't for the dirt and litter cluttering the sidewalk, she'd consider ripping her shoes off altogether.

"Cassandra, wait!" Unfortunately, his long strides allowed him to catch up to her in seconds. "Would you talk to me for a minute?" His hand closed around her elbow, forcing her to stop.

She whirled around. "How dare you!" she growled, wrenching her arm from his grasp. "You knew that was my design. You absolutely knew. Why didn't you stand up for me?"

"And say what?" He threw his hands up in frustration. "You know how powerful Adriana is. More than your job was on the line in there."

Cassie glared at him. "Whatever happened to supporting each other through everything? Why is your job security more important than mine?" Not to mention he'd been raised to work at his father's firm since birth. He could break the law and only receive a slap on the wrist. But she didn't say that out loud.

"I didn't tell you to confront your boss," Drew spat back. "You walked in there with fire in your eyes, expecting to burn bridges. Don't turn this around on me." He jabbed his finger in her direction.

She couldn't believe him. She'd always done her best to support him in his ambitions, to act as the listening ear when he was tired or stressed at work. For five and a half years, she'd put up with his mother's judgement to fight for their relationship, their dream life. And what had he done for her? The realization hit her hard, knocking the breath from her.

"You know what? I can't do this anymore. I'm done." She started to turn, catching the eyes of several passersby who'd slowed to watch the commotion. They all looked away and continued down the street.

Drew grabbed her arm again. "What do you mean you're done?" he asked forcefully. "That's it? We're not going to talk about this?"

He shook his head slowly with a bitter chuckle. "Fine. I have to get back to work anyway. One of us still has a job to do. Go calm down. We'll discuss it tonight at dinner."

Cassie squeezed her eyes shut. "No."

"No?"

Opening her eyes again, she forced her shoulders back, and her nose up in defiance. "No. I'm done talking." She wiggled the engagement ring from her finger, grieving not only the stunning diamonds but also the relationship she thought she'd had.

"What are you doing?" Drew asked, not taking the ring when she held it out to him.

Cassie reached for his hand and pried his fingers open. After placing the ring on his palm, she closed his fingers around it. "You were right. More than my job was on the line in there."

"You can't be serious," Drew said with a derisive laugh, pushing his free hand through his perfect dark brown hair. "After everything we've been through? Cassandra, we're getting married in three months. The invitations have already been sent."

She shook her head slowly. "The wedding is off. Goodbye, Drew."

Without another word, she turned, the adrenaline from their fight wearing off quickly, leaving her exhausted and close to tears. But she refused to let him see her cry.

"I don't believe you," he called after her. "You'll be back."

Cassie sniffed but kept walking, resisting the temptation to rub her nose.

"Where will you go?"

His question stopped her. The plan had always been to move in with Drew once her lease ended. With the wedding no longer happening, that possibility wasn't on the table anymore. And without an income, she couldn't afford to cover her portion of the rent for the cute apartment overlooking Central Park she shared with two of her college besties.

What *was* she going to do?

She took a deep breath in through her nose to squelch the rising panic. She couldn't let Drew see her worries. Besides, Gemma's wedding was next weekend. A little time away might help her think clearly enough to figure out her next step. And celebrating her sister's happiness would hopefully keep Cassie's mind off the fact that her own life had just blown up in her face.

She swiveled slowly back around, forcing a smile. "Don't you remember? I'm going to a wedding."

Chapter Three

By the time Brad Lucas reached the sign welcoming him to Buena Hills, he couldn't wait to get out of his Pathfinder. Despite the open window, the late July heat hovered in the vehicle as stifling as an oven, cooking him from the inside out. His head pounded—one of those steady, pulsing headaches that started right between his eyebrows. Fortunately, it hadn't turned into a migraine. Not yet anyway. Once that happened, it was game over. Hopefully, he'd be able to make it to his sister's house before it came to that.

The six-hour drive down from San Francisco was way too long to be trapped inside this sauna-on-wheels. Of course his car's air conditioning would decide to fizzle out on the morning he'd planned to leave for his cousin's wedding.

Tyler wasn't getting married for another week though. With any luck, Brad could find thirty minutes or so to drop the car off at the auto shop in town. Carlos, the owner, had helped him out with a few maintenance issues before, which had been a lifesaver when he'd lived here during his cash-strapped college years.

Granted, two years post-graduation, Brad was earning pennies compared to what he would've been making had the doc not recommended an end to playing football. If the amount of hype he'd received during his season and a half off the bench—he'd redshirted his freshman year—were any indication, earning a draft pick hadn't been an unrealistic possibility. Not that he'd ever go pro only for the money. And he definitely didn't care about the potential fame. He played for the love of the game, but he'd be a fool not to be enticed by the pay.

Leaning forward to release his back from the sticky leather seat, he grimaced at the sweat trickling down his clammy skin. Yeah, that was attractive. Good thing the only people he planned to see in the next hour were related to him. Sadly, they'd seen him looking worse than this.

He stuck his head out the open window, hoping to capture any breeze on his face to cool him down. Even the air rushing past him due to the movement of the car was so dang hot. Outside the vehicle, there wasn't even the tiniest flutter from the palm trees lining the main road leading through town.

It hasn't changed much, he thought, driving past the old theater, its flashing marquee advertising this week's showings. He was almost positive it hadn't been updated since being built in the 1950s. It only showed two movies at a time, and yet the weekend crowd wrapped around the front of the building exactly like he remembered. The high school was up the road a bit, and beyond that, the village center with all its mom-and-pop shops, parks, and community center.

Bringing his head inside the vehicle again, he slouched against the leather seat, tapping the fingers of one hand against his restless thigh. A sports radio show played from his car's speakers, and he only half focused on the roundup of last night's baseball games.

Once he reached the center of town, traffic slowed, and he eased on the brake as he drove past, leaning forward again to give his back a rest from the sticky leather. The pounding in his forehead had now spread to his temples. He massaged one side of his head, attempting to relieve some of the pressure.

Hoping to bypass the rest of the traffic, he turned off of the main road that split through the center of town. He knew these roads like the back of his hand, even though he hadn't visited since moving away. This alternate route would have him pulling up to the house in less than ten minutes.

The topic on the radio switched from baseball to football, and the Rams' preseason rookie camp. Brad reached over to turn the volume up.

"All eyes are on one of this year's top draft picks, Tyrone Miller, fresh off a remarkable senior season at USC," the analyst said. "Everyone wants to know if he can bring the same momentum and intensity he's built over his college career to the pro level."

Tyrone had been awarded the starting position at running back after Brad had left the team. And he deserved all the hype being served his way. He was a phenomenal athlete, and an even better guy. A coach's dream. Brad was happy for him. Still, it stung watching his old teammate living out the life that for *him* was now only a heap of failed goals.

Quitting the team had been the hardest decision he'd ever had to make in his life. But there'd been no other choice. One more concussion and he might've been handed way more problems than he had to deal with already.

What if he hadn't stopped though? What if he'd pushed through the pain like his high school coach had always drilled into him? Even after all these years, he could hear Coach Sanders yelling at him to toughen up, to show no weakness, to keep his eye on the end goal. Maybe the outcome would've been different than all the side effects his doctor had warned him about. Maybe instead of making a career out of talking about the pros, he'd be playing with them.

Brad sighed and jabbed the button to turn off the radio. He didn't need any more reminders of what could've been. He'd made his choice, and now he had to deal with the aftermath.

The hum of the tires against the road filled the car, though the peaceful lull didn't last long before his phone buzzed from the center console. Briefly taking his eyes off the road, he swiped to answer the call, putting it on speaker.

"Hey, Brook." He returned his hand to the wheel. "What's up?"

"Just calling to check in," his youngest sister, Brooklyn said. "Did you make it to the house yet?"

Brad flipped on his right blinker before turning onto another side street. "Not yet. I just got into town. I'm almost to Beej's." Beej was their other sister, the middle sibling in the pecking order. "When are you getting here?"

"We're not driving down until Tuesday. The district swim meet is on Monday, so I have to be here for that."

"That's right. Are you ready for it?" He rolled his shoulders, trying to find a more comfortable position.

"I think so," she said. "I have to admit though, I'm kind of nervous. There's more at stake for this one. If I do well enough, I'll qualify for the state meet. Will you come if I make it?"

"If?" He scoffed. "Don't be modest with me. You know you're a shoo in. You've had the fastest times all season."

Brooklyn was an incredible three-sport athlete, excelling in soccer and softball at the high school. But she'd always claimed swimming as her first love, and she competed both at school and in the summer league. He wouldn't be surprised to see her sign her letter of intent to USC before she graduated next year.

"I'm not a shoo in." The smile was obvious in her voice. "Upsets happen all the time in swimming."

"Just swim like a shark is chasing you, and you'll be fine."

Brooklyn laughed. "Will you come though? It's in two weeks."

Brad worked through the logistics in his head. He was starting a new job in three weeks, one that would require a cross-state move from San Francisco back to LA. After returning from the wedding, he'd have five days left at his current job. He'd planned to use the following week to pack up his apartment and tie up all the loose ends before driving back down here. But maybe if he planned it right, he'd be able to do all of that at the same time.

"I'll be there," he said, keeping his internal processing to himself. Brooklyn didn't need to know the logistics of how he'd make it work; she just needed him there. He'd been to so few of her events since he'd moved away from home. He wanted to be there for her this time.

They ended the call a minute later, but the screen didn't have time to go dark before it rang again. He groaned. It was probably Beej, calling to nag him about his "condition." Their relationship had improved somewhat since he'd moved away from Buena Hills, but it was still ... complicated.

Surprisingly, it wasn't Beej who responded when he accepted the call. Instead, his cousin's voice came through the line. Talk about a welcome surprise.

"Hey. What's your ETA?" Hallie asked by way of greeting.

"I should be pulling up to your place in about six minutes. Give or take a few."

Hallie lived with Beej. As did her sister, Elise, and Kendall, their best friend and honorary relative after living with them during high school. The house was a whole family affair pretty much. Even though Brad and his sisters hadn't grown up in Buena Hills, their connection to the LA suburb ran deep. Their father had been born and raised here, for one thing. After Granny and Granddad passed away several years ago, they'd left their home to Dad in their will. Rather than sell the house that had been in the Lucas family for generations, he'd rented it out until Brad and Tyler had started at USC. Once they'd graduated, Beej and their cousins had moved in.

"Perfect," Hallie said in her typical getting-the-job-done tone. "Are you hungry?"

"Starving." His stomach grumbled in agreement.

"Beej, Elise, and Kendall just left to grab teriyaki."

"At Tanaka's?"

She scoffed. "Is there any other place?"

"Touché," Brad said through a chuckle, then winced when the action intensified the throbbing in his head. Tanaka's served the best teriyaki within a twenty-mile radius.

"Beej ordered you a chicken and rice bowl, heavy on the chicken and light on the cucumbers," she continued. "Did you want anything else? I can text the girls."

"Not unless it includes a side of pain killers. Do you have any?"

"Of course. Migraine?"

Brad grunted in response. "Not yet. But if I don't get out of this car soon, I won't be surprised if it turns into one."

"That's rough." Hallie made a humming noise into the phone. "I thought you were taking something that's supposed to prevent them."

"I am," he responded. "And they're much better than they were. This heat is really getting to me."

Normally, conversation about his chronic migraines was enough to bring out his grumpy side. Especially how much Beej insisted on fussing over him. *He* was the older brother, for crying out loud. Getting a few migraines a month gave her no reason to treat him like an invalid. Even if she was a nurse. He was fully capable of taking care of his own health.

But Hallie had a practical, non-judgmental way about her that made it almost impossible to get on the defensive when talking to her.

"Well, the couch is all ready for you if you need to sleep it off. Unless you'd prefer to bunk with Tyler in the spare room." Her brother had been living with the girls since finishing his master's at Berkeley and moving back to Buena Hills a couple months ago.

Brad pushed out a sarcastic laugh. "That would be a hard pass. He snores like a foghorn." Not to mention the few times they'd had to share an air mattress during family reunions they'd spent the entire night taking turns pushing each other off. "The couch is fine."

"Great. Elise will be sharing with me for the week so there's room for Mandy to sleep in hers."

His throat constricted, and he swallowed slowly. "That won't be necessary. Mandy's not coming." Beej had called a few days ago to talk details about his trip. Had he really forgotten to tell her about Mandy?

On second thought, that didn't surprise him. His sister would've made a big deal over it. And knowing her, she'd make it her mission to pair him off with one of her friends before he even arrived in town.

"She's not coming?" Hallie asked in surprise. "How come?"

He hesitated, sticking his head out the window. Hotter than

blazes. "Because I don't think her boyfriend would be happy if she took a road trip down to Los Angeles with another man."

"What? She's dating someone else?"

"Yeah." He couldn't keep the bitterness out of the word.

Sadly, Mandy was only the most recent addition to his list of failed relationships. The reasons behind his inability to keep a girlfriend long-term had been a topic of hot debate among Beej and their cousins for years. He'd heard everything from commitment issues to pickiness being the cause of his dating problems. And maybe both of those were true. He did tend to date the same type of women. Or maybe there was just something wrong with him.

"When did you break up?"

"Apparently, a few days ago. I went over to her apartment, and *he* was there."

Hallie gasped. "She cheated on you?"

"Not exactly." Brad sighed, not wanting to get into the details but unable to withhold them. "It's more like he dumped her, and she decided to get back at him by dating me. He got jealous, and I had the pleasure of walking in during their very passionate make up scene."

Hallie was silent for a few seconds before answering. "Wow. Talk about a hot mess. Not to sound insensitive, but it seems like you've dodged a bullet with that situation."

"Tell me about it." What did it say about him and his dating history that he was more embarrassed than heartbroken over this most recent break up? He'd rather not think about that.

"At least I won't have to see her for a week." The only thing worse than finding his girl with another man was having to constantly run into them in the hallways of his apartment building. Never again would he date someone who lived on his floor.

In fact, would it be so bad if he stayed a bachelor forever? That life path sounded better all the time.

Hallie made a grunt of pure disgust, and Brad's frustration softened at her support. "And you won't be living in that apartment for much longer, anyway," she pointed out.

"True. At least there's that."

Who knew the relocation would come at such a perfect time? He'd been looking for a new job for months. One that would allow him to be in front of the microphone instead of taking care of the behind-the-scenes stuff for the small news station he worked at in San Francisco. Occasionally, he'd had opportunities to fill in for the sports reporters on the broadcasts, but he wanted more than a temporary gig. When a sports analyst position had opened up in LA, naturally he'd jumped at the chance to apply.

And once he returned from the wedding, he'd only have to run into Mandy and *Jack*—just the sound of his name sent nausea rippling in his stomach—for three more weeks before he'd be gone forever.

Good riddance.

"I'm sorry, Brad." Hallie's sympathy brought him back to the present. "It's her loss."

"Thanks, Hal."

He turned another corner and came only inches from plowing into a silver sedan parked at the curb, its back end jutting out into the street. Hissing a curse, he yanked the steering wheel, swerving to the right to avoid making contact.

"Everything okay?" Hallie asked.

"Yeah, fine. Uh, I gotta go. I'll see you soon."

He hung up before she could respond, then glared into his rearview mirror at the offending vehicle. The reflection of the setting sun created a blinding glow that made it difficult to see. But in the glare, he could make out the silhouette of a woman crouched on the sidewalk next to the car.

A groan rumbled in his throat as a debate waged inside him. He was so close to getting out of this heat trap. Five minutes away from food. And pain meds. Possibly a shower. He took an involuntary whiff, then made a face. No, not possibly. Shower first, then food.

He kept driving. A block later, something tugged at his conscience, and he slowed his car to a crawl. What if that woman needed help? What kind of person would he be if he didn't stop?

This is the twenty-first century, he thought, ignoring the temptation. If she truly were stranded, she could call someone. He sped up again, beckoned on by the prospect of finally getting some relief for his pounding head.

After one more block, however, the guilt had wiggled its way into his stomach, and one of his father's favorite lines entered his mind. *Are you part of the solution or the problem?* Brad hated when Dad used that tired old phrase. He'd said it a lot when Brad was younger, usually when he and Beej weren't getting along. It wasn't fair that, as the oldest, he was the one that always got in trouble even when she'd started the conflict.

With Dad's voice ringing in his head, he grumbled and pulled into a neighborhood, using the driveway of a one-story rambler to turn around. After backtracking the way he'd come, he passed the sedan still parked on the side of the road and made a U-turn, coming to a stop a few feet behind it.

The air was only slightly cooler outside his car, though it was nice not having to sit in his own sweat for a while. He pulled his damp shirt from his equally damp stomach as he enjoyed the sensation of fresh air on his flushed skin. He hadn't been out of the car since he'd stopped for gas near Santa Barbara over two hours ago. Letting go of the shirt, it immediately clung to his stomach again. Gross.

The woman was crouched next to the back passenger side tire. From a few feet away, Brad picked up on certain details he hadn't noticed while driving by. She wore dark jeans paired with strappy heels that made his arches hurt just looking at them. Her white top was already smudged with something that looked like dirt or grease from the car. Maybe both. A dented hubcap lay on the sidewalk a few feet away, like she'd tossed it aside in frustration after prying it off the vehicle. Her face hid behind an avalanche of golden curls as she strained against the weight of the wrench, trying unsuccessfully to loosen a lug nut.

Brad had a hard time pulling his eyes away from that hair. He'd never seen such perfect curls before. Like the sun had painted them itself.

He stopped in his tracks and rolled his eyes at himself. *What does that even mean?* And when did he start waxing poetic?

Dragging his gaze away from those golden waves, he reminded himself of his purpose and approached.

"Need some help?"

The woman startled, then lifted her head, giving him his first good look at her face.

Ah, crap. Now the designer clothes and perfect curls made sense. Brad hadn't seen the gorgeous Cassie Schalk since she'd flown in from New York to help her sister after their grandma's stroke two years ago. Her *twin* sister who happened to be Tyler's future sister-in-law.

Yet that hadn't stopped Brad from making a complete fool of himself in front of her when she'd joined them for a friendly bowling game while in town. He hadn't expected she could turn his harmless trash talking into a personal dig on his character as fast as she did. And she'd avoided him for the rest of her trip. Not that he'd thought about her or anything.

What was she doing crouched on the side of the road attempting to change her own tire? She didn't seem like the type to concern herself with dirty tasks such as that. She glared up at him, showing that the displeasure of being unexpectedly caught in his presence was entirely mutual.

He'd already established a habit of looking like a complete moron in front of her, so he shouldn't have been surprised about doing it again. He always had a talent of digging himself into even bigger landfills. And this time, he jumped right into another one by letting the curse out of his mouth before his underperforming brain could stop it.

Chapter Four

"Do you greet all your acquaintances by swearing at them?" Cassie asked with all the haughtiness of a royal addressing her least favorite subject. "Or do you reserve your best language just for me?"

He scrunched his eyes closed. *Nice one, fool.* For a moment, he'd thought the word emerged quiet enough to go unheard. Apparently he was destined to continue playing the idiot card in front of her.

Rubbing at his aching temple, he shook off his blunder. Instead of responding to her question, he said, "Well, well, well. Princess Cassie is back in Buena Hills."

Her expression darkened even more as she stood, brushing her hands together, which did little to help the black grease smeared across her palms. "Hey, *bro.*" Her eyes traveled down the length of his sweaty T-shirt, the side of her lip curling up like she'd spotted a rat crawling out of an overflowing dumpster. "What happened to you?"

Brad's jaw clenched as he forced himself not to deliver the uncharitable comment about *her* current state that came to his mind. As his cousin's best man, he had a duty to make sure Tyler's wedding day went off without a hitch. Starting out on the wrong foot with the maid of honor would do little to fulfill his role. Although by the way their time together had ended the last time, that might be asking too much.

"It looks like you're in a bit of a bind." He took a few steps toward her, stopping close enough that she had to crane her neck to meet his eye.

Shaking her head, she faced the tire again. "I can do it myself." She picked up the wrench and connected it to the lug nut, groaning as she used all her weight to push against it. The wrench didn't budge.

Pulling back, she took a deep breath and tried a second time. Again, nothing happened.

She was persistent. He'd give her that.

"Will you please let me help you?" he asked a little more impatiently than he'd intended. Every second he stood here increased the pain in his head. The sooner he could get this over with, the closer he'd be to finding some relief. He propped his hands loosely onto his hips.

Cassie continued struggling with the wrench. "No thanks."

He pushed out an intense breath. She was persistent *and* stubborn. Well, he could be stubborn too. Crouching next to her, he placed his hand on the tool she was holding. "At least let me loosen the lug nuts. They're pretty tricky to get off."

Shoulders drooping, she finally gave up and let Brad take over.

Every strain of his arm muscles aggravated the pounding in his head as he pushed down on the wrench to loosen the first bolt. He clenched his teeth to prevent his discomfort from showing. After a moment, he said, "Why don't you go get the jack while I take these off."

"The ... jack?"

Raising one brow, he turned to look at her sitting next to him on the curb. "You know, the thing that lifts the car up so you can pull the tire off? There should be one in the trunk."

"I know what that is," she said, staring him down for a long second before rising to her feet. "I just didn't know the name for it."

She trudged to the back of the vehicle which was most likely a rental. He'd glimpsed the sticker on the windshield before crouching down. Sounds of her rummaging through the open trunk met his ears as he returned to his task. Out of the corner of his eye, he caught flashes of movement while she pulled out two wheeled suitcases, a black garment bag, and another midsize bag without wheels. How much luggage did one woman need for a week?

As soon as the thought crossed his mind however, he pushed it away. Why did he even care? He went back to his work, wondering what could've caused the flat on a tire that seemed to be in pretty good shape.

Once he'd placed the final lug nut on the sidewalk next to the others, he shifted onto his knees to peer into the wheel well, looking for the culprit. Running his hand down the tire, his finger slid over a smooth, circular indent on the side toward the ground. He bent over to get a closer look and noticed a sizeable nail wedged all the way into the tire's tread.

Bingo.

By the time Brad finished inspecting the problem, Cassie still hadn't returned with the jack. With a frustrated sigh, he went to see what was taking so long. When he came up beside her, she was standing in front of the near empty trunk with her head bowed. One palm braced against the rim of the open trunk, her fingers tangled around a cell phone charger. Her other hand pinched the bridge of her nose with her thumb and forefinger. Was she crying?

His gaze lingered on her, an uncomfortable sensation tugging at his insides. He didn't need a reason to feel sorry for her. Had she even noticed his approach?

If he didn't do anything soon, they'd be standing here all night, and *someone* had to change the tire. He reached into the trunk and pulled out the metal crank.

"The jack," he said, holding it out to her.

Something that looked a lot like embarrassment flashed in her eyes as her head jerked toward him. But in the next second, it vanished, and she yanked the tool from his hand. "I knew that. I was just testing you." She marched back to the passenger side, stopping to open the door and toss the charger onto the seat. Her unnaturally high heels clacked against the cement as she returned to the back tire.

Oh, she was testing him, all right. He lifted his gaze to the darkening sky, praying for patience. This was exactly why Brad didn't bother going the distance when it came to women. His past relationships had been full of constant frustration. But that was a story for another day.

"Do you know where it goes?" he asked to keep his mind off both his current predicament and his complete lack of dating prospects now that Mandy had left the picture. He pointed to the jack she was helplessly staring at.

"Of course I know where it goes," she snapped. "I can handle it from here. Why don't you go back to wherever you came from?" She flicked a delicate hand in his direction like she was shooing away varmint. "Hopefully that includes a shower."

His jaw hurt from all the clenching he'd done to hold back the retorts he'd wanted to make. That didn't do anything to help his head. He seriously doubted her ability to change the tire herself, but if she insisted on being this stubborn, he'd just leave her to it.

"Whatever you say, your highness," he grumbled quietly. But obviously not quietly enough to go unheard, judging by the way her head jerked toward him, her eyes narrowing into slits.

He shrugged off the regret he didn't want to feel. If she couldn't appreciate his help, or the effort it took to offer it, then he refused to feel bad about leaving her here. Let her be stuck all night for all he cared. Shoving his hands into his pockets, he squared his shoulders and headed back to his car.

"Brad," Cassie's voice called out after he'd only made it a few feet.

He stopped. What could she possibly want now?

Her eyes were on him when he turned around, and in the soft light of the lingering sun, he could've sworn he detected some resignation in their depths. But that couldn't be right. Only a minute before, she'd been bracing for a fight. A fight that, after driving all day, the lack of air conditioning sucking all the energy from his soul, he had no desire to reciprocate.

They stared at each other for a few seconds. Brad almost gave in and asked why she'd called him back, but he resisted. He wasn't the difficult one here.

Finally, she sighed, the tension in her shoulders sagging. "I've only changed one tire in my entire life, and my dad did most of it." She kept her focus on his feet as she spoke, and it sounded as though the admission had been forced out of her. "Living in New York City, I rarely drive a car as it is."

He waited another second for her to continue, which seemed to aggravate her even more.

"Will you help me change the tire?" she asked, the measured calm in her tone obvious.

"That depends."

Her eyes flashed. "On what?"

Lifting a shoulder, he studied his fingernails as he said, "I didn't hear the magic word." He knew he was tiptoeing on thin ice with her, but she wasn't the only one annoyed about having to be together right now.

"Please," she pushed out through clenched teeth.

Resisting the urge to puff out his chest a little at that small victory, he swaggered back to her. For once, he held the upper hand. She needed him. He'd won this battle of wills.

"Why don't I show you how, so you'll be able to fix it yourself if there's a next time?"

She tilted her head to one side in confusion, and for a moment, he expected her to reject his offer. Apparently, all her insistence over doing it herself was only for show. How disappointing. She really was the princess she'd made herself out to be two years ago, willing to let everyone else get their hands dirty.

"Oh...kay," she said, surprising him.

Brad bit back a small smile once she'd turned away from him to crouch into position. He dropped to a squat next to her, but not near enough to touch her. She wouldn't appreciate getting up close and personal with a sweaty man.

"What do I do?" she asked, glancing at him, her hazel eyes wide with expectation. His stomach hitched a little. She really did have gorgeous eyes.

Nope, don't go there. Those eyes could burn a hole right through him with their fire.

Forgetting his momentary slip, Brad instructed her to feel underneath the car's frame until she found the smooth spot of metal that would fit the jack. She slid the tool in place and twisted the lever to raise the tire.

As she worked, he found his focus straying more to her face than to the car parts she handled. The hitch in his stomach returned. He couldn't deny she was a beautiful woman. And her determination to be independent a minute ago was hotter than sin, which made no sense for how prickly she acted toward him. But he'd always liked some spice in a woman.

He cut that train of thought before it could chug any further down the track. How did he go from wanting to leave her stranded to thinking about how hot she was? That was a dangerous leap he couldn't afford to make. He needed to remember that.

In order to distract himself from the ridiculous trail his brain had taken, he retrieved the spare tire from the trunk, grunting at the weight of it as he carried it back to Cassie.

"If you don't know how to change a tire," he said, thumping it onto the ground next to them, "why didn't you call roadside assistance? Or Gemma at the very least. I'm sure she and Tyler would've come to get you." His cousin would go out of his way to be helpful. Almost annoyingly so. But hey, that personality trait had helped win over his lady love, so who was Brad to judge?

Cassie sat back on her haunches and shrugged. "I wanted to, but my phone died."

Ah, so that explained the charger.

"It's been an awful weekend." She spoke the last statement under her breath, and he got the impression that she hadn't meant for him to hear it.

Do not feel sorry for her. She'd given him no reason to care about her bad weekend. He turned away from her to study the grease underneath one of his fingernails, attempting to brush away the sympathy tugging at his conscience.

She stared at the tire, and panic rose up Brad's chest as he studied her. This marked the second time in a few minutes she seemed close to tears. He could handle the icy side of Cassie Schalk, but he had no idea how to handle a crying woman who wanted nothing to do with him.

He cleared his throat. "Come on, I'll help you get the tire off."

That seemed to snap her out of it. They worked together to remove the flat before he showed her how to slide the spare tire onto the axis and screw the lug nuts back on by hand in a star formation. Then she lowered the car back to the ground.

"Why do they call these lug nuts?" she asked, accepting the wrench that Brad held out to her.

Sitting back onto the curb, he let his hands hang between his raised knees as he watched her tighten the bolts. "Because they're hard to get off. Lugging something usually implies using effort. It's laborious, you know?"

One side of her mouth slid upward. "Wow, laborious, huh? That's a big word."

"Ha ha." Brad shook his head. He'd always suspected she didn't think him particularly bright. But he couldn't help a smirk of his own at the well-placed zinger.

Once the lug nuts were back on, he took the wrench from her and made sure they were tightened before carrying the old tire to the trunk and placing it inside. Cassie followed with the jack, wrench, and bent hub cap.

"There you go," he said after helping her arrange her luggage around the tools. "Good as new."

They both faced each other, and his eyes met hers in the beat before her gaze darted away from him. In the next instant, it traveled back to his face, catching him still staring. He jerked his eyes to the ground. This continued for several long seconds, like some strange competition neither of them were trying to win.

Shoving his fists into his pockets, he rocked back and forth on the balls of his feet. This silence was even more uncomfortable than their feud had been.

"You'll want to call the rental company and tell them about the flat," he said, rubbing at some grease on the side of his thumb. "They'll need to send you a replacement so they can get that tire fixed."

Cassie nodded. "Are you sure you didn't sabotage the job? The tire isn't going to fall off as soon as I start driving again, right?"

Really? "Is this how you treat everyone who rescues you?"

Her posture stiffened, and she took a step toward him, her pert little nose lifting in defiance. She was several inches shorter than him, though her heels put her forehead level with his chin. "Maybe I don't want to be rescued all the time."

That statement held weight, but Brad was too annoyed to dissect what it meant. "Why is it so impossible for you to just say thank you?"

Fire flared in her eyes as she matched him stare for stare, and they stood that way for a long beat. He refused to back down. He'd tried being the gentleman. It wasn't easy to put his hard feelings for this woman aside when he found her needing help. He'd ignored his own needs a little longer for her well-being and yet she'd refused to give him the same courtesy.

Before he could walk away, her shoulders slumped, defeat filling her lengthy sigh. "Thank you," she said quietly. "I do appreciate your help."

Some of his indignation fizzled out at her apology. But not all of it. He released a long breath to calm himself enough to speak. Then he gave her a curt nod. "You're welcome. That wasn't so hard, was it?"

As soon as the words were out, he could've kicked himself. Why did his snarky mouth always get him in trouble when he was grumpy?

Cassie obviously didn't appreciate the comment either. Her eyes turned to steel right before him, and her teeth clenched so hard he could see the muscles in her jaw flexing.

With a haughty *hmph*, she whirled around, and those ravishing curls whipped his face. His head jerked back. Storming to the driver's side, she got in the car and slammed the door. The engine roared to life, and she peeled off, tires squealing against the pavement.

Alone on the sidewalk, he watched until her taillights disappeared in the growing darkness. Running his hand through his tousled hair, he walked back to his car.

The wedding week hadn't even started yet, and he was already in hot water with the maid of honor. That didn't bode well for the days to come.

Chapter Five

It had to be him, Cassie grumbled silently as she drove away from the curb. Clutching the steering wheel in a vice grip, she took a few deep breaths to calm herself. *Of course, it had to be him.*

Out of all the thousands of people making up the population of Buena Hills, why couldn't it have been a nice lady who'd stopped to help her? Or a mechanic. That would be the perfect scenario. Heck, she'd even settle for a policeman, even if he gave her a ticket for blocking traffic.

But no. This weekend had already proved she didn't live a charmed life. It had to be the one person she'd hoped not to run into on her first day in town.

If she'd had the foresight to pack her phone charger in her purse instead of somewhere in her checked luggage, she could've called a tow truck and avoided the whole embarrassing situation. She glared down at the white chord now plugged into the car and attached to her phone.

After the rotten twenty-four hours she'd had already, it was only fitting to add this to the list of disasters piling on top of her.

"Why is this happening to me?"

She tried to be a good person. Never once had she cheated on her taxes, and she was kind to everyone. Well, most people, at least.

You were a little rude to Brad back there. Where did that thought come from? Her subconscious had no right to call her out like that. Besides, he hadn't been much of a gem either. He'd proved to be as snarky and annoying as the last time they'd been together.

Why couldn't the universe throw her a bone by giving her some time to mentally prepare herself before running into him again? She wasn't unrealistic by thinking she could avoid him completely this week. Gemma was marrying into a close-knit family. As Tyler's cousin, of course Brad would be at the wedding. But was it really necessary that *he* be the one to stop?

With a rush of dread, her mind spiraled back to their one and only meeting two years ago. Cassie had flown to California to help Gemma after Gram's stroke. Granted, she was supposed to be in Mexico with Drew back then. He'd planned the whole trip, even convincing Adriana to give her the time off. Cassie had always suspected her boss had a soft spot for Drew, being the son of her attorney, and all.

She still remembered the giddy excitement swirling inside her leading up to that trip. In her mind, she had no doubt he'd planned the whole thing in order to give her the perfect proposal she'd dreamed of since childhood. The white sand beach at sunset. The gorgeous dress—blue, of course, because she always looked beautiful in blue—her skirt billowing out from her legs with the breeze. Tall, handsome Drew bending down on one knee in front of her.

It couldn't get much more movie-worthy than that.

That picture perfect engagement had come crashing down even before they'd left New York, thanks to the Covington family dinner two days before the trip. Cassie still hated those events. "Family" was a loose word. Theresa Covington's idea of family included at least a dozen of New York's upper elites bent on showing how much Cassie's average, middle class upbringing didn't belong with the rich and haughty. Drew's mother was always parading more eligible young women around her son, hoping one would catch his eye.

Whatever. Cassie could handle his mother's antics. Except when combined with Miss Eleanore Whitney—Drew's ex and Theresa's number one candidate for the crown of future daughter-in-law. Her flawless black hair and porcelain skin made her the epitome of a Disney Princess. She even sounded a little like Snow White, but she was no sweetheart with the way she shamelessly threw herself at Drew that night. He hadn't exactly encouraged her flirting, though he didn't shut it down either.

"I should've ended it back then," Cassie muttered as she came to a stop at a red light, still remembering the fight they'd had in the taxi on the way back to her apartment after the exhausting night. "I shouldn't have tried so hard to make it work."

But hindsight was twenty-twenty, and the next day, she'd hopped on a plane to California with the intention of reevaluating her life. What better place to have space to think about change than in the land of sunshine and palm trees?

Instead, she'd met compulsive trash talking, bro-dude Brad Lucas.

Lucky her.

Her face still burned with shame at the memory of showing the worst side of herself to a good percent of Buena Hill's young adult population, including Tyler and his sisters and cousins. Why hadn't she stayed back at Gram's when Gemma had invited her to go bowling that night? She clearly hadn't been in the right emotional state to be around people. Especially when it came to Brad's constant ribbing. The guy would. Not. Shut. Up. A person could only take so much of it before they snapped.

Everywhere she turned the whole night, there he was running his mouth, getting in her head each time she got up to take her turn, joking about her lack of bowling skills especially. Who even bowled anymore, anyway?

"Bet you can't get those spares, princess," he'd muttered during the eighth frame as she passed his seat to pick up another ball from the return.

Cassie had done her best to keep her growing frustration from showing on her face, even grinding her teeth to keep from offering a retort. She hated that nickname, no matter who called her that. And no, he hadn't been the first. It always sent her right back to high school when all the kids in her expat community treated her like some kind of royalty. She still had no clue what she'd done to give them the impression that she was better than they were, but she'd constantly felt set apart from everyone else. Isolated and lonely.

Shaking off Brad's annoying trash talk, Cassie picked up the blue and purple swirled ball and approached the foul line. She stared down the three pins at the other end of the lane before raising the ball in front of her. Then she took one step forward and swung her arm back. Another step forward and another before releasing the ball, watching it spin down the lane, and ...

"Gutterball!" Brad hollered in a deep voice as she turned back toward the rest of the group. He caught her eye and winked, the amused smirk snapping the last bit of patience she had in reserve. "Too bad, princess."

Heat creeped up Cassie's face at the reminder of what came next. Even two years later, the mortification still felt as fresh as it had immediately after the fact. She shouldn't have lost her temper. It didn't matter how annoying someone was. In no universe was it ever okay for her to pluck the drink out of his hand and dump it over his head. Her only explanation for why she'd lost her cool so entirely was that her already heightened emotional state over Drew had clouded her judgment.

A lame excuse, for sure, but still an excuse. And she continued to feel the shame of it.

But instead of owning up to her outburst and apologizing, she'd stormed out of the bowling alley, praying she'd never have to see his infuriating face ever again.

She'd run away.

Evidently, she was good at that.

"In five-hundred feet, turn right."

Cassie startled at the sudden voice given by the car's navigation system. She flipped on her blinker.

It was silly that she still needed a GPS to direct her to a house she knew so well. She'd been visiting her grandparents in Buena Hills her whole life. Growing up in another country, she loved spending several weeks here during the summer. But hey, she hadn't been paying attention to directions as a kid. And sadly, her visits now were few and far between.

Attempting to push her frustration with Brad from her mind, she turned onto a street with picture-perfect lawns. She counted the houses until she arrived at Gram's two-story home. Two cars were parked in the driveway, so she came to a stop at the curb and shut off the engine, remaining in her seat for a few long minutes to let the stress of her day drain off her.

After a few deep breaths, she grabbed her purse from the passenger seat, unplugged her phone, and stepped out of the car. Leaving the rest of her bags in the trunk to get later, she made her way up the driveway toward the three figures occupying the front porch.

Gemma and Gram sat on opposite sides of the hanging swing that Tyler had put in shortly after Gram's stroke. A woven blanket was draped across the matriarch's lap. Someone had dragged out one of the kitchen chairs, which Tyler now occupied at his fiancée's side, leaning forward with his forearms resting on his thighs. He wore his usual easy smile as he listened intently to something Gram was saying.

Cassie's grandmother had a soft spot for him, and for good reason. The way he continued to help care for her even two years after her health scare won over not only herself and Gemma, but the rest of the Schalk family as well.

"Cassie!" her sister shrieked, hopping up from the porch swing and jogging down the walk to greet her. Her dark curls bounced behind her as she threw her arms around Cassie's neck. "You're here early!"

Returning the tight embrace, Cassie beamed for the first time all day.

"Where's Drew?" Gemma asked after pulling away. She turned toward the car, squinting for a closer look inside the vehicle. "Did he come with you?"

The warm feeling spreading from Cassie's heart died quickly. "Um, no, he's still in New York." She left it at that and turned to her future brother-in-law. "Hi, Tyler."

"You made it," he said, wrapping an arm around her shoulders in a side hug. "It's good to see you."

"What happened to your clothes?" Gemma asked in alarm.

Cassie glanced down at her favorite white blouse, grimacing at the grease stain she'd earned from brushing up against the flat tire while trying to get the lug nuts off. Ruined clothing was becoming her new way of life.

Fantastic.

"I should get this shirt in the wash before the stain sets." If it hadn't already. "But first I want to say hi to Gram." She continued to the porch with Tyler and Gemma following behind.

A pleased smile formed on Gram's face as Cassie approached, and she held out her hands. "Hello, my child," she said, her voice slightly shaky but much stronger than the last time Cassie had talked to her in person. "I'm happy you're here. It's been too long since you've come to visit."

A twinge entered Cassie's heart. "It really has." She dropped onto the bench next to Gram, careful not to jostle the swing too much. Sliding one arm around her grandmother's bent shoulders, she leaned in close, pressing their cheeks together. Gram's skin was soft and wrinkly against hers, the touch warm and comforting. "You look good. How are you feeling?"

"I'm still here, aren't I?" Gram asked, her green eyes sparkling with mirth. "You can't get rid of me quite yet."

Cassie laughed. Though Gram's mobility hadn't entirely returned since her stroke, her sense of humor was still sharp as a tack. "And thank goodness for that. You're not allowed to go anywhere."

Gram chuckled as she patted her granddaughter's thigh with a weathered hand. Cassie dropped her hand on top of it, gently weaving their fingers together. One of the most difficult parts of living in New York was not being able to see Gram as often as she'd like. Every visit was a hard reminder that her beloved grandmother wouldn't always be with her.

"So, what happened?" Gemma asked again. She lowered herself

to perch on Tyler's lap, who'd reclaimed his seat on the kitchen chair. "That looks like a nasty stain."

Cassie let out a dramatic sigh, all the frustration rushing back in the sound. "I got a flat tire. My phone was dead, so I had to do it myself."

"You changed a tire?" Gemma's eyes—the exact shade of hazel as Cassie's—widened in shock. "By yourself?"

Cassie tried not to be offended at her twin's disbelief. Car repair, or anything that required her to get dirty, was never her first choice of activities. Honestly, if there'd been any other way, she'd never have attempted the task.

"Not exactly. I had help," she admitted reluctantly. She turned to Tyler. "Your cousin drove by when I was in the middle of trying to get the lug nuts off." She couldn't keep the bitterness out of her voice.

Tyler's blond eyebrows rose. "Who? Beej?"

Beej was his only cousin currently living in Buena Hills, so it wasn't an unrealistic guess. But Cassie couldn't imagine Brad's sister changing a tire either. She shook her head slowly. "The other one."

"Oh boy," Tyler mumbled, realization dawning on his face. "Did Brad behave himself?" Both he and Gemma had witnessed Cassie's ill-timed outburst at the bowling alley.

"That's debatable." He'd shown his true annoying self, that was for sure. But he *had* helped her.

She groaned. Why did he have to be the one to stop?

"Is he always this frustrating?" she asked, her question accompanied by an exasperated moan. "I still don't know why you didn't pick your brother to be your best man."

She'd posed her statement in a tongue-in-cheek way, but there was more than a little truth to it. She'd much rather walk down the aisle on the arm of Tyler's seventeen-year-old brother than his twenty-five-year-old cousin. Not to mention, she'd probably have to dance with Brad at the reception too. She shuddered at the possibility.

Tyler, leaning his cheek against Gemma's arm from behind, gave her a sympathetic look. "I'll talk to him when I see him. I promise."

Cassie nodded, though she was ready for this line of conversation to be over. "So, what still needs to be done as far as wedding prep?"

"I'm really glad you came early," Gemma said. "My final dress fitting is tomorrow morning."

That was yet another drawback of living so far away. Cassie couldn't be here in person when her twin had found her perfect wedding dress. Tyler's sisters had made sure to include her in the appointment by video chat, but it wasn't the same.

A wide grin spread across her face. "I wouldn't miss it for the world."

A soft buzzing reached her ears. Sliding her purse from her shoulder, she opened it and pulled out her phone, which still sat at the top from when she slipped it inside before hugging her sister. She frowned at Drew's name on the screen, wishing she hadn't taken the time to locate her charger from her suitcase while Brad was unscrewing the lug nuts.

> Drew: Cassandra, we need to talk about this.
> Call me.

Cassie glanced up to see Gram watching her intently. Could she read the text from where she sat?

Clicking off the screen, Cassie dropped the phone back into her bag before turning to her sister again.

"I'm here for anything you need me to do. Just name it. Your wedding will be absolutely perfect."

Throwing herself into the final wedding prep was just what she needed to wash her hands of all the emotion of the weekend. By the time Tyler and Gemma said *I do*, Cassie would be asking, "Drew who?"

Chapter Six

Aside from some noises in the kitchen, the house was mostly quiet when Brad woke the next morning. Breathing in a warm vanilla aroma, he picked his phone up from the coffee table and lit up the screen. The time blinked back at him: 6:45. Hallie must have a client if she was up baking already. His cousin had started her home bakery last year to help bring in a little extra cash to supplement her college scholarship.

Pushing himself into a sitting position, he straightened his legs, flattening the bottoms of his feet against the opposite arm of the couch. He hadn't had the most comfortable sleep last night, but it was a far cry better than the floor in Tyler's room.

After stretching the cricks out of his back, he left the living room and headed past the front entryway, down the hallway next to the stairs and pushed through the swinging door into the kitchen. Hallie stood with her back to him, her blonde hair gathered in a low ponytail, pouring flour into the electric mixer on the counter. A metal sheet of already prepared cookies sat on top of the stove, and more were cooling on a wire rack set up on the center island behind her.

"Morning," he said groggily, rubbing a hand down one side of his face.

She paused in her task to glance at him. "Hey. Are you feeling better?" she asked, setting the empty cup down on the marble countertop before picking up a container of baking powder.

He nodded, though she couldn't see it now that her attention had shifted to measuring out the white powder with a metal measuring spoon. "Much better. There's nothing a good meal, cold shower, and sleep can't fix."

He'd taken her invitation from last night to heart and crashed soon after he'd eaten and showered. Driving all day always exhausted him anyway, so it was just as well.

"You're at it early this morning," he said, leaning his hip against the stove. His dad had put in a brand new one shortly after he and Tyler had left. In fact, the counters and microwave were fairly new as well. It figured he'd wait until the girls moved in for an upgrade. Brad had nearly set the kitchen on fire—by accident, of course—after only living here a few months, so he couldn't really blame his dad for waiting.

Hallie's focus didn't stray from her work. "My mom called from the airport to tell me they were boarding." Her parents and younger brother were flying in from Miami this morning to help with the final wedding prep. "When I got off the phone, I thought I might as well get started on these. They have to be baked, frosted, and decorated by eleven so I can deliver them to an anniversary party on our way to lunch. You're invited, by the way. My parents are paying."

"How can I say no to free food?" Brad teased, lifting his eyebrows. "Need some help?"

She pursed her mouth to the side, seeming to think it over. "Thanks, but not right now. I could use an extra hand when it comes to packaging and delivering them though. Nine dozen cookies are more than my arms can carry."

"Sure. I'm at your disposal. Besides getting my car fixed, I don't have any definite plans this week anyway."

"Except your cousin's wedding," she said dryly.

Brad's mouth lifted. "Oh, is that why I'm here?"

Hallie laughed at his feigned memory lapse. "Help yourself to anything you can find for breakfast," she said, measuring out some salt and dumping it into the mixing bowl along with the flour and baking powder.

"Thanks." Reaching for one of the cookies on the metal sheet, he received a quick whack on the back of his knuckles with her measuring spoon. He snapped his hand back and winced.

"The cookies aren't included," she scolded, grabbing a hot pad and moving the pan out of his reach. "They're not for you. And don't even think about sneaking one when I'm not looking. I'm counting every single one of them."

He walked to the fridge, massaging his knuckles. "I was just teasing you. I wouldn't really take one."

"Yeah right. I know you better than that. Your guilt is written all over your face."

That brought a small laugh out of him.

"When is the rest of your family getting in town?" she asked, apparently satisfied that her warning had come through.

Brad pulled eggs, hash browns, cheese, and milk out of the fridge and set them on the counter. "Tuesday. Brooklyn has a swim meet tomorrow night, so they can't drive down until after that."

"I bet you're excited to see her," Hallie said, adding two sticks of butter to the mixer.

Brad nodded. "We talk on the phone at least once a week, but I haven't been home since Christmas."

Hallie turned on the mixer, and the grinding noise filling the kitchen made further conversation difficult. As he waited for her to finish, he nudged the cookie sheet to the side so he could free a single burner, then set to work cracking the eggs into a small bowl.

After adding all the other ingredients, he whisked them together and dumped the mixture into the skillet. With his eyes away from the door, he didn't notice a third person enter until two hands clasped his shoulders from behind, startling him. He turned his head to see who it was, and a wide smile broke onto his face.

"There he is," he said, setting the spatula down on the counter and turning fully to face his cousin. "The man of the hour."

"Hey, buddy." Tyler's short blond hair stuck out in several places and the creases on one side of his face showed that he'd barely fallen out of bed. "It's good to see you. You couldn't even wait up for me to get home last night before passing out? What's with that?" He smiled as they embraced.

Brad gave him a hearty slap on the back before letting go. "Hey, you were the one who had the audacity to be gone when you knew I was coming. This one's on you." He winked at Hallie, who watched the exchange, her mouth tipped up in amusement.

"Sorry, man. I had to take a few things over to Gemma's and ended up staying longer than I intended." A mischievous glint appeared in his blue eyes. "But let's face it: I'd rather be with her than you. No offense."

"You are committing to spend forever with her," Brad said, stirring his eggs before they burned. "It would be a little problematic if you didn't, don't you think?"

Despite growing up on opposite sides of the country—and even on two different continents for several of those years—he'd always considered Tyler one of his best friends. A lot of his core childhood memories involved getting into scrapes with him at family get-togethers. He couldn't be happier for his cousin.

"Speaking of the wedding..." Hesitation entered Tyler's expression, and he backed up a few steps, pulling out one of the bar stools tucked under the center island and lowering himself onto it. "Cassie showed up while I was over there. She told us about running into you."

Oh boy, Brad thought, adopting a casual air as he flipped off the burner. "What did she say about it?" She'd probably gone into great detail about how much he'd ruined her day by stopping.

"She seemed ... frustrated." Tyler placed his hands between his knees. "Look, I know you two don't like each other, but she's Gemma's sister. Could you please put whatever feud the two of you have to rest until I'm safely on my honeymoon? I love you, man, but the last thing I want to think about while lying on a beach in Hawaii is how you messed up the wedding."

Did he really think Brad would let his feelings for Cassie come to that?

"What happened between you two, anyway?" Hallie asked, grabbing the smaller spatula and beginning to move the cookies from the baking sheet to another wire rack. "All I saw was her dump her drink over your head and storm out. What made her so mad? She's usually such a nice person."

Brad shook his head, just as confused as Hallie as to what had made Cassie so mad. Sure, he did hassle her a bit throughout the night, but he'd teased everyone else too, and none of them had taken offense to it.

He retrieved a plate from one of the upper cabinets to the side of the stove and slid the scrambled eggs onto it before turning back to Tyler. "Did you give her this same speech?"

"I'm leaving that up to Gemma," Tyler said. He clasped a hand on Brad's shoulder when he claimed the stool next to him. "Look, pal, I'm not asking you to like her. Just please promise you'll try a little harder to get along until the wedding is over. That's all. Once Gemma and I are married, you can go back to hating each other's guts."

Hate was such a strong word. There were very few people, if any, that Brad actually hated. And despite his grudge against Cassie, she didn't make the list. Was he confused at why she was so disgusted by him? Yes. Annoyed by the way she always acted like she was better than him? Yes. A thousand percent.

Yet he was also self-aware enough to know that he could be a bit much for some people.

But so could she. And he didn't love the idea of being in the same room with her. Or having to work closely together to pull off this wedding. That was part of being an adult, though, taking the high road even when he'd rather not.

"I promise," he said with a shrug. "I'll try harder to be nice to her."

"Thanks, man." Tyler patted his shoulder again and rose from his stool. "That's all I'm asking."

As his cousin went about the kitchen making his own breakfast,

Brad dove into his eggs, though his mind was far from food. His cousin's request seemed like an easy ask while his unintended nemesis was out of sight. But with Cassie's spitfire personality and ability to hold a grudge, he suspected that once they were in the same room again, it would be a lot harder to fulfill his promise.

Chapter Seven

When her sister emerged from the changing room in her wedding dress at Behind the Veil Boutique, Cassie realized she hadn't adequately prepared herself for the overwhelming sadness that would pummel her heart. Biting her cheek, she did her best to blink away the tears while Gemma stepped onto the pedestal facing the line of mirrors at the back of the shop.

She was a vision of loveliness in the deep V-neck gown. The cap sleeves were made of sheer lace, which also ran along the inside of the neckline. A layer of chiffon ruching crisscrossed down the bodice, ending at her waist.

Pull yourself together, Cassie thought as she placed the simple veil over her sister's dark curls. Now was not the time to cry over Drew. *This week isn't about you. You can fall to pieces when she's on her honeymoon.*

She could always confide in Mom if the emotions became too desperate to carry alone. But Cassie wasn't ready to tell her parents of her broken engagement. They'd be sympathetic, of course, though they also had the frustrating tendency of finding the silver lining in everything. And right now, Cassie just wanted to feel. Besides, their plane wasn't scheduled to land in Los Angeles for several more hours.

Stepping back from the pedestal, she studied her twin in the full-length mirror in front of them. "Oh, Gem. Look at you!" Her hands flew to cover her mouth.

"Isn't she lovely?" Lena, the shop owner said from Gemma's other side, talking to them both through the reflection in the mirror. "Your fiancé is a very lucky man."

"Absolutely gorgeous." Cassie smiled up at her sister, her eyes still stinging with tears.

Gemma took in her reflection, touching a finger to the elegant beading that lined the waist, then running her hand down the flowing chiffon skirt. "Thank you." Pink tinted her cheeks. She'd always had a hard time responding to compliments. The blush only added to her radiant aura.

Lena crouched down and began arranging the hem of the dress to check for any last minute adjustments that needed to be made before the wedding. From up on the pedestal, Gemma bent slightly to grab Cassie's hand.

"I can't tell you how glad I am that you came early." Her face fell when she looked at her sister. "What's wrong?"

Cassie couldn't keep her breakup a secret forever. Her family would know something was up when the wedding she'd been obsessing over for a year didn't happen. But if she opened up now, it would only bring down Gemma's mood.

"I'm just so thrilled for you and Tyler." She meant that with every piece of her soul. Gemma had won the heart of the man she'd loved since their childhood. A perfect wedding day would be the icing on the cake of her beautiful love story.

But immersing herself in all the last-minute details only reminded Cassie of everything *she'd* lost in the last forty-eight hours.

She blinked more moisture from her eyes. She hadn't allowed herself to fully cry over Drew. It was only a matter of time before the dam broke. And if she started now, she wouldn't be able to stop.

Choking out an embarrassed laugh, she said, "Are you glad I talked you out of wearing your sweats to the ceremony?"

Gemma tilted her head side to side, pondering the question. "I would've been more comfortable, that's for sure. But I'm only getting married once. I guess I can suffer through one day of wearing a dress."

Cassie smiled. Thank goodness her sister had come to her senses.

"I'm all done here," Lena said, rising to her feet and scrutinizing the gown's hem with her hands on her hips. "I have a few minor adjustments to make, but I'll have it ready well before Sunday."

"Thank you for all your hard work on it. I love it." Gemma shook her head in amusement. "I never thought I'd say that about a dress."

"That means I've done my job," Lena said. "A bride should always be in love with her wedding gown. It's almost as important as the man, I say."

Cassie and Gemma shared a chuckle, which was interrupted by a tinkling of the bell above the door at the front of the shop. Lena turned in that direction, though the partition dividing the fitting area from the sales floor prevented her from seeing who'd entered.

She glanced at her watch. "That's probably my next appointment. Go ahead and change. You can leave the dress hanging in the fitting room. I'll grab it after you leave."

With a few parting words, she hurried away, and Cassie slid the veil off her sister's hair, draping it neatly over her forearm.

"Do you need help getting out of this?" she asked, walking with Gemma to the three dressing rooms behind the line of mirrors.

Her sister opened the door to the middle room, revealing her clothes draped clumsily over the small chair in the corner. "No, I think I can get it. But will you undo the button?"

Cassie unhooked the pearl at the nape of Gemma's neck. Much of the back was open down to the waist except for a sheer lace lining held together by a single pearl.

"I'll be out front when you're done," she said before walking out to the sales floor.

A petite woman stood across the room, her face glowing with new-bride excitement, piercing the knife deeper into Cassie's splintering heart. Lena held a clipboard in her hands, jotting down notes as the young woman talked animatedly.

Cassie turned away from them. Pretending to browse through a rack of bridesmaid dresses, she tried to push away the deepening sadness at the reminder of the day she'd walked into Kleinfeld's in search of her perfect gown.

She blinked back more tears as she pictured the gorgeous Vera Wang dress she no longer had use for. She'd found *the dress,* with all its lace, the sweetheart neckline and fitted bodice that flared out halfway down her legs. Now she'd never get to wear it. Even if she ever did find another man, it would always remind her of Drew.

"You ready?"

Cassie startled at Gemma's voice right behind her.

Her sister gave her an odd look, then held up her phone. "Tyler texted me a minute ago. He just picked up Gram at the house, and they're heading for the restaurant now." His parents had graciously invited Cassie and Grandma June to join them for their family brunch.

"Yep, let's go," Cassie said, leading the way outside, the bell above the door chiming their farewell way too loudly.

"When is Drew getting in?" Gemma asked once they were in the car. She turned in the driver's seat to check behind her as she backed out of the parking spot. "He's still coming on Tuesday like you originally planned, right?"

Cassie had hoped to avoid that question for at least another day. She cleared her throat. "He's not coming."

"He's not?" Gemma braked before turning out of the parking lot. She looked at her sister, confusion written plainly on her face. "Did something come up at work? I remember you said he was in the middle of a huge case."

Cassie didn't answer right away. Her chin wobbled, and she could already feel the tears welling in her eyes again.

Gemma reached across the center console for her hand. "Cassie? What is it?"

The concern in her tone cut right through Cassie's core. There was no point in fighting the sorrow any longer, so she hung her head and gave in to the ugly sobs gripping her body. Tears raced down both cheeks, dropping onto the black and white flowers of her sundress. Gemma gripped her hand tighter, offering what little support she could while strapped in a car.

"I called off the wedding," Cassie finally squeaked out. "It's over for good this time."

Her sobs were the only sounds inside the car. They started moving again, and for a moment, she thought her sister somehow knew that she didn't want to talk about it. But then they stopped again, and she heard the click of a seatbelt before arms came around her from across the center console.

"What happened?" Gemma asked softly.

Cassie rested her head on her sister's shoulder, savoring the comfort of having her twin to help her work through her grief. There was a time in their lives when this wouldn't have been the case. "I found out some things that made me realize I didn't want to spend the rest of my life with him."

Gemma was silent for a beat, like she didn't know what to say. But she continued her tight hold on her sister. "I'm so sorry. Why didn't you tell me earlier?"

"We're supposed to be celebrating you and Tyler. Your wedding should be the happiest day of your life." Cassie hiccupped a sob. "I refuse to ruin that by making it about me."

Her twin placed her hands on Cassie's cheeks. "I love that you want to make my wedding so perfect. But you're my sister, and I'm here for you whenever you need to talk. I mean it. Even if I'm on my honeymoon."

Cassie felt her lips curve up a bit. "I think Tyler would have some objections to that."

"Well, he can deal with it." Gemma laughed. "When you marry one twin, you marry the other."

Cassie dabbed under her eyes with the back of her hand. Her waterproof mascara was going the distance today. "Thanks, but we should get going. We don't want to keep the Abernathys waiting."

Gemma nodded, and they finally left the parking lot. The drive to Trattoria d'Italia was done mostly in silence. Cassie appreciated the time to pull herself together before they met up with everyone else.

When they pulled into the parking lot at the bistro located on the outskirts of town, they found a spot near a bubbling spring in the corner of the lot. A blanket of trees surrounded the rustic building on three sides, blocking the street behind it from view, like a fairytale haven hidden inside a modern suburb. Even after countless visits as a child, it never failed to surprise Cassie how different Buena Hills felt from other big city suburbs. It was a refreshing change from the craziness of urban living. She could see herself settling down in a place like this if she ever got her fill of New York.

"There's Tyler," Gemma said, throwing open her door.

He stood near the entrance chatting with his parents and younger brother. If Cassie did the math correctly, Wes had to be a senior in high school now. She hadn't seen him since his family had moved away from their expat community in Chile. He'd grown a lot from the little boy he'd been back when the Abernathys had lived next door. Only an inch or two shorter than Tyler's six feet, his facial features resembled those of his three older siblings. All the Abernathy kids had inherited their father's smile and their mother's blond hair. His waves were long enough to swoop out to the side, reminding Cassie of a surfer.

Gram stood at Tyler's other side, her arm resting in the crook of his elbow for support. In his free hand, he held her folded-up walker. She despised that contraption and took any opportunity she could not to use it. Only a few hours ago, Cassie had walked in on her shuffling around the kitchen, attempting to make breakfast for everyone, her walker nowhere in sight. It had taken Cassie and Gemma a full thirty minutes to find it stashed in the small gap between the washing machine and the wall.

"How am I supposed to use my hands when I have to hold onto this thing?" Gram had grumbled after the walker had been found and she was safely seated in a chair at the kitchen table.

"By letting us be your hands," Cassie had responded while asserting control of the breakfast prep. "You've taken care of us our entire lives. Now it's our turn to take care of you."

She smiled, thinking about Gram's fierce independence. Oh, how she missed her grandmother, living so far away.

Gemma hurried off to greet Tyler and Gram. After stretching onto her toes to kiss her fiancé, she pressed her cheek against Gram's. Cassie turned away from the happy scene, pulling a compact mirror from her bag to check the damage her little sob session had done to her complexion. Her eyes were still lined with red, and she'd cried off most of her mascara.

Apparently, the waterproof label didn't apply to uncontrollable crying in the car. Good to know. At least the blotches had pretty much faded, and there weren't any black streaks running down her cheeks. But she'd still need to sneak to the bathroom to touch up her makeup once they got inside.

Dropping the mirror back into her purse, she walked over to Tyler's parents to say hello. Before she reached them, someone caught her attention on the other side of the parking lot. She turned toward the new arrivals, and her gut twisted when she met Brad's eye. Why hadn't she realized he'd be here? Tyler's humongous extended family had a tight-knit bond. Of course this lunch invitation would be extended to those relatives already in town.

Cassie held back a groan as he crossed the parking lot followed closely by his sister and cousins. *He must be staying with them,* she thought, wondering why she cared.

He greeted his uncle with a firm handshake, clapping his other hand on Mr. Abernathy's shoulder. Against her will, her eyes traveled from the short wave of Brad's dark blond hair downward, stopping at the way his pressed blue dress shirt and chinos showed off his stocky but muscular build. So different from the rumpled, sweaty look she'd seen him in yesterday. It would be difficult for any woman not to notice that he was an attractive man. But he didn't carry himself in the refined, powerful way that Drew did.

Her eyes went wide. What was she doing comparing Brad to Drew? Brad's laid-back, California vibe didn't hold a candle to her ex.

Ugh, why did Drew still have such a hold over her? She had to stop thinking about the qualities that she'd once seen as turn ons. Correction: she needed to stop thinking about him, period.

As Brad bent to hug Tyler's mom, his eyes landed on Cassie and the affectionate smile intended for his aunt dropped. But he didn't look away. Wariness entered his expression as he watched her watching him.

Brad Lucas, wary? She never would've thought that possible. He'd always given the impression of being overconfident.

Just then, the maître d' came out to usher them all inside, breaking the tentative connection between Brad and Cassie. Everyone filed in by twos and threes, led by Mr. and Mrs. Abernathy. Tyler, Gemma, and Gram went next, followed by Wes and Beej. And right behind them, Tyler's sisters and their friend, Kendall, whom Cassie had met the last time she was in town.

Brad shoved his hands into his pockets as he fell into step beside Cassie at the back of the group. "Hey," he said in a tone that couldn't be considered unfriendly but didn't give off any vibes that he was happy to be in her company.

She nodded to him, keenly aware that the evidence of her emotional breakdown was all over her face. "I see you took my advice about that shower." *Smooth one, Cassie.* Why did he always bring out her snarky side? She wasn't normally a mean person.

Contrary to the verbal barb she expected from him, he just shrugged. "I thought I'd try it to see if I liked it." His mouth twitched, drawing her attention to his full lips.

I bet those would be fun to kiss.

Whoa!

What?

Where had that come from? She hadn't made out with a guy for kicks since high school. Okay, early college. Definitely not since she'd met Drew.

Silence fell between them, though the conversations in front of them mingled with the Italian music playing low throughout the open room. The processional wove past tables covered in white cloths. Single red roses in glass vases made up the simple center-pieces at each table. Off-white twinkle lights strung along the ceiling created a cozy ambiance in the dimly lit space.

As the group reached a separate room in the back of the restau-rant, Cassie's phone buzzed in her clutch, vibrating against her side.

Why is Sylvie calling? she thought after pulling it out and noticing her friend's name on the screen. She dropped back from the others to answer.

Sylvie's frazzled voice greeted her as soon as she held the phone up to her ear. "Where've you been? I stopped by your apartment this morning and you weren't there."

"I'm in California for the wedding," Cassie said. "I needed to get away from the city for a while, so I decided to come early."

"California?" Sylvie's voice grew pitchy. "What about the party? You promised you'd help."

The party? Cassie brought a hand to her forehead. *The party!*

After the horrible events of Friday morning, she'd been so focused on getting out of New York that she hadn't given Adelaide's birthday a second thought. "Oh, my gosh. I completely forgot."

"Yeah, I think you did," Sylvie whined.

Cassie pinched the bridge of her nose with her fingers, guilt churning her stomach. Her friend had come to her rescue the other day when she'd needed her most. How could she forget one of the few times Sylvie asked for help?

With a sigh, Cassie raised her head, inadvertently looking into the room where the first course was already being served. Multiple conversations were going on at once, many of them punctuated with laughter. No one noticed Cassie, again on the verge of tears, in the doorway.

No one except Brad.

Just perfect. Of all the people who could've noticed her emotional breakdown, it had to be him. Brad Lucas surely wouldn't let her forget about this. In fact, he'd surely find some way to use it against her.

She turned away, pressing her back against the wall. "I'm so sorry. Was it terrible?"

Sylvie sighed. "No, it wasn't that bad. I talked my sister out of the pony, thankfully. But still, I could've really used your help."

Should Cassie tell her bestie why she'd left New York in such a hurry? She wanted to. Sylvie's hype-girl attitude was exactly what she needed right about now. But that would only be making excuses for forgetting about the party.

"I'm really sorry, Sylv," Cassie said again. "How can I make it up to you?"

"Well..." Sylvie drew out the word as though she already had something in mind. "I've never been to the West Coast. You can bring me back something authentically Californian. And I'm not talking about a T-shirt."

Cassie laughed, despite her heavy heart. "You got it. Prepare to be amazed. I'll find something perfect for you."

By the time they hung up a few minutes later, Cassie's broken commitment was water under the bridge. And yet, she still felt awful. She'd come to Buena Hills to step away from everything for a while, but the problems kept piling on top of her. First, she'd blown up her job. Then she'd taken a pickaxe to her future marriage. And on top of it all, she'd let her best friend down.

She used to have everything she could've wanted. Now, her life lay in crumbled pieces at her feet.

Chapter Eight

Cassie had been crying. For the life of him, Brad couldn't wrap his head around why that bothered him. And the fact that it did made him grumpier than he cared to admit.

Grumbling silently to himself, he picked up his fork and pushed the lettuce around the decorative plate in front of him. This bland salad didn't help his mood. Was it too much to ask for a nice, medium-rare steak to magically appear as the main course?

Lively conversations danced around the table, as it always did whenever his family got together. Brad caught a few words here and there, but his position toward the middle of the table made it hard to focus on a single one. Across from him, Hallie whispered something to Elise, who registered her comment with a barely detectable smile and nod. She'd been so mopey since he'd arrived in town. What had caused his usually happy cousin to lose her zest for life?

He took a bite of leafy greens, absentmindedly chewing as his mind returned to Cassie. It made no sense to be so drawn to her. Though considering all the women he'd pursued with disastrous results—including Mandy—she fit the pattern. He needed to remind himself that the flashy, popular girls never made good dating material. They might provide a nice distraction for a while, right up until the moment he realized he was their pawn in sticking it to their preferred man. Brad was tired of being someone else's rebound. He'd rather be single for life than risk putting himself through that one more time. A guy could only take so many shots to the ego before bowing out of the dating game completely.

Next to him, Beej's laughter rang out above the murmur of voices. He glanced at her, shaking his head at the way she shamelessly flirted with the dark-haired waiter refilling her water glass.

The man winked at her, his smile revealing deep dimples in both cheeks.

"What?" she asked after the waiter had walked away and she noticed Brad watching her.

"I thought you were dating someone. That architect. Parker? Percy? Or was it Patrick?"

"His name was Peter," Hallie said, joining the conversation. "And he's an accountant. Jeremy was the architect."

Brad pointed his fork at her. "That's the one. I knew it started with a P. He didn't last long."

Beej speared a few pieces of lettuce onto her fork. "It just didn't work out." She slid the bite into her mouth, seemingly unconcerned with the fact that they were talking about her most recent ex. They could be discussing the weather, or what they'd had for breakfast with the nonchalant way she acted right now.

Brad squinted in confusion. Finding Mr. Right, getting married, and raising a bunch of babies had always been her biggest aspiration in life. And she was borderline adamant those things were the ticket to making everyone else happy too. She'd already suggested multiple friends she thought would be a "good match" for him.

Not in a million years.

"Don't look at me like that," she said, matching his narrow-eyed expression. "I know what you're thinking. But I have my standards too, and he didn't cut it. So now I'm single again, and you can bet I'm ready to mingle." She shimmied a little in her seat.

"Of course you are," he muttered with a smirk, stabbing at a strawberry on his plate.

It never took her long to get back into the dating scene after a breakup. She'd be attached to someone new by the end of the week. Maybe even that waiter. He was still making googly eyes at her from across the room. She did a little finger wave, and he smiled.

Brad rolled his eyes and looked away from the love connection his sister seemed to be making. At least *she* was having a good time in the dating market.

As he focused again on his food, the seat on the other side of him slid away from the table, and Cassie sat down in it. His gut clenched.

It makes no sense, he reminded himself. She'd made it crystal clear from their first meeting that she didn't like him. He shouldn't still be so drawn to her.

"Hey, everyone," she said cheerfully. "What did I miss?"

Brad didn't bother answering. If he opened his mouth, he'd probably say something to offend her, and this was neither the time nor the place to engage in verbal warfare. Not to mention he'd promised Tyler he'd be on his best behavior around her.

"Just the first course," Hallie responded. She gave Brad an odd look when he met her eye. Could she tell he was holding something back? She had a tendency of being frustratingly perceptive in her ability to read people. "I'm sure if you asked, they'll bring you out a plate."

"That's okay, I can wait for the main course." Cassie unrolled her cloth napkin and placed it neatly in her lap, laying the silverware back on the table. "I saw them getting ready to bring it out on my way back from the restroom."

Brad peeked at her from out of the corner of his eye. She'd applied a fresh layer of mascara on her long lashes, covering up the last remnants of tears as if she hadn't been crying before they'd entered the restaurant.

"Brad, I talked to your mom a few days ago," Tyler's dad said from one end of the table as waiters came by to clear the empty salad dishes. "She told me about your new job. It sounds like a nice gig."

Uncle Jason was Mom's older brother. Brad wouldn't be surprised if she'd bragged about his job change to all her siblings through their group text thread. Which meant he'd have to prepare himself to be bombarded with all sorts of questions once the rest of the family trickled in for the wedding. They were always up in everyone's business, which was both a good thing and a bad thing.

"You got the job?" Tyler asked, from the opposite end of the table. "Congrats, man!"

"It's in LA, right? So you'll be moving back down here?" Elise asked, before taking a sip from her water glass.

He felt Cassie's attention on him as he answered his cousin's question. "That's right. I'll be working as a sports analyst for USC. I'm hoping I'll have some time to look at a few apartments while I'm here this week."

"You should," Tyler said. "We have our tux fitting tomorrow, but besides that, I don't think we'll need you until later in the week." He glanced at his fiancée seated beside him, her hand tucked into his, for confirmation. Gemma nodded in agreement.

Hallie crossed her arms on the table and leaned forward. "Are those the guys who talk about the games on TV?"

Brad blinked at her, and it wasn't until she looked around the table that he realized Tyler, Uncle Jason, and Wes were all giving her equally appalled glances.

"Oh, come on," she scoffed. "You all know I'm clueless when it comes to sports."

Brad chuckled. "Yes, I'll be commentating. Not football, unfortunately, but hopefully after I get some more broadcasting experience, I'll be able to slide into the big-ticket sports. I'm also teaming up with two other analysts to start a new sports radio show on campus."

"It'll be nice to have you close by again," Tyler said after the chorus of congratulations from the rest of the group had died down. "Maybe we can grab lunch every once in a while." He'd recently started his new job as a journalist for a travel website based in Los Angeles.

The serving staff arrived again with the main course. Brad bobbed his head in thanks when Beej's hunk set the plate of chicken in front of him. He turned his attention to his food, eager to dig in. Ignoring the sounds of his sister's flirting, he took his first bite.

He had to admit, it was pretty good, bursting with lemon and tomato flavor. And the Italian spices added a nice kick. It wasn't the steak he'd hoped for, but it would do as a substitute.

Next to him, Cassie quietly cut her meat into neat little bites. She speared one onto her fork and placed it daintily into her mouth. Man, she even ate like a princess.

In the middle of chewing, she noticed him watching her and swallowed. Her eyes narrowed. "Is something wrong?"

"No," Brad said, going back to cutting his chicken.

After a beat of silence, she spoke again. "It's good, isn't it?" She placed another politely sized bite into her mouth.

He bobbed his head slowly, though he could tell out of the corner of his eye that her attention hadn't wavered from her food as if she, like him, was trying to be civil. Maybe Gemma had made the same request that Tyler had given him. "Yeah, it is."

More silence followed before she said, "Of course, it's not the burger I'm really in the mood for, but I guess it will do."

Brad snorted, and his fork froze halfway to his mouth. He put it down on his plate and turned toward her, trying to hide his amusement. She didn't seem like the kind of woman to settle for something like a burger. Wouldn't that be considered peasant food for royalty like her?

She met his gaze, a comically innocent look entering her hazel eyes. "What? Am I not supposed to say that here?"

"You're allowed to say whatever you want." He broke off a sizable bite of chicken. In an undertone, he said, "I was hoping for a steak," before popping it into his mouth.

What happened next took him by surprise, and he almost choked on his food. Cassie grinned. And not a pity grin, or one of indulgence. No, this was a full smile that transformed her entire face into a masterpiece of radiance because of something *he'd* said. He didn't know why but his chest swelled. For once, her beauty didn't make him grumpy.

"Congratulations on your new job, by the way," she said after they'd gone back to eating quietly. "It sounds like you're really moving up in your career."

Brad swallowed hard, an unexpected trickle of disappointment settling in his stomach. Sure, he was moving up. He had every reason to be thrilled. But he couldn't seem to make peace with the way his life had turned out. A few years ago, his path was destined for greatness. Now he was a washed-up has-been, forced to settle for his fallback plan.

"Thanks," he said after chasing his bitter feelings down with a long swig from his water glass. "It'll be nice to do something other than the behind-the-scenes stuff."

"Yeah, I get that." Her tone spoke of sadness, and she kept her focus on her food.

"You do?" He couldn't help asking the question, though he found himself wanting to return their conversation to lighter things.

She looked at him, and her eyes held a dissatisfaction that he'd never seen on her before. "Sorry, I just have some things on my mind. It's nothing."

"Your phone call earlier?" he asked before he could catch himself.

Her head jerked his way again. "What about it?"

He shrugged, realizing from her tone that he needed to proceed with caution. "You seemed ... tense. Everything okay?"

She watched him warily for a few seconds, making Brad even more curious about what had bothered her earlier.

"Of course," she said finally. "Everything's ... fine. Just a silly disagreement with a friend. But we worked it out."

There was definitely more to it. But why would she tell him? They weren't bosom buddies. They weren't even casual acquaintances. She'd never choose to confide in him any more than he would in her.

"Listen," Cassie started again after a few minutes. "I ... uh ... think I owe you an apology."

Well, she was full of surprises today. "For what?"

She blew out a tense breath, then squared her shoulders as she shifted to face him again. Her bare knee brushed against his thigh, sending a wave of goosebumps traveling up his leg.

"Getting that flat tire yesterday was the final straw to an already terrible weekend, and I wasn't acting like myself. You happened to come along when I was looking for a fight. I'm sorry. And ... thank you." Her brows turned down as she frowned. "For showing me how to do it myself, instead of automatically assuming I didn't want to learn."

Brad's jaw almost dropped. Women like Cassie Schalk never admitted they were wrong. And he should know based on the women he'd dated. Apparently, the princess had a humble side, after all.

"Glad I could help." He picked up his fork again. "Now you'll know what to do if it ever happens again. Maybe just work on parallel parking closer to the curb next time."

She gasped, bumping his upper arm with her elbow. But for the first time since they'd met two years ago, she didn't look like she wanted to kill him.

His mouth stretched into an answering smile before he cleared his throat. "I'm sorry too. I may have said some things that weren't very nice. Sometimes my mouth runs away from me."

She studied his face for a minute, and Brad couldn't begin to guess at the thoughts running through her mind. Then she bobbed her head once. "Apology accepted."

Just like that? Maybe this week wouldn't be so bad after all.

But it couldn't be that easy.

Could it?

Chapter Nine

"Thanks for driving me over here," Gemma said from the passenger seat as Cassie parked across the street from Tyler's house. An agent from the rental company had dropped off her new car earlier, assuring her that there wouldn't be an extra charge on her bill since the flat hadn't been her fault. What a relief.

Cassie shut off the engine and removed the keys from the ignition before turning to her sister. "It's no problem. But I thought you were meeting Tyler at the estate." He and Gemma had an appointment with Sydney, their wedding planner, for a final walkthrough of the venue before the big day. "Why'd he ask you to come here first?"

"Hallie wanted to show me the cake, so I told her I'd stop by this morning," Gemma said, opening her door. "Tyler and I agreed it would be easier to drive together anyway."

As they walked up the pathway toward the two-story bungalow with the wide front porch, Cassie's phone vibrated in her Louis Vuitton handbag. Digging through her things, she pulled it out and frowned when Drew's name flashed across the screen.

Seriously, what did he want? She'd given back his ring. Washed her hands of him completely. Well, not completely. She still had to notify the invitees not to show up for the wedding, cancel the venue, and the caterer, etcetera, etcetera. But those could all wait until she got back to New York and was more equal to the task.

The fact that he'd waited three days to call her had made her think he'd gotten the hint that she was serious this time. That maybe he'd finally realized he'd really blown it by throwing her under the bus.

"Is everything okay?" Gemma asked, her brows furrowing when

Cassie dragged her eyes away from her phone. "Do you need to take that?"

Cassie forced a smile onto her face and clicked off the screen to send the call to voicemail. "No. Everything's fine." She dropped her phone into her bag and followed her sister up the stone steps to the front door.

While they waited for someone to answer, Cassie rested her arms across the stone balustrade, admiring the small but neatly trimmed rose garden below her while she tried to push Drew out of her mind. This week was about getting away from all her problems. Recharging from her traumatic last day of work. That wouldn't happen if she let one little phone call from her ex rattle her. From now on, all thoughts of Drew were strictly off limits.

Tyler answered the door in the next minute, his wide grin immediately falling on his fiancée. "Hey!" he greeted them, bending to give Gemma a quick peck on the lips. "Your timing is perfect. Come on in."

He tucked an arm around his soon-to-be wife, ushering her inside. Cassie followed them down the hall, past the stairs on their right side and the living room on their left. Morning sunlight streamed through the front picture window casting a spotlight of warmth on the couch where a blanket had been tossed haphazardly across the cushions. A pillow was propped against one end. That must be Brad's bed while he was in town. She could imagine his stocky frame crammed onto that couch, and she felt sorry for him. She'd sat on that couch. It was comfortable enough, but not to sleep on.

She tilted her head to one shoulder, confused at her sudden interest in his sleeping arrangements. Why should she care whether he slept comfortably or not? Having one relatively normal conversation with the guy didn't make them all buddy-buddy.

Speeding up her steps, she pushed through the swinging door of the kitchen behind the almost-newlyweds. Elise and Kendall sat on stools at the marbled center island, while Hallie, bent at the waist, stood in front of an elegant three-tiered cake. Holding a piping bag with both hands, she carefully dabbed little blue buds onto the edge of the bottom layer. An elaborate blue orchid with its petals open rested on top of the highest tier.

"Wow!" Gemma exclaimed, approaching the cake for a closer look. "Hallie, it looks even more beautiful than you described."

Hallie set the piping bag on the island and stepped back, smiling proudly. "Do you like it? I kind of messed up on this part right here —" She turned the cake on its stand to show the spot where the white waves of icing were a little smashed. The mistake was barely noticeable. "—but I won't do that on the real thing."

"This isn't the real cake?" Kendall asked, propping both elbows on top of the counter.

"Not unless you want to eat cardboard." Hallie picked up a leveling knife and tapped the broad side of the blade on the bottom tier. A hollow thunk sounded underneath. "This is just so I can practice decorating. I've made a bunch of cakes for birthdays, a couple for graduation parties, and there was that one for Carmen Jimenez's quinceañera a few months ago. I've never had to make a wedding cake though. Unless you count that one I did back in culinary school, but that was a while ago. I want this one to be perfect."

Tyler squeezed his younger sister's shoulder. "It's going to be great." He reached around her to swipe his finger through the buttercream of the middle tier, then licked it clean. "Mmmm, if the rest of the cake is as good as this frosting, it'll be a hit."

Hallie shoved him away gently, laughing. "Stop ruining my decorating."

"I wish you'd let us pay you for this," Gemma cut in before Tyler could sneak his finger back for another swipe. "I don't want to take advantage of you."

Although Hallie had only been eleven when the Abernathys moved away from their expat community in Chile, Tyler's youngest sister had dreamed of owning her own bakery even then. As their next-door neighbors, the Schalks had often been the recipients of

Hallie's creations. The fact that she'd finally started her own business didn't surprise Cassie at all.

Hallie waved away Gemma's comment. "I already told you. This is my wedding gift to you. But since you mentioned it, I'd love a glowing review on my social media profiles. And I wouldn't say no if you were to name your first child after me."

Laughing more dramatically than the situation warranted, Tyler draped an arm around her neck as though placing her in a headlock. "I'll have to discuss that with my co-conspirator over there." He wiggled his brows suggestively at his fiancée and winked. Gemma threw a look of exasperated amusement back his way.

"Let's keep the bedroom door firmly closed with this conversation," Kendall said, shutting down the implied topic. "I'd rather not have images of what you'll be doing on your honeymoon stuck in my head."

"You mean watching hours of baseball while stuffing their faces with pizza and donuts?" Elise's mouth lifted in the first smile Cassie had seen from her since she'd arrived. Tyler's usually chatty sister had been rather subdued at lunch yesterday too. So different than Cassie remembered from when they were kids.

She didn't have much time to contemplate the change in Elise before the kitchen door swung open with a whoosh, and Brad walked in, dressed in basketball shorts and a solid white tee, his hair still damp from a shower. Cassie's stomach gave an involuntary flip, and she silently groaned. *Don't start now.*

He crossed the kitchen with his phone to his ear, putting up one finger when Tyler started to say something to him. His clean scent permeated Cassie's senses as he passed her, an inviting mix of masculine body wash and peppermint.

"Hey, Carlos!" he spoke into the phone, disappearing into the mud room. A light flipped on in the garage a second later. "How's it hangin', man?"

He left the garage door open, his muffled voice carrying into the kitchen, though his words weren't clear enough for Cassie to understand. Unable to dismiss her curiosity, she found herself inching toward the door to better hear him.

What am I doing? She snapped her attention back to those occupying the kitchen.

"We better go, Ty." Gemma slid her arm around Tyler and gave his waist an affectionate pinch. "We don't want to be late for our appointment. And don't forget, you have your last tux fitting afterward. You told your groomsmen about it, right?"

"They all said to tell you they can't wait," he said dryly, though he didn't seem too put out about the task. Tyler was every bit the besotted groom that Gemma deserved. He bent and kissed the top of her head.

"Awwww," Hallie sighed. "You guys are so cute."

Cassie sighed for a different reason. She hadn't received that kind of adoring affection from anyone in a long time. Not even from Drew. She missed it, especially since coming here and being surrounded by so much happiness and love.

And that just made her mourn Drew all over again. Great. Telling herself not to think about him obviously wasn't enough to get her to stop thinking about him.

Tyler touched his temple with two fingers of his free hand and flicked them forward in a peace sign. "See you guys." Gemma waved at them as the happy couple left the room.

"Since when did the garage turn into Picasso's Playground?" Brad asked, stuffing his phone into his pocket as he reentered the kitchen. "And who's the dude in all those paintings on the card table?"

His eyes fell on Cassie, and he cocked his head to one side as if he'd only just noticed her there.

Hallie and Kendall both looked at Elise, whose cheeks had turned a rosy shade of pink. "I thought I put those away," she mumbled to her hands, taking a sudden interest in her cuticles.

Hallie went back to her decorating. Bent at the waist, she

squeezed more decorative flowers onto the cake. "Elise turned the garage into her own personal art studio."

"That explains all the cars in the driveway." Whether on purpose or not, Brad stopped right next to Cassie, leaning his back against the counter by the sink. His scent filled her space again, and she felt a strong urge to move a little closer, or maybe stick her nose into his shirt. When he cleaned himself up, his pheromones would get any woman excited. He smelled even better than Drew.

Ugh... She had to stop comparing him to her ex. Maybe this was her heart's way of working through its grief over her broken wedding plans. Or maybe she was just lonely. Sadly, it wouldn't be the only time she'd latched onto the first attractive man she came across after a breakup. She used to bounce around from guy to guy all the time back in high school.

But she wasn't that silly teenaged girl who always had to have a boyfriend anymore. Cassandra Schalk was now a mature woman, willing to be comfortable being single.

"But who's the dude?" Brad asked again.

Kendall glanced at Elise as if waiting for her to answer. She didn't, so her best friend spoke for her. "That's Elise's long lost Irish love, ripped from her by distance and broken dreams."

Elise rolled her eyes. "Thanks for that. You don't have to be sarcastic about it."

"Really? You met a guy over there?" Brad pushed off the counter and dropped onto a stool next to his cousin. "It must've been serious if you're still obsessed enough to paint creepy pictures of him."

"I really don't want to talk about this right now." Elise hopped off her stool. "I need to get ready for work." Without another word, she left the kitchen, the door swinging shut behind her.

A weird silence filled the room with her exit. So that explained her subdued mood. Cassie understood completely. The poor girl had to be heartbroken.

"Was it something I said?" Brad asked.

Cassie scowled at him. His inability to recognize why his words would come across as insensitive was another reason why she couldn't stand him. But she'd expect nothing less from Brad Lucas.

"You could've used a little more tact," Hallie said calmly, looking up from her cake. "She's questioning a lot right now."

"But she's been back from her semester abroad for a year. She hasn't moved on?"

Kendall shook her head. "Beej tried to set her up with a guy a while ago, but Elise immediately put him in the friend zone. She's not interested in moving on. I think she feels guilty about the way it ended and can't let it go."

Brad stared at the door Elise had exited, his mouth pursed to one side as though he had something on his mind. Cassie didn't miss the concern in his expression. He'd given *her* that same look when they'd met eyes across the parking lot yesterday.

After a few beats, he cleared his throat. "Anyway," he said, a lingering heaviness in his tone. "I have to take my car into the auto shop here in town. Can one of you girls come with me? I'll need a ride back."

"Sorry, no can do." Kendall stood and patted him on the shoulder on her way to the door. "I have work too."

Brad directed an expectant look toward Hallie.

"I can't either," she said. "I'm helping my parents finish planning the family bonfire today."

"You can't spare a few minutes?" Annoyance crossed Brad's face.

She shrugged. "They're going to be here any second, and I don't know how long it will take. If you wait until this afternoon—"

"I'll go with you," Cassie volunteered, immediately wishing she hadn't.

Brad glanced at her, obviously as surprised as she was. "Really?"

She silently asked herself the same question. But despite her annoyance with him a minute ago, she sadly didn't have anywhere else to be right now, and she'd begun to feel a little awkward now that Gemma had left. "Yeah, sure. You helped me with my tire. I guess I owe you a favor."

Right, she'd go with that.

He held her gaze for a long moment, and she couldn't ignore the warmth spreading through her core. Why did Brad make her want to strangle him one moment, then go weak-kneed by a look the next?

Finally, he stood, rapping his knuckles on the countertop. "Thanks. I'll go get my keys." He swaggered from the kitchen, taking Cassie's breath with him.

Chapter Ten

Brad pulled into a spot in front of Buena Hills Auto Repair and shut off the engine, hopping out before the inside of his Pathfinder could get any hotter. A few other vehicles were scattered around the small parking lot of the old brick shop, all in various stages of disrepair. The sounds of clanking metal and the grinding of an electrical tool carried to him from around the side of the building.

He wandered over to Cassie's car in the next spot, opening the driver's side door a little. "I'm hoping this won't take too long. You can stay here if you'd prefer. I'll be right back."

"That's okay," she said with a shrug. "I can come in."

Once again, she surprised him. He didn't think she'd risk soiling another outfit with car grease. She wore a puffy-sleeved top that ruffled out a little at the waist and showed the tiniest amount of her stomach above her distressed jean shorts. The look gave off a more down-to-earth country girl vibe than high-end New York fashion designer, but it suited her.

Backing up a step, he held the door open wider as she grabbed her purse from the passenger seat and slid out gracefully. Everything she did was graceful.

Instead of leading her to the entrance of the waiting area at the front of the building, Brad headed straight to the open garage around the side, a privilege of being on a first name basis with the owner. A slight breeze ruffled his T-shirt, cooling the air enough to make the July heat pleasant as opposed to stifling. Seriously, where was this breeze on Saturday during the drive down?

The smell of exhaust fumes and rubber accosted them as soon as they stepped inside the garage. He scanned the space, searching for someone who could help him. Finding no one, he cupped his hands around his mouth to be heard over the hip hop beat blaring from the speakers. "Yo, Carlos!"

A few heads poked out from behind the two cars currently being worked on, one of them suspended above the ground on a two-post lift. Carlos wasn't among them. In fact, none of the guys seemed familiar.

"Maybe we'd have better luck if we tried the front desk," Cassie suggested, gesturing to the plexiglass window looking into the waiting room.

"You're probably right. Let's go."

Before they'd taken a step, a tall, lanky man in dark gray coveralls exited a small office on the other side of the shop from where they stood. He laughed when he saw them standing there.

"Well, well, well, if it isn't Brad Lucas," he said, shaking his head. "I was wondering if I'd ever see your ugly mug back in Buena Hills."

A wide smile split the bottom half of Brad's face. "Gimpy Stevenson. Don't tell me you still work in this old dump." He gave his college friend a crushing handshake.

Gimpy's full belly laugh echoed off the concrete walls of the garage. "I have to work my way through grad school somehow." That was an ironic thing to say coming from a guy who graduated top of his class in accounting. There had to be better paying jobs available to him than making minimum wage at an auto shop.

"Is Carlos around?" Brad asked. "I talked to him on the phone earlier and he said he'd be here."

Pushing his glasses further up his nose, Gimpy said, "Yeah, he's here. I think he's in his office. I'll go grab him." He turned back toward the same room he'd come out of a minute ago.

"Thanks, man," Brad called after him. "It's good to see you."

Gimpy paused to give a quick wave before disappearing behind the door.

"Gimpy?" Cassie asked from Brad's side, the word wobbling a little in her surprise.

"It's a nickname. His real name is Paul."

She arched one of her perfect blonde eyebrows. "How in the world did he earn such a horrible nickname?"

Brad chuckled. "Back in college, I sometimes got together with some guys to play touch football on the weekends."

That was after he'd quit USC's team. A twinge of sadness settled over him. Once he'd recovered from his last concussion, those afternoons were the only connection he had with the sport he still loved. But it hadn't been the same as playing in front of a packed stadium for points that really mattered.

He pushed the lingering grief away and continued. "Gimpy would usually come along. He wasn't much of an athlete, but he made up for it in enthusiasm." Brad smiled at the memory. "Unfortunately, after one too many injuries, his roommate started calling him Gimpy, and the name stuck."

"Guys can be so weird," Cassie said through a laugh.

"You have no idea how weird we can be."

She crinkled her nose as her smile grew, her hazel eyes squinting adorably.

Wait, did he just think of Cassie Schalk as adorable? Nah, she was about as adorable as a stray kitten with rabies. She might look cute, but she'd bite his hand off if he got too close. Their interaction on Saturday had proved that, even if she'd apologized for it.

"He seems to take it in stride, at least," she said.

Brad shrugged. "Gimpy's a good one. I don't think he's capable of getting offended about anything."

"Hey, Brad." Carlos' familiar voice calling above the cocktail of noises interrupted their conversation. He walked toward them, looking almost the same as the last time Brad had seen him two years ago, except for the number of grays peppering his dark hair.

They shook hands, then Brad bumped the older man's shoulder with his. "Hey, man. It's been a long time, hasn't it?"

"Would you take a look at you?" Carlos clapped a grease-stained hand on Brad's shoulder. "San Fran has been good to you. How're your folks? I haven't talked to your dad in a while."

"Both are doing well," Brad said. "They're driving down with Brooklyn tomorrow."

Carlos folded his arms over his chest. More grease streaked across the olive skin of his arms where his coveralls were rolled up to his elbows. "Ah, for the wedding? Tell them to stop by the house for dinner while they're here. You and Beej too, of course. Sofia would love to see you all again."

"I'll tell them. Thanks."

Carlos' attention fell on Cassie, then switched back to Brad. "Who's this lovely lady? Your girlfriend?"

Cassie's brows shot up in surprise when Brad looked at her. He barked out a quick laugh that he stifled immediately. Cassie, his girlfriend? *Maybe in an alternate universe.*

"No, she's a..." How did he even classify what he and Cassie were? Not friends, certainly, despite the weird sort of truce they seemed to have forged. "She's actually Tyler's soon-to-be sister-in-law. She's here for the wedding."

Carlos stuck his hand out to her. "Carlos Rivera. Nice to meet you."

At first, Brad thought she'd balk at having to shake hands with a man with more grease under his nails than she'd probably dealt with her entire life. But she didn't hesitate before accepting the welcoming gesture.

"Cassie Schalk. It's nice to meet you too."

With the introductions complete, Carlos got down to business. "You said it was an air conditioning problem you want me to look at?"

"Yeah," Brad said. "The fans seem to be working fine, but when I turn on the AC, nothing cools down. I think the air might even get hotter."

Carlos nodded, pursing his lips as though he were pondering what the issue could be. "It could be a problem with the compressor. Or maybe a clog somewhere is preventing the fan from cooling the air. I'll take a look at it. How long are you in town?"

"I'm hoping to drive back to San Francisco next Monday. Do you think you can have it done by then?"

Shoving his hands into the pockets of his coveralls, Carlos shrugged. "Most likely. Unless there's a bigger issue that requires me to order a part. I'll give you a call after I'm able to get in there to diagnose the problem. And I'll make sure to give you the family discount."

Brad clapped him on the back and laughed. The man hadn't changed. "I'd appreciate that."

"Anything for my best friend's kid."

That was another thing about Carlos. It didn't matter that Brad was halfway through his twenties. He'd always be a kid to the man.

Carlos turned to Cassie once again. "It was very nice to meet you."

She rewarded him with another of her stunning smiles, and Brad couldn't resist enjoying the sight of it just a little.

"You, as well," she said, then turned to go, leading the way toward the entrance of the garage.

Carlos walked alongside Brad behind her. "She's really not your girlfriend?" He spoke in an undertone, tilting his head closer to Brad so she wouldn't overhear.

Brad shook his head. "She hates my guts," he answered just as quietly.

"That's too bad. She's cute."

Brad couldn't stop the quiet laugh that choked out but gave no other response. She was more than cute. She quite possibly topped the list of the most beautiful women he knew.

That was the problem. Why was he constantly attracted to the women who refused to give him the time of day? The few times he'd allowed himself to get fully invested in a relationship, he'd always ended up with his heart ripped out of his chest and stomped on by those same tenacious bombshells. And their jealous boyfriends.

How did he constantly miss the signs with these women? He wasn't an idiot. He'd never been at the top of his class in school, but his grades hadn't been terrible. He had good street smarts. His radar for detecting these things must be broken. That had to be the reason he kept falling for those who only wanted a good time at his expense.

Either that or *he* was the shallow one.

Um... He'd rather not dwell too deeply about that.

"How are the migraines?" Carlos asked as they stepped outside. Coming from the artificial lighting in the garage, the sun almost blinded them. "Still giving you trouble?"

"I'm ... managing." Brad stole a glance at Cassie still walking a few feet ahead of them. She didn't appear to have overheard their conversation. Thankfully.

He hadn't been lying. Compared to the last time he'd seen Carlos, he *was* managing. Back then, he'd still suffered from episodes a month. Now they'd dwindled to only a few, though he hated having to admit they were still an issue at all.

Carlos made a small grunt like he didn't quite buy Brad's unconcerned tone. "That's good. Listen, my buddy is the head football coach over at the high school. He was telling me the other day that one of his assistants is retiring at the end of this season. They're looking for someone young to take his place. Someone who could really understand the players better than the rest of those old guys. Since you're moving back down here, I told him I might know someone." He nudged Brad's elbow. "Of course, you'd have to enroll in the coaching certification course, but if you got started soon, you'd have plenty of time to finish it before next fall."

"Coaching?" Brad stopped walking, squinting his eyes against the gleam of the sun reflecting off one of the cars in the parking lot. "I don't know about that, Carlos. I'm not much of a role model for kids."

"Sure you are. You've got a lot of experience in the sport, a lot of playing time. Plus, Mike was telling me it's really difficult getting some of his players to care more about their schoolwork. You're the perfect guy to help show these young kids that there's more to life than football."

Brad read the meaning behind that statement. His role would be to act as living proof of the importance of a fallback plan. "Thanks for the recommendation, but I think I'll pass." He didn't need yet another reminder of his failed dreams.

"Hey," Carlos placed a hand on his shoulder. "Just think about it. It could be a really good opportunity for you."

Compassion hung in the older man's face when Brad met his eyes, and he immediately felt some regret for his quick offense. Carlos had been a huge support back when he'd first left the team, becoming like a second dad since his own father lived so far away. He'd never use any opportunity as a slight on Brad's situation.

"I'll think about it."

Carlos slapped him on the back. "'Atta boy. I'll call you soon about that air conditioning unit."

Brad thanked him and met Cassie at her car, his mind still heavy with that parting conversation. He folded into the passenger seat as she turned the key in the ignition.

"I didn't know you grew up here," Cassie said, sliding her sunglasses onto her face.

Brad pulled his focus away from his depressing thoughts. "I didn't, but my dad did. He grew up in the house my sister lives in now. My grandparents added the second story back when he was a kid. After they both died several years ago, they left it to him. He almost sold it, but my mom convinced him to rent it out instead. Turns out that was a good move now that all the cousins are getting old enough to go to college."

"Tyler told me about your family tradition of going to USC," she said, turning to look behind her as she backed out of the parking spot. "It's really cool that there's so much history here for you all. And it's so nice of your dad to let everyone live there. I'm not sure my parents would be so trusting of such a beautiful house."

Brad braced his hand on the door handle as Cassie peeled out of the lot. He threw an alarmed look at her, wondering if he'd made the right choice in accepting a ride back to the house. But he kept his thoughts to himself.

"It's definitely given him a few more grays," he said, relaxing his grip. Especially when he and Tyler occupied the house. Dad probably slept better at night now that Beej lived there. She'd always been the goody two-shoes of the family. "Buena Hills is a great place to live, even if it's not glamorous like New York City."

"Why do you say that like it's a bad thing?" Cassie said sharply.

"Huh?"

She groaned in disgust. "Just because I live in New York and like fashion and shopping doesn't mean I'm this stuck-up snob."

Man, she had a talent of switching from being civil to jumping down his throat quickly. Not to mention how easily she twisted his words. "Hold up. Don't get those cute shorts you're wearing in a knot. I wasn't trying to offend you. But while we're at it, maybe I wouldn't think you were a snob if you hadn't immediately written me off as someone worse than the mud on your designer shoes."

His words and tone seemed to stun her. She didn't say anything for a minute, though her mouth opened as if she wanted to. Then she closed it again, her lips pursing into a thin line.

A thick, suffocating tension filled the car, but Brad refused to take back his words. He stared out the window at the passing buildings leading away from home.

He turned back to Cassie. "This isn't the way to the house."

"We're not going to the house."

"Then where are we going?" he asked, biting back the frustration, not wanting to upset her even more. She'd started this most recent battle but that didn't mean he cared to continue it.

She took her eyes off the road long enough to study him, though her oversized sunglasses prevented him from reading her expression. "You have to be fitted for your tux."

Brad groaned. He'd completely forgotten about the appointment Tyler had told him about yesterday. "I'd rather go dumpster diving for loose change."

"I could arrange that," she said haughtily, and a smirk tugged at her mouth as though she were picturing that very thing.

Brad rolled his eyes.

"However, you're the best man. Which means that *I* have to walk down the aisle with you in a few days, and I refuse to be escorted by Trashy McTrasherson."

"Trashy McTrasherson? We're back in grade school now?"

She glared at him but didn't retaliate. "Besides, it's my duty as the maid-of-honor to deal with all the ... problems ... that arise leading up to the wedding."

"I'm a problem now?" he asked dryly. "I can't decide if that's a step up or down from *bro*."

Her exasperated sigh filled the car. Brad waited for her to deliver the next barb, but she didn't. Only her deep breathing interrupted the tense silence that followed. She was obviously working to regain control. Either that or creating his very violent demise in her mind. That seemed more likely.

"My life isn't as easy and privileged as you seem to think it is," she said quietly, sadness tainting her words.

That was cryptic. Brad studied the way her jaw clenched, not out of anger, but like she was trying not to cry. She'd been crying yesterday too. Some of his frustration faded, even as he wondered what could've happened to cause the emotion for such a high and mighty princess.

"And I'm not the dumb jock you seem to think I am." He didn't know why he insisted that she realize that.

She refused to look at him as she turned into the parking lot of Behind the Veil. She found a spot next to Tyler's old Honda and put the car into park, letting it idle as she stared out the front windshield.

As they sat in tense silence, Brad recalled the conversation he'd had with his cousin yesterday morning. It would've been nice if he'd remembered that stupid promise before he'd come to verbal blows with Cassie just now. Again.

He pushed out a heavy sigh as he ran a hand down one side of his face then shifted in his seat to face her. "Look, I know we started off on the wrong foot. And I'm sorry for my role in that. But Tyler is my cousin, and my best friend. I really want his wedding to be a good day. Can we at least try to get along?"

She lifted her chin in a defiant gesture and Brad's jaw tensed.

"Please?" he asked through clenched teeth.

Several seconds ticked by before the rigidity in her posture softened and she pushed out a breath. She slid her sunglasses onto her head before placing her hands in her lap and turning to him. "You're right. Believe it or not, we're in agreement here. My sister deserves her wedding to be perfect, and she shouldn't have to worry about us fighting the whole time."

Brad studied her face, her flawless skin, dainty nose. And especially the resigned look in those gorgeous eyes that already had his defenses slipping. "Do we have ourselves a truce?" He held out his hand.

She stared at it for a long moment, then bobbed her head once in finality. "Yes, we do," she said as she took his hand.

Her skin was soft against his palm, and Brad's pulse picked up speed the longer he allowed the connection to go on. What was happening? They'd just argued about how much they didn't like each other, so why did one handshake make him all warm and fuzzy inside?

He let go quickly and cleared his throat. "Well, thanks for the ride. I'm sure Tyler can take me back to the house after we're done."

"Sounds good." She refused to meet his eye, and a light blush appeared on her cheeks. If he didn't know better, he'd think she'd been a bit affected by the contact too.

Nah, that couldn't be right.

He ignored that thought and pushed his door open.

"I guess I'll see you at the bonfire tomorrow night," he said.

Technically, it was a family get-together for everyone who

arrived over the next twenty-four hours, but Brad couldn't see how Gemma's family wouldn't be invited too.

"Yeah." She lowered her sunglasses over her eyes before facing him again. "I'll be there."

Brad got out of the car and headed toward the entrance to the bridal shop, still unable to process the sensation overload he'd experienced holding her hand. And even more confused about the realization that he wouldn't mind doing it again.

Chapter Eleven

By the time Brad made it down to the sand on Tuesday evening, his arms strained under the weight of the table he and Wes carried on their shoulders. Before leaving for the bonfire, they were somehow selected as the lucky fools tasked with getting the fold-up piece of furniture from Wes's parents' SUV down to the shore. That wouldn't have been much of a problem, except they'd parked a good half mile away from the beach, and this was no ordinary card table. The thing must've weighed at least a hundred pounds. Was it even made of wood? It felt more like solid lead disguised as wood.

Aunt Amy followed a few steps behind, carrying a large bin of beach activities. She'd sent Brad digging through the cavernous closet underneath the stairs at the house for anything he could find. Kites, shovels and buckets, various kinds of balls and frisbees ... name it, and it was probably in there. He'd even come across his dad's old golf clubs from high school, though those didn't make the trip.

Uncle Jason walked at her side, carrying several beach chairs. Hallie, Elise, and Kendall came up last, their arms full of foil serving platters and blankets.

"Where do you want this, Aunt Amy?" Brad asked in between grunts.

His aunt set the bin down on the sand. "I think this is good enough. We can set up the chairs and blankets here for now—" She pointed to the spot she indicated. "—Then move them when we have the fire going." A shallow bonfire pit stood a few yards away.

On the count of three, both guys dropped the table onto the sand, and Brad immediately shook out his arms with a wince. What a relief.

"Geez, Mom," Wes said, massaging his own shoulder. "You couldn't have found a lighter table?"

Aunt Amy laughed lightly. "It was the only one in the closet that would work. The others were too small."

"A little hard work is good for you," Uncle Jason said, coming up to stand between Brad and Wes, slinging his arms around both their shoulders. "It builds character."

Brad rolled his neck around a few times to relieve some of the tension there. "It wouldn't have been so bad except for those stairs. I was sure I'd biff it a few times."

"I'm not looking forward to carting this thing back up at the end of the night, bruh," Wes said, pulling out the table leg closest to him. "Especially in the dark."

Brad extended the other leg, locking it into place. "We'll make Tyler do it by himself." Except not even the strongest man on the planet could possibly lift it alone. "Ready? On three."

He counted to three and with matching grunts, they turned the table upright in the sand.

"Where is Ty anyway?" Brad asked as he helped the girls unpack the containers of food.

"We forgot to pick up cups when we did the grocery run this afternoon," Elise said. "Tyler and Gemma ran to the store to get some on their way over here. They're probably driving around looking for a parking spot right now."

The beach wasn't too crowded due, in part, to the bluffs wrapped around the perimeter of the sand, making this area of shore a little more secluded than others nearby. But parking was still hard to come by around here.

"Are the Schalks with them?" Aunt Amy asked, unfolding a flannel blanket and spreading it across the sand.

"I think Tyler said they were coming separately," Hallie said.

Mention of the Schalks brought Brad's mind back to the truce he'd made with Cassie yesterday. More specifically, it reminded him of the handshake they'd sealed it with right before he'd left the car. Why had her touch affected him so much?

Sure, he was attracted to her; he could admit that much. Maybe two years ago he would've seen this connection as a sign to pursue her. But that sign vanished as soon as he'd found himself drenched in soda, watching those luscious curls bouncing around her shoulders as she stalked out of the bowling alley. He'd never be an Einstein or receive admission to Mensa, he knew that. But not even the multiple concussions he'd received while playing football could make him dumb enough to willingly place himself in the line of her quick temper again.

Nope, that handshake meant nothing. He just had to bite his tongue through this week. By Monday, she'd be out of his life again, and he could push their whole feud out of his mind until the next time they were forced to be together. Or maybe there wouldn't be a next time.

All the better.

Someone colliding with his ribs jolted Brad from his thoughts.

"Sack the quarterback!" a girl's voice yelled as he got knocked sideways a few steps. He looked down to find his baby sister grinning up at him.

"Oh no, you don't," he said through a laugh. He wrapped his arms around her and wrestled her to the ground, turning his body so he landed underneath. After all, he didn't want to hurt her. "Only I'm allowed to play that game."

Brooklyn smirked as she sat up, running a tan hand through her long, caramel-colored hair. "You're just mad I'm big enough to come up with my own plays now."

"You two never stop, do you?" Mom asked, her attempted scold missing the mark due to the amused look on her face.

Brad stood and brushed the sand off his shorts before reaching out a hand to pull Brooklyn up too. "You never got me a dog or a brother. I had to find an alternate wrestling buddy." He winked at his mother before wrapping her in a hug. She was shorter by several inches, the top of her blonde head reaching underneath his chin.

When she stepped back, she kept her hands lightly clasped around his elbows, commencing her usual inspection with a fond expression, though her eyes shone with concern. "Are you feeling well?"

He gave his typical response. "Yeah, I'm great." Any references to his headaches only made her worry, and he'd rather save her maternal fretting for another time. "Where's Dad?"

"He's looking for a parking spot. He dropped Brook and me off at the entrance." She scanned the beach, her face turning eager. "So where's this girl you said we'd be able to meet?"

Right, Mandy. He shouldn't have told his family about his plan to bring her to the wedding. He hadn't brought a girl home to meet his parents in a long time. Too long, according to his mother.

He cleared his throat. "Uh, it didn't work out."

Mom's mouth turned down in a sympathetic frown. "Really? I had a good feeling about this one."

Brad remained silent, chewing on his bottom lip.

"That's too bad, son. Well, she didn't deserve you, anyway." He could tell she was trying not to let her disappointment show. She reached up and patted his cheek. "I know you're going to find someone amazing one day."

Brad didn't have the heart to disagree with her. She always got so excited whenever he admitted he'd met someone new. He sensed that his newfound choice of eternal bachelorhood wouldn't go over well with her.

"You know," Mom continued, "one of the other hygienists at the new dental office I work at is about your age. Maybe I can introduce you the next—"

"Nope," he said forcefully. "Uh ... no. I think I've got the whole dating thing under control, thanks." This conversation, on the other hand, was quickly getting out of control. He needed a topic change stat.

"Hey, guess what?" Brooklyn asked, coming to his rescue.

Brad pursed his lips. "You decided to blow all your savings on a boat and circumnavigate the globe by sea?"

His sister tilted her head from side to side as though contemplating the idea. "No, but that would be awesome. I should get to work on my sales pitch to convince Mom and Dad."

"I heard that," Mom said as she walked past them to greet Uncle Jason. "And it's never going to happen."

"I saw that coming." Brad casually draped his arm around his sister's shoulders. "So, what's up?"

She took a few seconds to respond, her face obviously still contemplating a way to convince Mom of the idea. Then she shook her head a tiny bit, forcing herself back to the conversation. "I qualified for state."

"Way to go, baby sis!" He raised his free hand in the air for a high five. "See, what did I tell you? I knew you'd make it."

She slapped his hand. "Thanks. I'm really excited. You're coming right?"

"Of course. I'll be the one in the front row holding the sign with your face blown out of proportion."

"Just don't do anything to embarrass me."

Brad scoffed and mussed the back of her hair. "For that, I'll be extra embarrassing."

She groaned and rolled her eyes so big that her irises almost disappeared. Then she squinted toward the water line where Wes was spinning a frisbee on top of one finger.

"Oh, look. There's Wes." As the only cousins in the same grade, they'd developed a close friendship over the years, similar to the one Brad shared with Tyler. "I still owe him for that prank he played on me last Thanksgiving."

She sprinted off toward Wes and Brad chuckled when she jumped on the poor guy's back. That girl had more energy than she knew what to do with.

A second later, someone clapped him on the shoulder. He turned to find his dad next to him.

"Hey, Pops," Brad said, returning the warm embrace he received and patting Dad on the back. "You made it."

"It's good to see you, son." Dad pushed his glasses up on his nose. "I talked to Carlos yesterday. He said you stopped by the garage."

"Yeah. He's helping me out with a faulty A/C vent in the Pathfinder."

"He also told me about the coaching position he recommended you for. You're really not interested in it? It sounds like it'd be right up your alley."

Leave it to Dad to get right down to business. Brad shrugged, unsure of what to say. He'd promised he'd think over Carlos' recommendation, and he had. In fact, it seemed when he wasn't puzzling over why Cassie constantly dominated his mind, he was contemplating his conversation with Carlos.

But why? Coaching didn't interest him in the slightest, even if it were only part time, so there was no reason it should take up so much real estate in his brain. Too much bad blood lingered surrounding his own high school coach to even consider putting himself in a position to be a role model for impressionable youth. Coach Sanders pushed him to excellence, sure, but what the man did on the field didn't make up for the borderline abusive way he treated his players. If Brad hadn't been so focused on making a career out of football, he probably would've quit.

None of that matters anymore, he thought bitterly.

"I told him I'd think about it." He left it at that.

Dad scrutinized him with concern in his eyes. "You sure everything's all right?"

"Yeah, I'm fine."

His words didn't reassure his father in the slightest, and he continued to watch him behind his glasses.

Why did the man always assume something was wrong? Ever

since Brad had been forced to walk away from football, Dad always seemed to want him to open up about how he felt. It was awkward constantly having to sidestep conversations or change the subject abruptly. He used to be able to talk to his dad about anything.

But despite him being one of Brad's biggest role models, he couldn't confide in him about his anger over the way his life had played out. Couldn't talk about the fact that if it hadn't been for those concussions, he'd probably still be playing. Couldn't admit to his worry over the migraines and the future of his health.

Because if he opened up about that, the little control he had over his sanity would crumble to pieces.

He was barely holding onto it already.

Chapter Twelve

"Watch your step." Cassie clutched her grandmother's elbow tighter, assisting her off the last concrete stair onto the beach. "The ground is uneven here. I don't want you to fall."

"I've endured a lot harder things than going down a few stairs." Gram's green eyes twinkled with mirth.

Cassie laughed, wrapping an arm around her grandmother's bent shoulders. "All the same, I feel better being able to help you."

"Thank you, dear," Gram said, leaning toward her in a side hug that Cassie readily reciprocated. "It's so good having you here. Would I be too selfish to say that I wished you'd come visit more often?"

If it weren't for the constant demands of her job, Cassie *would* visit more. But Adriana was always a stickler about vacation time. And when the boss was working, she expected her assistant to be at her beck and call.

Sadness pricked at Cassie. She had all the vacation time in the world now.

Pushing aside the reminder of her jobless state, she squeezed her grandmother tighter. "I don't think you have a selfish bone in your body."

The sun had already begun its slow descent toward the horizon, bathing the scene in front of them in a warm glow. Little sequins of light danced along the ocean waves. Cassie's flip flops sank into the sand, which made walking difficult. She kicked them off and wiggled her toes, enjoying the soft, grainy texture sliding through them. Days spent at the ocean were a rarity for her in New York. She wouldn't consider herself a beach bunny by any definition of the term, but she understood the appeal of the Southern California lifestyle. There was something relaxing about watching the sun go down over the water.

She bent to pick up her flip flops, making sure not to dip too low so she wouldn't bring Gram down with her. The beach bag Cassie carried on her other shoulder slipped onto her elbow, and the pale pink sweater bulging out the top tumbled onto the sand. She hurriedly picked it up and slung it onto her bare shoulder before snatching her sandals and righting herself again.

"I'm so sorry about Drew. And this close to the wedding too," Gram said, allowing Cassie to lead her a few paces behind Mom and Dad toward the group of people congregating near a picnic table filled with food. Though Cassie didn't know everyone scattered along the somewhat secluded beach, she suspected they were all Tyler's extended family. It appeared that many of them had already arrived from out of town for the wedding.

Cassie shrugged in response to Gram's comment. During breakfast that morning, she'd barely held back the tears while breaking the news about ending her engagement. Considering how much she'd fallen apart while confiding in Gemma only two days before, however, she counted the fact that she'd had any control over her emotions at all as a win. Who knew how much longer she'd be able to hold back the waterworks?

Especially considering that Gram wasn't done talking. "In my experience, it's better to find out that a man isn't right for you before the ceremony. Lost deposits and a few uncomfortable conversations might seem like the end of the world right now—and understandably so, don't get me wrong—but they're nothing compared to the difficulties of suffering through an unhappy marriage."

Cassie stopped suddenly and faced her grandmother. "What do you mean *in your experience?* How many men have you married?"

Gram pursed her lips in barely suppressed humor. "Just your grandpa. But that doesn't mean no other men asked me."

A laugh bubbled up in Cassie's throat. All her life, she'd looked at her grandparents' relationship as one out of a fairytale. Never in her wildest dreams did she ever consider that there could've been others before Grandpa Will. "Does Dad know you were engaged before?"

"Of course not." Gram gave her a withered look that Cassie could tell wasn't at all serious. "And you're not going to tell him. I'll never hear the end of it."

Cassie smiled over at her grandma. "Yes, ma'am."

"I will say this. It doesn't matter how many frogs you've kissed once you meet your real prince. Remember that, dear."

Laughter carried to them over the crashing waves and the few squawking gulls circling high above the water, waiting for an opportunity to swoop down for a snack. Off to the left of the picnic table, Tyler's parents bent over a shallow cement basin full of firewood. Another couple about their age crouched next to them, the woman pointing toward the basin like she was giving directions. They all looked up as Mom and Dad joined them. The rest of the family were already scattered around the beach, their silhouettes darkened against the backdrop of the setting sun.

Cassie and Gram arrived at the meeting spot where Beej sat cross-legged on a beach towel locked in a deep conversation with the dark-haired waiter from Trattoria d'Italia.

She looked up from her date as Cassie eased Gram into one of the empty beach chairs. "Hey, you guys." After offering a quick wave, she started lifting herself off the towel.

Cassie held a hand up to stop her. "Don't get up. We didn't mean to interrupt."

"Not at all. We're glad you could make it." Beej pointed at a pile of various objects in the sand in front of them. "There are frisbees and kites if you're interested. And I'm not sure what's in that bin over there, but you're welcome to dig through it. Help yourself to some food, too, but save room for dessert. Once the fire's going, we'll break out the s'mores stuff."

Cassie dropped her bag onto the sand. "This is quite the setup you've got here. You must throw these kinds of parties a lot, huh?"

"When you live in Southern California, it's what you do, I guess."

Beej turned back to the hunky waiter, and they resumed their conversation.

Stepping behind the line of beach chairs, Cassie placed her hands on her grandmother's frail shoulders. "Are you hungry, Gram? Let me get you some food."

"That would be lovely. Thank you."

Cassie gave Gram's shoulders a squeeze, then walked to the table. As she scooped the usual picnic favorites—potato salad, barbecue chicken, corn on the cob, and watermelon—onto a paper plate, her natural curiosity took over, and she lifted her eyes to scan the beach. Tyler and Gemma were over by the water line, tossing a baseball back and forth. Not far away from them, Hallie, Elise, and Kendall were in the middle of sculpting an impressive fortress out of sand, complete with a mote and two turrets.

Further up the beach, Cassie spotted Brad, clutching a football with both hands in front of his chest.

His completely bare chest.

She held back the urge to fan herself. With his arms flexed like that, he sure had a nice set of biceps. And triceps. And every other kind of 'ceps.

He dropped back a few steps before launching a perfect spiral toward the group of guys—including Tyler's younger brother, Wes—and one girl jockeying for position to catch the ball.

Once his full chest was on display, she had a hard time pulling her eyes away. Because not only his arms deserved recognition. He had a great body; about six feet if Cassie guessed correctly, with abs straight out of every woman's fantasy. He clearly spent a lot of time working out.

Yuck. A gym rat? That should've been another tick against him. So why did she have the sudden desire to snuggle up to those muscles?

Cassie's cheeks burned. She shouldn't be ogling him like this. Looks weren't everything. Especially when his personality left so much to be desired. Yet for some reason, he seemed different now.

More carefree than she'd seen him before. Maybe the magic of the ocean had something to do with that. She certainly felt more relaxed, so near the soothing rolling of the waves as the soft glow of the setting sun kissed her skin. It must have the same effect on him. Or maybe his family brought out a different side of him. A less abrasive side. Or maybe he simply hadn't noticed *her* yet.

Whatever the reason, the change in his demeanor intrigued Cassie. Especially by the way he threw his head back and laughed when Wes leapt for the ball, then ate a mouthful of sand when the girl pushed him on his way down, causing him to faceplant on the ground. Brad's easy posture painted a completely different picture than the guy she knew.

Look away, she instructed herself, finally managing to pull her eyes from the fine specimen that Brad Lucas had turned out to be.

But no sooner had she dished out a small helping of potato salad onto Gram's plate, her gaze strayed back in time to see him jump, his whole body fully stretched from feet to hands, to snag the football the girl had thrown back to him. His fingertips grazed the laces, slowing the momentum and making it pop higher in the air. He caught it on its way down.

"Surprise!" a voice said in her ear as long arms wrapped around her from behind.

Cassie flinched, almost screaming bloody murder in her shock. The serving spoon dropped from her hand, clattering to the table and splattering potato salad all over the chicken next to it. Whirling around, she dropped the plate as she darted backward out of Drew's arms, ricocheting off the wooden table. He reached out and caught her before she lost her footing completely.

"Drew! What are you doing here?" Had he noticed her checking out another man? She rubbed at her side to mask her shame.

But why should she be ashamed? They weren't together anymore. She'd done nothing wrong.

His mouth lifted in a crooked smile. "I'm here for the wedding, of course." He said it as though it should've been obvious.

"The ... the ... wedding?" Cassie's brain refused to catch up with her eyes. She'd called off the wedding. "How did you even know where I'd be tonight?"

Drew shoved his hands into the pockets of his khaki slacks. Seriously, he looked more like he should be on his way to a client meeting, right down to his brown loafers. "You emailed the schedule to me two weeks ago with a note in bold letters to make sure I'm there."

Shoot. She *had* done that. Still, her confusion grew. She'd given back his ring. The automatic assumption would be that he no longer warranted an invite to Gemma's wedding.

Right?

RIGHT?

"But ... but ... we're not together anymore," she managed to get out.

The look he gave her caused Cassie's skin to crawl, tempting her to clasp her hands behind her back like a repentant child. She'd seen that expression on him several times, but for some reason, had never put the pieces together before.

"You can't seriously still be mad about what happened," he said, arching a condescending eyebrow. "I've given you a few days to calm down. I didn't push when you didn't return my calls. Now we really need to work this out. I refuse to lose you this way."

Her jaw clenched. Ever since arriving in Buena Hills, she'd been forced to take a hard look at the past five years. All this self-reflection had led to a single realization. Drew Covington always had a game plan for winning her back. How had she not seen it before?

This was step one: Authoritative reasoning.

She took several deep breaths, eyeing the people milling about the sand nearby. Beej and her waiter friend had pulled Gram into their conversation. Mom and Dad were helping Mr. and Mrs. Abernathy with the bonfire, and everyone else was still engaged in their chosen activities. No one had noticed the tense conversation at the picnic table.

All the same, Cassie pulled on Drew's arm, dragging him far enough away that they wouldn't be overheard.

"I don't want to work it out," she hissed, crossing her arms over her chest. A slight breeze passed between them, rustling her curls off her shoulder, though her current posture had nothing to do with the chill permeating her skin. "We're over."

"Cassandra, I don't know why you're making such a big deal about this. It's just a dress."

Ah, and here came step two: Minimizing her feelings. Piggy backing on that would be the apology and grand gesture involving expensive gifts. That last one always got her. But not this time. She wouldn't let him make it that far.

"It's more than the dress," Cassie insisted. "You betrayed my trust. We were a team. A partnership. That means sticking up for each other. You were so worried about your own job that you completely threw me under the bus when I just wanted you to tell the truth. How can I be certain you'll stand up for me with anything else?"

Drew opened his mouth to speak but she didn't let him get a word out. She wouldn't give him the opportunity to logic his way out of this one.

"And another thing? Your job wasn't on the line. You work for your dad. He would've given you a little slap on the wrist and lectured you about looking good for the firm, then sent you on your way."

He sighed, running his fingers through his perfectly combed dark hair. "I get it. You're still mad. Tell me how I can make this up to you."

"You really want to know?"

"Yes."

"You can leave. It's really over this time." She turned away from him, facing the water. Unfortunately, that only brought her right in the sight line of Brad's game, which had morphed into some kind of touch football now that Hallie, Elise, and Kendall had joined in. "I've moved on."

"What do you mean you've moved on?" he asked skeptically. "Honey, a week ago you were obsessing over flower arrangements for our wedding. You can't have moved on so quickly."

"Believe it," she said, holding her head high. "Because I have."

Out of the corner of her eye, she noticed the football game end, smaller groups breaking off in separate directions. Brad headed toward the picnic table by himself.

"In fact, I've met someone new." As soon as the words were out, she wished she could take them back.

"You've met someone new?" Drew parroted doubtfully.

"Uh-huh."

A weight dropped into her gut. Drew wasn't one to give up easily. The same qualities that made him an excellent attorney also guaranteed that he wouldn't let this go until he came out the victor. And now that the words were out, she had no choice but to own her lie. As much as she hated herself for the idea forming in her mind, she needed reinforcements. Desperate times and all that.

"In fact, he's here tonight," she said, attempting to keep her words light, instead of the pitchy way she always sounded whenever she told a lie.

In a weird twist of fortune, Brad's path to the picnic table led him right by Cassie and Drew. Before she could talk herself out of it, she swallowed her hesitation and pasted on a smile.

"Hey, honey," she said sweetly once he'd gotten close enough to hear. Yikes, that sounded cringey.

Brad froze, then hesitantly lifted a hand in a small wave. "Hey... baby?"

The question in his greeting didn't bode well for the believability of her plan. But she walked over to him and latched onto his elbow with both hands anyway. His eyes went wide.

"Play along," she hissed after stretching onto her tiptoes to reach his ear. She kissed his cheek. *"Please."*

He blinked at her a few times before speaking. "Oh...kay."

Good enough. Cassie dragged him the few steps over to where Drew was watching them, his mouth stretched into a thin line.

"Drew, this is Brad." She ran her hand up Brad's delectable biceps, giving his arm a little squeeze.

Woah.

Ignoring the flip of her heart, she smiled up at him. "My new boyfriend."

Chapter Thirteen

Ooooooh no.

Uh-uh. No way.

Brad gaped at Cassie, using all his control to keep his mouth from dropping open in shock. What did she say? He must've heard her wrong. There was no possible way she just introduced him as her boyfriend.

But then why was she staring back at him like that? Was she expecting him to say something?

This had to be a joke. There was no other way around it. Any minute now, a guy with a camera would pop out of his hiding spot to film Brad's reaction. The video would probably end up online for the whole world to see. Sadly, it wouldn't be the first time.

That honor went to Kendra Jacobson during his junior year of high school. He shuddered thinking of her again. It was never a good idea to pursue the senior captain of the cheerleading squad right after learning she'd broken up with her college-aged boyfriend. Falling hard and then professing his feelings for that girl over the loudspeaker at a home basketball game with their cross-town rivals had been an even worse idea.

Unknown to him, one of her friends had gotten the whole thing on video and posted it all over social media. Brad hadn't needed to hear about that from his friends. He'd seen the proof himself. Along with the hundreds of comments from the rest of his high school branding him as The Rebound Guy.

He thought he'd learned his lesson. It had been beyond humiliating for a seventeen-year-old boy still trying to figure out his place in the world. Especially because his teammates were some of the worst offenders when it came to the teasing. And thanks to all the lectures Coach Sanders gave the team about being tough and invincible to pain, his "buddies" would've hassled him even more if they knew how much the whole experience had traumatized him. Football players were supposed to have thick skins. A little embarrassment shouldn't have been enough to break him. So, he'd always pretended not to care.

But he had. Oh, how he'd cared.

Unfortunately, even seven years and a hundred and fifty miles from Jefferson High hadn't given him the space he needed to shake that label, however unintentional the situations he'd found himself in were.

Brad eyed the guy—Drew, if he'd heard Cassie correctly—putting the pieces together. Stiff posture, check. Puffed out chest, check. Jealous gleam in his eyes, definite check. This guy had to be the ex.

Oh, man! Brad thought, wishing he hadn't allowed Cassie to drag him over here. *How is this happening again?* And he'd just gotten out of his last bad situation, too. The image of walking in on Mandy swapping spit with her real Mr. Right resurfaced in his mind, fueling his frustration with women everywhere.

No. He refused to let another one use him. He was putting his foot down. Brad Lucas would no longer play the role of the rebound guy.

He turned to Cassie and opened his mouth to set her straight. The way she stared back stopped him. An almost desperate pleading pierced those striking hazel eyes, making it obvious how unhappy she was about Drew being here.

No, not just unhappy. Uncomfortable. It had only taken Brad a second to determine he didn't like this chump. If she'd been mistreated in any way, he couldn't leave her hanging. He was no knight in shining armor, but at least he had a conscience. Dang it.

"You've got to be kidding me." Drew practically spit the words in disgust, interrupting Brad's internal debate. "Him?"

Why is that so unbelievable, pal? The incredulous comment sealed

Brad's decision, and he wrapped an arm around Cassie's shoulders. Underneath his weight, he felt her relax and take a breath. Something definitely wasn't right. He bent to press a kiss to her hair in order to make the ruse more believable. His mouth lingered there for a few seconds longer than necessary. For dramatic effect, of course. It was absolutely not because her curls were every bit as silky as they looked.

Keeping her close to his side, he turned to Drew, wearing the smile of a man head-over-heels for the woman beside him. "That's right. It took me some time to win her over, but somehow, I managed it. Hi, Brad Lucas. And you are?" He stuck out his hand.

Drew eyed it, the suspicious gleam in his eyes lit up by the glow of the bonfire now roaring against the darkening sky several yards away. He accepted the handshake, his grip firmer than necessary. An obvious challenge.

Brad tightened his own grip as he sized the guy up. Drew's dress shirt and loafers screamed investment banker. Or maybe corporate attorney. The exes were almost always one of those two things.

"Andrew Covington," Drew said pompously, finally dropping Brad's hand. "Cassie's fiancé."

Fiancé? *The plot thickens.*

"What's he talking about, princess?" Brad asked, capturing her attention by tightening his one-armed embrace.

Cassie stiffened, and the smile she directed toward him held a noticeable tightness. "We're not engaged anymore. I don't know why he's even here."

"To win you back." Drew spoke like it should've been an obvious assumption. "Why else would I be here? You can't throw away five years for the first random guy you come across." He eyed Brad like he was a stray dog sniffing around at an upscale picnic.

"He's not some random guy," Cassie insisted. "We met a few years ago when we—" She gestured between herself and Drew. "—were on that break. You know after I caught you cozying up to Eleanor at dinner? Or don't you remember that?"

Her whole body was like a tight ball of tension under Brad's arm. His head spun trying to keep up with the information coming his way. They'd broken up before? Because of another woman? That made him like Drew less and less as the conversation continued.

"I wasn't cozying up to her," Drew countered, a muscle in his neck popping as he clenched his jaw. "You totally misread the situation."

Cassie ignored his argument. "Anyway, when Brad and I saw each other again a few days ago, there were immediate sparks."

She snuggled into Brad, lifting her face to look at him. If he couldn't still feel the tension in her body, he would've believed the adoring smile she directed his way.

"Isn't that right, honey?" she asked, her tone sickly sweet.

It wasn't a complete lie. Sparks did fly, but not the romantic kind she referred to. For whatever reason, she needed Drew to think they'd fallen hard, and though he knew it wasn't smart to put himself in this situation, Brad could play along.

He tapped the tip of her nose with his finger. "More than sparks. Fireworks, really. I'm just lucky you finally decided to give me a chance."

"Awww, you're so sweet!" She stretched on her tiptoes and kissed his cheek. Tantalizing prickles danced across his abs when she placed her hand lightly on his bare stomach.

Focus, dummy, he reminded himself. *This is all for show.*

"Isn't he the cutest?" Cassie asked Drew.

"Adorable," he muttered, his voice cracking with the lack of humor. Frustration illuminated in his face as his eyes bounced back and forth between her and Brad. "Nice try, but I'm not buying whatever you're selling."

"I already told you it's over, Drew," Cassie responded, the sappiness in her voice from a moment ago replaced by ice. "I said it in New York, and again tonight. We won't be getting back together, there will be no wedding, and I want you to leave. Now."

Her fingers dug into Brad's skin where they wrapped around his back, her nails biting his flesh. He could feel her other hand shaking as it rested on his stomach. What could've happened between her and Drew to cause such an intense reaction to his presence? That alone pushed away the last of Brad's reservations.

Shifting so they faced each other, he joined his other arm around her waist in an embrace, partly to show his support, but mostly to stop her nails from drawing blood.

"Hey, man," he said to Drew. "She told you to leave. It's time you listened to her."

Drew stared at them with his mouth partly open like he was about to say something. He shut it, then opened it again. This went on for a few long seconds. Open, shut. Open, shut. Like an ugly old fish gasping for air.

Finally, he pushed out a breath. "This isn't over, Cassandra. I will find a way to win you back. Before the wedding."

He turned and strode off down the beach, his expensive loafers slipping and sliding in the sand. Brad watched him leave, his awareness of Cassie's lingering closeness heightening the longer she stood in his arms. He should let go. That would be the smart thing.

Except for some reason, he didn't.

After a moment, all the tension drained from her body. "Thank you," she mumbled, dropping her forehead to his chest. "You keep saving me."

He swallowed the chuckle rising in his throat. "Soooo..." he drawled, dropping his arms and stepping back. "Would now be a good time to ask how we went from a tentative ceasefire of hostilities to suddenly dating in a little over twenty-four hours? I've worked out some of the details myself, but after that Oscar-worthy performance, I think I deserve the full story."

That drew a small, breathy laugh from her. "Fine. But not here." She grabbed his elbow and turned him around, pushing him gently to get him to start walking. "Hold my hand. Drew might still be watching."

"I thought he was leaving." Brad wove his fingers through hers anyway.

"I wouldn't put it past him to find a reason to stay." She said nothing else until they'd rounded a bend where the rocky cliffs jutted out closer to the water line. A strong breeze nipped at his bare skin, sending a few goosebumps up his arms. Next to him, Cassie shivered. Her cut off shorts and tank top probably didn't provide much warmth now that the sun had all but gone down. It might be July, but this close to the ocean, it still cooled off at night. If only he'd had a chance to grab his sweatshirt back at the table.

They stopped at a spot a little out of reach of the waves. Laughter and loud voices carried to them from the group, though he couldn't see them from their position behind the bluffs.

She faced him, raising her arms out to her sides in an exaggerated shrug. "So, you want the whole story? Go ahead, ask me anything." She lowered herself to the sand.

Brad dropped down beside her, wondering where to start. "What did you even see in him?"

She was silent for a moment, staring out at the moonlit ocean. "I used to think his assertiveness was attractive. Two years ago, I tried ending things with him. We were supposed to be leaving for a trip to Mexico. I had no doubt he was planning to propose. But then I caught him flirting with his old girlfriend at a dinner with his family and half of New York's swankiest residents."

"Yikes."

Cassie laughed bitterly. "Tell me about it. His mother had always been vocal about how much she *loves* Eleanore. I know she's always wished that Drew was still dating her instead of me. I heard it every time I had the pleasure of being in the same room with her. When I saw him with Eleanore, I couldn't take it anymore. I broke up with him. That was right around the time my grandma had her stroke, so I came here to get away for a bit."

Brad nodded slowly, processing the timeline. A small prick of guilt plagued him as he thought back to their first meeting. Perhaps he'd been a little unfair by judging her so quickly back then. After all the times he'd allowed himself to fall for a woman, only to have her let him down, he definitely understood the emotional toll that experience would have on Cassie.

"Why'd you take him back?" he asked.

Cassie paused a few beats before responding. "Drew can be very persuasive. He told me that she'd come on to him, that it wasn't his fault."

"And you believed him?"

Her head snapped in his direction. "I had no reason not to. He'd never done something like that before."

Brad held his hands out in front of himself as a show of apology. "I'm not judging. I'm only trying to understand."

She sighed, her defensiveness slipping. "I wanted to believe him. Maybe I was naïve, but the way he fought for me, I thought he really cared. Now, looking back at the last two years, and how distant I've felt from him, I wonder if he just said that to keep himself out of trouble."

"You're probably right," Brad said, unsure if agreeing with her helped the situation or made it worse. He knew guys like Drew. The ones who'd say anything to cover their own skins.

Pulling her legs up to her chest, she hugged her knees. He slid his hand underneath his thigh, resisting the unexpected desire to wrap it around her shoulders. Being co-conspirators in this plan to fool her ex didn't change the fact that out here, where no one else was around, they were still Brad and Cassie, two people who barely tolerated each other. No matter how good it felt to have her in his arms earlier, he couldn't allow himself to hold her again.

"He used to be so different," she continued. "I was in my second year at FIT when I met him at this big Christmas party in the city. We spent the whole time together, dancing and making up these goofy stories about all the other people there."

Even in the descending darkness, Brad noticed her mouth lift slightly as though she were enjoying reliving the memory, even though it made her sad.

"When it was over, he asked me out for coffee. We ended up talking the whole night in this little twenty-four-hour café near Times Square. I knew right then I was going to marry him."

She broke off after that, the silence drowned out by the waves crashing onto the surf a few feet away. The tide carried the water up to them, lapping over Brad's feet. He picked up a handful of sand, letting the grains fall through his fingers as he waited for her to continue.

When she didn't, he glanced at her out of the corner of his eye. "What changed?"

"I don't really know. His mother's expectations maybe. Or work. Once he finished law school and started at his dad's firm, it seemed like he stopped trying as hard." She shifted quickly toward Brad, crossing her legs in front of her. "You know, he used to take the subway from NYU to FIT every day just to bring me my favorite latte after class. But once he got his job, he buried himself in his work. I kept telling myself he was overwhelmed, that eventually he'd adjust and be able to find more time for me. Especially after he helped me get the position as Adriana's assistant."

"Adriana?"

"She's my boss. Well, my former boss." Cassie brought her hands up to cover her face. "I got fired last week."

Oh man, a broken engagement and losing her job on top of it? No wonder she was so prickly when he'd come across her last Saturday. Brad would be too. "I'll bet there's a story there."

"Ding ding ding," she said, her words devoid of enthusiasm. "You win the jackpot."

Then she told him everything. How she'd attempted to show her boss her design at Drew's encouragement, only to have it be written off as nothing special. And how, a few weeks later, Adriana had stolen that same design without so much as acknowledging it was Cassie's.

It took guts to stand up for herself, knowing it would most likely cost her job. With everything she told him, he found his opinion of her shifting from barely concealed annoyance to sympathy, maybe even a little admiration.

"Now that it's over, it's not even really about the dress." The more Cassie talked, the less inhibited she seemed to become. "I mean, yeah, I'm still angry. Who wouldn't be? But I can design another one. It's more the implication that I wasn't worth anything as a designer that bothers me, not the deception."

"Yeah," Brad agreed. "That's shady."

"But I guess it was for the best," she said in resignation, staring back at the sea. "When Drew humiliated me in front of my boss, the red flags I'd been ignoring all this time became too big. I finally realized I didn't want to be married to him for the rest of my life. Or worse, go through with the wedding and end up with a nasty divorce a few years in. So, I ended it for good. Unfortunately, he can't accept that."

They morphed into silence again, and Brad thought about everything she'd told him. Something she'd said in the car yesterday clicked into place.

My life isn't as easy and privileged as you seem to think it is.

No, her life clearly wasn't as perfect as he'd originally thought. Maybe it was time to let go of the grudge he'd held onto for the last two years and turn over a new leaf.

"So," she said at last, "will you help me out with this? Will you be my pretend boyfriend to get my ex-fiancé off my back?"

Brad caught his bottom lip between his teeth, pulling his thoughts away from his shifting perception of her. He mulled over her proposal. It wasn't smart. He'd always been attracted to her, which aggravated him more than he could articulate. And he still didn't understand how he'd landed in yet another plot to get back at an ex. At least this time, he was going into it knowing their relationship was fake.

Still, he couldn't afford to let Cassie get too close to him. He couldn't allow himself to discover why he felt a pull toward her in the first place. Because experience had taught him that playing with fire ultimately led to him getting torched.

She must've taken his hesitation as a no by the way she grabbed his bicep with both hands and brought her face close to his. "Please, Brad. I wouldn't ask you to do this if I wasn't desperate. Drew isn't going to take a simple no for an answer."

He spared her only the smallest glance before returning his focus to the ocean.

"I'll pay you."

"With what money?" he asked through a snort. She shot him a glare and he cleared his throat. "Too soon?"

"I think so."

"Sorry." He forced out a breath, then muttered, "Fine. I'll do it."

She shrieked, throwing her arms around his neck. "Thank you, thank you, thank you! I owe you big time."

Yeah, she did. Yet, he couldn't ignore the thrill pulsing through him at the feel of her so close to him. "So, does this mean we get to make out now?"

A long groan emanated from her. "Don't be like that."

"What?" he asked a little too innocently, his mouth spreading into a wide grin. "It was a joke. After what you're asking me to do, I should at least be allowed to laugh about it."

Even looking at her profile, he could tell she was rolling her eyes. But he also noticed the slight lift of her lips.

He stood up, offering his hand to her. She accepted it, and he pulled her to her feet. "Come on, let's go test out our acting skills." He slung his arm around her shoulders.

Flinching, she threw it off her and hopped back. "What are you doing?"

"Do you want to make this look believable or not?"

She sighed, then tucked herself closer to his side, sliding her fingers around his back. "You're right. Let's do this."

Brad pretended not to notice how perfectly she fit under his arm as they slowly walked back around the bluffs, in full view of those now gathered around the bonfire. The sun had all but disappeared behind the horizon, leaving a sliver of light kissing the line where the water met the sky.

To a casual observer, they looked like any couple enjoying a romantic walk on the beach. But inside, Brad's mind whirled. *It's only for a few days,* he reminded himself. They just had to keep up the act until after the wedding. Then Cassie would board a plane back to New York, and Brad could return to his life of pathetic bachelorhood.

Easy, right?

What could possibly go wrong?

Chapter Fourteen

"Wait, you've never had a s'more before?" Brad asked a little later as Cassie sat next to him near the fire, holding a metal stick over the flames. "Seriously, who raised you?"

"Richard and Libby Schalk. They're sitting right over there." She pointed at her parents, who were in the middle of a humorous conversation with his aunt, uncle, and Gram a few yards away from them.

As her focus swung back to Brad, she caught Gemma's stare, and a warmth trickled out from her chest. And not the good kind of warmth. Her sister was looking at her as though she'd sprouted two heads, and her wide eyes signaled danger in Cassie's brain.

Why wouldn't Gemma be alarmed? Or surprised at the very least. Only a couple days ago Cassie had complained about how frustrating she found Brad. Now they were getting all cozy in front of the bonfire?

I'm confused too.

Forcing her eyes away from her sister, Cassie refocused on her conversation with Brad. "I don't really camp," she admitted. Not to mention indulging in frivolous calories was frowned upon in the fashion industry. She really admired Sylvie's ability to push all the pressure to look a certain way aside and eat what she wanted. Her bestie was a total foodie, and proud of it, but Cassie struggled to let go of the expectation to be perfect. A gluttonous assistant reflected poorly on a fashion designer.

She shuddered at the reminder of Adriana's words. The pressure to look a certain way was one of the reasons Cassie loved coming to California, even though it didn't happen as often as she'd like. Being here allowed her to take a break from the toxicity of the New York fashion scene. She felt more of herself shining through with each day here.

Not that she'd ever tell anyone that. Every profession had its downsides. One day, she'd love to be in a place where she could encourage women to embrace clothing styles that made *them* feel good instead of putting so much focus toward the size written on the tag. But until then, she'd endure the negatives of her job and cling to her dreams for the future.

If she still had a chance in the industry at least. That looked more and more like a very big if with every passing day.

"Get ready, Cassie," Brad said, preventing her thoughts from taking more of a downward turn. "You're about to get an education about the perfect way to make a s'more."

"How hard can it be?" she asked with a shrug. "You stick some chocolate and a marshmallow in between two graham crackers, and voilá, you're done."

His mouth dropped open, and he scoffed so dramatically that it had to be fake. "Honey, I'll have you know, it's more complicated than it seems. And it all starts with the marshmallow." He pulled his stick out of the fire and held it out to her. "You want to make sure it's perfectly roasted around the whole thing."

He squeezed it with his thumb and pointer finger before returning it to the top of the flames.

"If you don't roast it long enough, it'll be too hard and won't flatten between the graham crackers. But if you leave it in too long—"

Cassie gasped at the flames exploding onto her stick.

"—it'll catch on fire," he finished with a chuckle.

She drew back the stick quickly and blew at the flaming marshmallow to distinguish the small inferno. She huffed and puffed until all that was left was a smoking clump of ashes with some sticky white poking out underneath. "Well, I guess I ruined that one."

"See, it's not as easy as it looks." He bumped her side. "Thanks for the object lesson."

His smug smile held a hint of playfulness, and she found her mouth stretching into an answering grin.

"I concede," she said, lifting her shoulders to her ears. "Now what am I supposed to do with this?"

"We'll give it to Brooklyn. She likes her marshmallows charred," he said, pulling his stick out of the fire again. Smoke rose from the top of a perfectly golden-brown marshmallow that had bubbled a little at the bottom corner. "Perfection. Here, hold this. I'll take that one."

They traded sticks and Brad pushed himself off the blanket they shared.

"I'll be right back." He strode off toward the fold-up table a few yards away. Cassie's eyes followed him as he approached his youngest sister.

She'd seen them together a few times over the last hour or so since she and Brad had rejoined the group. Their mutual teasing and ready laughter spoke to their close bond and painted him in an even more positive light than Cassie had seen before. In fact, the way he interacted with the majority of his family proved that beneath the macho charisma that he so often resorted to Brad Lucas had a goofy side with a heavy dose of snark.

Perhaps the brash rudeness he'd shown at the bowling alley two years ago hadn't been intentionally mean-spirited after all. It was still annoying, of course. She wouldn't excuse him from that. But maybe it was past time she gave him the benefit of the doubt and let it go.

Cassie watched them joke around, and after a minute, both siblings turned to look at her, leaving no doubt about their topic of conversation. Her face flushed at being caught staring, and she broke her eye contact, pretending interest in the dancing flames of the bonfire.

What had Brad told his sister? Cassie couldn't expect him to keep silent about this ill-conceived plan to fake date, especially after the way they'd both showed their distaste for each other up to this point. She hadn't thought through what they'd tell their families about this thing, and sitting here an hour removed from her encounter with Drew, she couldn't deny the unbelievability of the whole idea.

Was it too late to take it back? To declare a do over of the entire night?

But even if she did, she'd still have Drew to contend with, and this whole mess came about because of him in the first place.

"Get ready to have your mind blown, Cassie."

She jumped as Brad dropped onto the blanket beside her, an open package of graham crackers and a chocolate bar in his hand. Where had he come from? His knee rubbed against her thigh as he crisscrossed his legs. Pulling one of the crackers out, he broke it in half, then proceeded to place half of the chocolate over it.

"Just stick that bad boy right on top," he said, nodding at the stick she still held in her hand. "The chocolate won't melt as much since we waited so long, but it'll still be amazing."

The marshmallow had cooled significantly already but still squished when he pushed the remaining cracker over it. Gooey, white goodness oozed from the sides as she slid the stick out of the sandwich, making her mouth water.

"Perfection." He held it toward her. "Go ahead, try it."

Cassie bit into it and ... wow! Rich chocolate and sweet marshmallow mingled delightfully with her taste buds as she chewed, the graham cracker adding a satisfying crunch. With that one bite, she fell in love.

With the s'more.

Not the man. Because that would be ridiculous.

"What do you think?" Brad asked, pulling the tasty treat away from her mouth. Swirled brown and white strings dangled from the end of it.

She looked at him, nodding her head vigorously and giving him a double thumbs up. "This is really good," she mumbled through her mouthful, then giggled apologetically and swallowed.

He chuckled. "Now you know what you've been missing. Here, you can have the rest." He handed it to her before leaning back on his hands.

"Don't you want some?" she asked, pushing it toward him again.

He shook his head. "I can always make another one."

She bit into it again, enjoying this bite as much as the first until she saw a familiar figure pass a few yards away from them. Tingles zipped up her spine. "Ugh, he's back."

As she'd told Brad earlier, Drew didn't leave the beach after their confrontation. Instead, he'd passed their gathering a few times in the last hour. After she and Brad had rejoined the group, Gemma had pulled Cassie aside and asked about Drew's purpose in being here. She'd spotted him by the picnic table earlier. Cassie may have been slightly elusive in her answer when she'd said she didn't know why her ex had decided to show up.

She did know why. Drew didn't think their relationship was truly over. But that didn't stop the confusion taking over Cassie's brain.

And now her sister was too busy flirting with Tyler a few feet away to realize that Drew had stuck around.

Each time he passed, he stayed far enough away to prevent the others from noticing him. It wasn't like anyone else expected him to be here anyway. In the dark, he looked like someone enjoying a nighttime stroll on the beach. Just minding his own business.

But Cassie noticed him. Sensed him, really. After five plus years of dating, she had the ability to pick out his silhouette and the rhythm of his gait in any crowd from yards away.

But she didn't recognize this stalker persona he'd adopted. She'd never felt unsafe around him before, but the big-time creeper vibes he exhibited right now gave her a bad case of the icks.

She clenched her free hand into a fist, tension fizzing up inside her. A few choice words entered her mind, words she'd love to spit out at him. None of them were at all nice, and her parents definitely wouldn't approve of her language, but the longer she sat here, the more his continued presence stoked the fire of her indignation. She needed to blow off some steam, and Drew provided the perfect target of her wrath.

Before she had the chance to get up, Brad leaned over and muttered something out the side of his mouth.

"What?" she asked, turning to him. Her pulse raced at finding his face only inches from hers.

"Don't do it," he said in an undertone so only she could hear. His breath tickled her ear, causing tingles of a different variety to dance across her skin. "I know guys like him. Going over there would only be playing into his hands. It's exactly what he wants."

How did he know she was contemplating confronting Drew again? "I just want him to go away," she muttered.

"I know," he whispered. "But if you want him to believe that this thing between us is real, you can't let him see that he's getting under your skin."

He shifted closer to her—so close that his body was right up against hers. The warmth of his firm torso seared her side even through his sweatshirt. His arm came around her. "Put your head on my shoulder."

She complied, forcing herself to appear relaxed as she curled into him. With her cheek against his clavicle, his heartbeat thudded against her ear, and nerves flitted through her.

Brad continued in an almost inaudible tone. "We're sitting here, enjoying each other's company."

His fingers found the end of her hair, running down her curls. The gesture would've been comforting if not for the fact that with each gentle stroke, she became more aware of his closeness.

"Nothing else matters but us," he murmured, his breath chasing more goosebumps down her skin.

She unclenched her hand, immediately pushing it against her bare thigh to keep it from shaking. Her pulse drummed in her neck, rapid and unsteady.

What is happening right now? And why did she like it?

Her reaction to Brad didn't make sense. The words he said were completely insignificant. He literally whispered sweet nothings in her ear. Well, maybe not so much sweet as nothing. Still, she shouldn't be responding this way.

Brad's fingers continued their slow, rhythmic trail down her curls. "We're just having a nice romantic moment by the fire ..."

The jitters doing a tango in her stomach no longer correlated to Drew being nearby. Cassie was sure of it.

It's not real. It's not real. It's not real. But that didn't stop Cassie's breaths from shaking. Warmth radiated to the tips of her extremities.

"...in front of both our families."

Cassie giggled, though it sounded a little pitchy to her ears. She glanced around her, suddenly remembering they weren't alone. Brad had woven his magic through her with his attentions, almost convincing her that they really were a couple enjoying a romantic night on the beach.

Gram sat on a beach chair a few feet away, watching them with keen interest. Her sharp eyes trained on them sent the magical spell Brad had woven evaporating into thin air.

Cassie's gaze darted away, only to land on Brad's sisters. Both women were staring in their direction with matching curiosity. The flames illuminated Beej's face to show her giddy excitement.

Swallowing hard, Cassie forced her attention elsewhere, refusing to even look at Gemma. She didn't want to know whether her twin had noticed, or what her reaction would be.

This plan she'd concocted had seemed like a good idea when it had first come to her. But she hadn't thought through the fact that she'd also have to face her family.

And that realization brought more butterflies than the idea of confronting Drew.

Chapter Fifteen

The next morning, Cassie called Sylvie and finally told her about the events that had led her to flee New York. She hadn't been trying to keep it from her best friend. But she still felt bad for bailing on her and couldn't find the heart to admit to the reason she'd skipped town early. After what happened last night though, Cassie needed a round of girl talk.

"He actually stayed?" Sylvie asked indignantly after Cassie finished describing how Drew had hovered on the beach, not quite part of the group, but close enough to keep an eye on her. "Even after you told him to leave? What a creep."

"Yep," Cassie said, surveying herself in the mirror on her vanity. Her phone, which she'd put on speaker while she got ready for the day, was propped up against the mirror's iron frame. She added one more swipe of mascara to her lashes.

"Don't those beaches have any kind of security? Why didn't you go to them?"

"And tell them what?" Cassie asked. "It was a public beach, and he wasn't doing anything illegal. He was just … existing."

"Giiirrrl," Sylvie groaned, "you know I love you to the moon and back, but I'm fighting hard to hold in this big 'I told you so' that's bursting to come out."

Cassie's laugh was devoid of humor. "Apparently not too hard because you just said it."

"Oops." Sylvie didn't sound at all apologetic. "I've said it before, and I'll say it again loud and proud. You deserve so much better than that jerk."

She was right. Cassie saw that now. Drew had made her feel so small last night, so … disrespected. No part of her wanted to be attached to a man like that for the rest of her life. She fumed thinking about the way he constantly ignored her wishes and minimized her reasons for them. And now that she could see their entire relationship more clearly, she wondered why she'd put up with it for so long.

"Tell me more about this other guy in the equation," Sylvie said, pulling Cassie out of the memory of last night. "He sounds hunky."

Thank goodness they weren't on video chat right now. Sylvie wouldn't witness the bright shade of red stealing across Cassie's cheeks. No amount of foundation would ever cover up that blemish. And she didn't need her friend knowing how much last night had affected her.

Brad had been very good at this game they were forced to play. The way he flirted with her unabashedly right there in front of everyone almost made her forget they weren't really dating. It was a little unnerving at first, but also kind of ... fun.

And the tantalizing way his fingers played with her hair as his low voice whispered in her ear? Last night was the most romantic non-date she'd ever had in her life.

"Sylv, there is no equation," she said, squashing the smile creeping onto her face. "Brad is just helping me get rid of Drew. That's all."

"Mmm-hmmm," Sylvie hummed. "That's how it starts."

Cassie tossed her mascara into her makeup kit before picking up her phone and taking it off speaker. "And how it will end. I really don't want to date anyone right now. Everything is still too fresh." She refused to resort to her old ways. Flitting around from guy to guy was the old her. The young, immature her.

"I'm just saying, there's nothing wrong with seeking comfort in the arms of a scrumptious man. After being shackled to Mr. Stick-Up-His-Butt for so long, you should get out and have some fun."

"Sylvie!" Cassie laughed hard. She should be used to the fact that Sylvie had no filter, but sometimes her friend still took her by surprise. "You're horrible."

"Someone had to say it." Sylvie groaned. "I have to get back to the studio before the dragon lady wonders why her precious cappuccino isn't on her desk yet. Now that you're not here, guess who she has running her errands? I don't know how you put up with it for so long. If she gets any more demanding, she might find a little something extra in her drink that's not supposed to be there. You get what I'm saying?"

Cassie held back a laugh. The situation wasn't funny. As Adriana's former errand runner, she knew how demanding the boss could be.

"Thanks for packing up my desk for me," she said instead.

"Don't worry about it. It's at my place, waiting for you when you get back. What will you do now that you're not working here?"

Panic pricked in Cassie's veins. Though she still had the Drew situation to sort out, being in Buena Hills for the past five days had given her a little break from the worry about her jobless state. Talking about it again brought the unwelcome anxiety back to the surface.

"I have no idea," she admitted, dropping onto her bed. "I need to find a new position, but I can't shake the fear that my chances of working in fashion aren't very great after what happened. Adriana will no doubt try to smear my reputation in the mud." Cassie had seen that pettiness used against others before.

Sylvie hummed into the phone. "I'm sure you could find something. Or ... *oh!*" Her voice rose like it always did whenever she'd hit upon a brilliant idea. "You should start your own fashion line. I don't care what Adriana thinks. You'd take New York by storm. Move over suckers! Cassie Schalk is in the *house!*"

"I don't know." Cassie had always wanted to branch out on her own, but not while in a desperate position, like right now. Not to mention the fact that she didn't have the funds saved up yet to support herself, let alone a business on top of it. But she appreciated her bestie's fierce support all the same.

"I miss you," she said, sidestepping that conversation. "I wish you were here."

"Right back at you. But I gotta run. Let's talk soon, okay?" Sylvie made a kissing sound into the phone before hanging up.

Cassie set her phone on her vanity and left her bedroom, heading down the hall. A sweet aroma wafted up from the kitchen as she knocked on Gemma's door. Mom and Dad must be up already. It was only a little after six, but they'd always risen early. Cassie, still operating on New York time, hadn't been able to sleep past four since landing in California.

Gemma, on the other hand, hadn't yet responded to Cassie's knock. No surprise there. Aside from sharing a birthday, they had very little in common, especially when it came to their sleeping habits. Cassie was always up with the sun, while Gemma preferred to take her time in the morning, easing into the day.

When she didn't answer after a second knock, Cassie cracked the door open and poked her head inside. She could barely make out the top of her sister's dark hair under the blankets.

Opening the door a little more, she winced when the hinges creaked. Gemma still didn't stir. Cassie tiptoed to the bed, careful not to upset the cardboard boxes stacked along the wall. They belonged to Tyler, who'd be moving in after they returned from their honeymoon to help Gemma care for Gram.

Once Cassie reached the bed, she crawled under the blankets, cuddling up next to her twin like they used to when they were younger. "Good morning, sleepy head," she said brightly, pulling the blue patchwork quilt off her sister's face.

A muffled moan emerged from Gemma as she threw the blanket over her head again. "Uh-uh. It can't be time to wake up yet," she mumbled. "I'm positive I barely went to sleep."

"That's because you were out with your man last night," Cassie said. "Where did you guys go after the bonfire? It was pretty late when I heard you come in."

Gemma rolled over and blinked her eyes open. "We were talking out on the porch swing."

Cassie waggled her eyebrows. "Just talking?"

"Stop," Gemma laughed. "Yes, talking. And ... maybe some other stuff mixed in." A flush appeared on her cheeks, and she moved on quickly. "It's been so crazy with all the last-minute wedding prep and Tyler's new job, plus all the family coming into town. We haven't had much time for *us* lately. We have to grab it when we can. Even if it means staying up late to get it."

If anyone understood not getting enough time with their future husband, it was Cassie. Although the many red flags were glaringly obvious to her now, she still wondered if Drew's busy schedule had contributed to their downfall.

"It's a hectic time," she said, snuggling closer to her sister. "But a bride needs her beauty sleep."

Gemma rolled her eyes. "I'll keep that in mind, thanks."

"What?" Cassie protested. "It's true. Getting adequate rest is one of the most important things you can do to prepare for the big day. You need to be refreshed and energized, so you're less likely to get sick from all the stress."

"You sound like one of those wedding blogs," Gemma said through a wide grin.

Cassie felt her own mouth lifting. "I may have read one or two. Or hundreds."

That quip didn't have nearly the effect she'd hoped for. Instead, her sister's face fell. "I'm really sorry things didn't work out with Drew."

Cassie propped her head onto her hand. "And I'm sorry about last night. I had no idea he'd show up at the beach. I hope he didn't ruin everything."

"It was a little weird the way he hovered nearby," Gemma admitted hesitantly. "Mostly because I worried about how you'd feel with him being there. But I guess you were a little preoccupied with Brad."

Cassie's face grew hot, and she sent a silent prayer to the universe that a blush wouldn't appear on her cheeks.

"What was that anyway?" her sister asked. "I didn't think the two of you were on friendly terms."

Rolling onto her back to stare at the ceiling, Cassie mumbled, "I'm starting to warm up to him."

She felt the suspicion in Gemma's expression as though she were looking at her straight on. But her comment wasn't a complete lie. After last night, she *was* warming up to him. And not only because of his cuddling skills. Which, for the record, should be given all the recognition. Cassie wouldn't mind snuggling up to him again.

But that wasn't the only reason her heart had softened toward him. This deception she'd dragged him into was a huge ask, and he'd played his part perfectly.

After a few beats of silence, Gemma sat up quickly, looming over Cassie. "Don't you dare use him as your rebound," she said more sternly than her usually good-natured tone. "Brad is Tyler's cousin. Which makes him my soon-to-be cousin-in-law. If something goes south between you two, I'll still have to see him at family gatherings, even if you won't."

Cassie scoffed, offended at her implication. "I haven't had a rebound boyfriend since high school."

Her sister's composure immediately softened. "I'm sorry. Just ... please be careful, okay? I like Brad. He might be a little rough around the edges, but deep down—sometimes very deep down—he has a good heart."

Before last night, Cassie would never have believed her. But he'd shown a different side of himself from the macho, bro-dude persona he'd played so far. He hadn't been faking his concern for her while she confessed the whole pathetic story of blowing up her job and life all in five minutes. She had no doubt about that. And he'd jumped right into the middle of this twisted situation, willing to go along with it to help her out. Maybe there was something more to Brad than she'd originally thought.

"It's not real," she mumbled, more to remind herself of that than to come clean to her sister. The way her stomach dropped to her toes with the admission surprised her.

"What?"

Cassie sat up, resting her back against the headboard, her shoulders sagging. "We're not really dating. I asked Brad to pretend to be my boyfriend, so Drew would think I've moved on."

The confusion in Gemma's face didn't fade, so Cassie continued.

"I'd already told Drew multiple times that it was over between us, but he wouldn't listen. I knew he wouldn't go away unless he had good reason to believe he had no chance of getting back together with me. So, I panicked, and Brad stepped in to help. By the way Drew hung around the beach last night, I doubt he accepted it. He'll probably be back."

Her sister didn't respond right away, and Cassie could see the wheels of thought turning in her head. "I didn't realize things had gotten that bad between you two," she said finally. "Why didn't you break up with him sooner?"

Bringing her legs up to hug her knees, Cassie said. "I guess I kept hoping our relationship would get better. And it was for a while after the charity auction—"

"What charity auction?"

For the second time in twelve hours, Cassie explained about catching Drew with his ex at his mother's auction and how that had led to their breakup before. Each time she dwelled on it, the shame of continuing with the relationship grew even deeper than before. Had she really been naïve enough to think she'd be able to change him?

"That was why you cancelled your Mexico trip?" Gemma asked, her voice soft. She rolled over onto her stomach to meet Cassie's eye. "Why didn't you tell me?"

Cassie swallowed the lump in her throat. "Gram had just had a stroke. You were working through all your stuff with Tyler. And we still weren't all that close back then." They'd only recently developed the kind of relationship that allowed them to talk about things like this. "I'm so happy with how far we've come, but by the time we got to a better place, there wasn't any point of talking about it since Drew and I were already back together. But I can't ignore the warning signs anymore."

"Well, I can't say that I like the idea of faking a relationship," Gemma started, pinning Cassie with a serious look. "This has bad news stamped all over it. But if it will help get Drew to leave for good, I guess I'll go along with it. Just ... please be careful. I don't want to see you get hurt again."

"I won't. Trust me." She clapped her hands on top of her bent knees, closing the book on this conversation. "So, what's on the schedule for today?"

"I have to pick up the bridesmaids' gifts, and Tyler asked me to go into LA to get the Dodgers tickets, since he forgot to check the e-ticket box when he ordered them online. He can't do it because he's packing up the rest of his things at the girls' place today."

In true Tyler and Gemma fashion, they'd both insisted on skipping the traditional bachelor and bachelorette parties and treating the entire wedding party to the Dodgers game Friday night instead. Cassie had resisted at first; as maid of honor, she had some amazing ideas for the girls' night out. But eventually, her sister had convinced her to get on board with the plan. Tyler and Gemma's entire friendship began years ago because of their mutual love for baseball, so the change in tradition made complete sense for them.

"I can pick up the bridesmaids' gifts," Cassie offered. "I already know what they are anyway, so it wouldn't spoil anything." She'd been the one to suggest the monogrammed robes for everyone to wear as they got ready together. The fabric was the same slate blue shade as their dresses, and so silky soft.

"Would you, Cass?" Gemma asked. "That would save me a lot of time. Why does it seem like there's still so much to do and not enough time to do it? I swear I'm going to forget something."

Cassie placed her hands on her sister's shoulders. "You're not going to forget anything. I'm here to help you. Your wedding day will be perfect."

As long as Drew doesn't go out of his way to mess it up.

"You're nearly there," she said, pushing thoughts of Drew from her mind. "Only a few more days, then you'll be happily married to your dream man, and any small mishaps that could've happened—they won't, though—won't matter anymore."

Gemma gave her a close-lipped smile, then leaned forward to hug her. "Thanks for constantly talking me off the ledge. Seriously, I keep thinking it would be so much easier if we eloped."

"Don't you dare," Cassie laughed, squeezing her twin tighter. "Besides, that's what sisters are for." Swinging her legs over the side of the bed, she placed her bare feet on the floor. "Okay, so I'll pick up the robes from the boutique this morning. I need to find a gift for Sylvie anyway. Text me if you need anything else while I'm out. And if you can think of something that screams California for someone who's never traveled west of the Mississippi, let me know, because I'm drawing a blank."

"I'm sure Brad would have some ideas." Gemma crawled out of the bed, her dark curls cascading over her shoulders in gorgeously messy waves, hiding her face. But Cassie didn't need a glimpse at her expression to see right through the casual tone.

She bumped her sister's side on her way to the bedroom door. "I thought you didn't like this idea."

Gemma pursed her lips but that didn't hold back a smirk as they stepped into the hallway. "I don't. I think it has the potential of turning into a disaster. But Brad *is* from California. And maybe spending a little time with him will help you both put the past behind you."

Why did the possibility of spending time with Brad send goose-bumps rippling up Cassie's arm? A few days ago, she and Brad couldn't get through ten minutes without bickering about some-thing. Now, after one night of cuddling under the stars, she was looking forward to spending time with him?

Get a grip, girl. These feelings aren't real. She was just lonely. After being with Drew for so long, she missed having that connection with a man. That had to be it, but she hated how desperate it made her seem.

Had she really not changed since high school?

Chapter Sixteen

As Brad folded the quilt he'd slept with last night, his phone vibrated in his back pocket. Tossing the blanket onto one end of the couch, he pulled out the device, accepting the call without looking at the screen.

"Hey," he said, bending to pick up the pillow from the floor and setting it on top of the blanket. He tilted his head to one shoulder and then the other as he tried to work out the crick in his neck.

"Hey, yourself." Cassie's bright tone came through the line. "Are you up for an outing with me this morning?"

He bit down on his bottom lip to prevent the smile brought on by her unexpected question. One night of pretending to be a couple did not give his subconscious permission to act like a sappy, lovesick puppy.

For the record, he wasn't sappy. Or lovesick. And definitely not a puppy.

"That depends. What did you have in mind?" He pulled his prescription bottle from his luggage by the window and dropped one of the little white pills into his hand. This particular beta blocker had become a lifesaver in his ability to lead a somewhat headache free life. It didn't prevent all migraines, but those he did have didn't last for days like they used to.

"I have to pick something up for Gemma," she said. "And then I need to find a gift for a friend back in New York. How does a little shopping trip sound?"

He doubted a shopping trip with Cassie could ever be considered little. And why would she ask *him* to go? The whole point of their plan to fake date was to fool Drew. She wouldn't want to hang out with Brad unless ...

"Are you with Drew?" His shoulders went stiff, an uncomfortable tightness gnawing in his chest. If her ex was bothering her…

"Nooooo." Cassie paused for a second. "Why would you think that?"

Brad shrugged one shoulder, even though he knew she couldn't see it. "You've made it pretty clear I'm not your first choice of people to hang out with."

"Maybe that opinion has changed after last night."

Was that a little flirty something in her voice? He clamped down his jaw again to keep the smile from creeping back onto his face as he walked into the kitchen. Tyler, Hallie, Beej, and Kendall all looked up from the island, where they were talking over their cereal bowls.

"In that case, you've talked me into it," Brad said into the phone. "What time do you want to pick me up?"

After filling a glass half full with water, he popped the pill into his mouth and chased it down his throat with a long drink. He set the empty glass onto the counter and pulled a bowl from the cupboard next to the stove while making a mental note to call Carlos later to check the status of his Pathfinder. Being forced to rely on others to drive him everywhere while his car was getting fixed had been a major pain the last few days.

A door shut in the background on Cassie's side of the line. "Are you ready now? I'll be there in five."

"How'd you know I'd say yes?" he asked, placing the bowl back in the cabinet. He'd have to settle for a grab-and-go breakfast. Ignoring the curious glances of his family members, he plucked an apple from the fruit basket next to the fridge, telling himself he'd get something more substantial while he was out.

Cassie made a small humming sound before answering. "Why wouldn't you? I'll see you soon. Tootles!" She hung up before he could formulate a response.

Pushing out a quiet chuckle, he shook his head slowly as he pulled the phone away from his ear. He stared at the screen until it went dark. She was a handful, he'd give her that. She'd definitely keep him on his toes.

You're going soft, pal, he thought, shoving his phone back into his pocket. He took a bite from his apple before looking up to find everyone's eyes on him. He swallowed hard, a piece of fruit scraping his throat all the way down. "What?"

"Something tells me you weren't talking to your roommate just now," Tyler said with a smirk.

"No." Thank goodness for that. Damien was a six-foot-five, three-hundred-and-fifty-pound former offensive tackle for Stanford. Not a beautiful, alluring, *confusing* woman who made Brad want to pull his hair out one minute and explore the idea of kissing her the next.

Uhhhh ... kissing? How'd he make that mental leap?

He dropped onto the stool next to his sister. *It's not real.* And there would be no kissing. He couldn't allow himself to get attached, no matter how much she captivated his interest. Situations like this one never ended well for him. After Mandy especially, he'd finally learned his lesson that falling hard and fast for a woman was a reckless flaw in his personality. Now that he realized that about himself, he could work on changing it.

"I know who it was." Beej spoke with a giddy trill in her voice, poking at his bicep with her pointer finger. He glared at her before moving his arm out of her reach.

By the knowing looks his cousins and Kendall shared with Beej, they *all* knew who it was. Of course they did after last night's acting job. Which, if anyone asked, deserved a Golden Globe. Brad had played the part of the besotted fool so well that no one even questioned the weirdness of the entire situation.

Sure, there'd been some odd glances now and then, but only Brooklyn had mentioned anything about it, and only because she mistook Cassie for Mandy. The rest of his family had been too busy with their own conversations to voice their curiosity out loud. Or maybe he was too wrapped up in Cassie to notice. How could he not be with the perfect way she fit snuggled in his arms as they roasted marshmallows in front of the fire? With the intoxicating scent of her perfume filling his space, and their whispered flirting, it had been almost impossible to pay attention to anything else.

The clattering of a spoon on ceramic jolted Brad's thoughts away from the beach. He cleared his throat, hoping it didn't show on his face how much he'd enjoyed last night.

"What I want to know," Hallie said, pushing her bowl to the center so she could cross her arms over the countertop, "is why Cassie would spend the whole night flirting with *you*."

Kendall snickered behind her hand.

"Ouch," Brad muttered before biting into his apple again. "That's a little harsh."

Tyler's amusement was less discreet. "It's a valid question. Three days ago, you couldn't stand her. You've switched your tune so fast you're giving me whiplash."

"What can I say? Women find me irresistible."

The laughter that followed stung a little but wasn't all that surprising. Everyone in the room had witnessed how often he'd struck out when it came to dating, even if only Beej had heard about the whole Mr. Rebound nickname. And she only knew because she'd been there for the incident that led to it. Brad had sworn her to secrecy, and surprisingly, she'd kept his humiliation to herself.

"Wow, guys," he said dryly. "It's nice to know you have such a high opinion of me."

Hallie shook her head, though even she appeared to be holding back a laugh. "I only meant that I thought she was engaged."

"Not anymore," Tyler clarified. "Gemma told me they broke up last week. I'm not sure why he even showed up last night since she's apparently into Brad now. I take it you've both moved past whatever happened two years ago?"

Brad didn't bother responding.

Had he moved past the bowling alley incident? He was working on it. And as far as Cassie's breakup went, he kept the reasoning to himself. That was her story to tell.

"Maybe she prefers the men in this family." Kendall shrugged offhandedly.

Loud coughing punctuated her comment as Tyler choked on the bite he'd put into his mouth. Hallie thumped him on the back. Leave it to their honorary family member to bring up the unfortunate incident between Cassie and Tyler during their teenage years that had all but destroyed his friendship with Gemma.

"We don't speak about that anymore," he said in a raspy voice, pounding a fist against his chest to clear his airway. "That's water under the bridge now. Besides, we were talking about Brad."

All eyes returned to Brad, and he ran his hands down his face, searching for a way out of this conversation. "I'd rather talk about anything else."

"Are you kidding?" Tyler asked, his voice finally back to normal. "After all the flack you gave me when I was pursuing Gemma? I've got one word for you, pal. Payback."

Beej and Kendall both laughed out loud as Hallie tossed an exasperated look at them. "Come on, guys. Leave him alone."

Brad gave her an appreciative nod. "Thank you, Hal. You've always been my favorite cousin."

"I think it's sweet that you're so giddy about her," she continued, a cheeky smile splitting her face. "And don't tell me you're not. We all saw how your phone conversation went. You have a terrible poker face."

His groan rivaled the sound Brooklyn always made when their dad droned on and on about golf.

"I take back my comment about you being my favorite. And she's not really into me." The admission brought heat to his neck, but knowing his relationship history, his family shouldn't be too surprised. Besides, when Cassie went back to New York after the wedding and never talked to him again, they'd find out the truth anyway.

"She seemed pretty into you last night," Tyler mumbled out of the side of his mouth. "I was almost expecting the two of you to start locking lips right in front of everyone. Thank you for not doing that, by the way."

His comment brought more heat to Brad's face. There was a moment last night when he'd been tempted. But he'd managed to hold himself back. Acting like her new boyfriend still didn't give him the right to take that step, no matter how much he'd enjoyed the ruse.

Brad finished chewing the last of his apple and got up to toss it into the trash can under the sink. "Her ex doesn't want to admit their relationship is over. When he showed up last night she panicked and asked me to pretend to be her boyfriend to get him to go away. I agreed to help her out."

"Why you?" Kendall looked at him as though he were something disgusting that had crawled out of the sewer.

He rolled his eyes at her. "You just love tormenting me, don't you?"

Her only response was to aim a sarcastic smile at him. She'd never been silent with how much she disliked the majority of men in the world, and she reserved a lot of her prickly attitude especially for him. He always got the impression it bugged her that he enjoyed sparring with her from time to time. It was kind of fun in a twisted sort of way.

"Well, I think it's great that you're helping her," Beej said, and the look on her face made him uneasy. It was the same look she always got right before sliding into the matchmaker role. "And you never know. It might be fake now, but I'd be willing to bet you'll be dating for real by the end of the week."

Brad shook his head slowly before swiping his empty glass from the counter to put it in the dishwasher. "Not everything ends with a happily ever after." He knew that better than anyone.

The doorbell rang. He slammed the dishwasher door closed a little too forcefully, eager to leave this conversation behind.

"Have fun with your boo," Beej called after him on his way from the kitchen. "Don't do anything I wouldn't do."

"And remember," Kendall added with a snicker in her tone, "no means no."

Brad growled back at them. "You guys are the worst."

The swinging door shut out most of their laughter. He slowed his steps as he reached the entryway.

"Hey," Cassie said when he opened the front door. Her mouth turned up in an easy smile, sending shockwaves of pleasure zipping down his spine.

Man, she was beautiful.

"You ready to go?" she asked.

"Yeah." He stepped onto the porch, a strange uncertainty replacing the pleasure. Did she expect him to go in for a hug? Or maybe he should grab her hand.

He shoved his hands into his pockets instead. They headed to her sedan parked on the street. So, she did know how to parallel park, he noticed, though why his brain felt the need to point that out was a mystery to him.

"What's so funny?" she asked, walking beside him down the front steps.

Had he been smiling? "I was noticing your parking job," he said with a noncommittal shrug.

"Really? We've been together for less than a minute and you're already criticizing my driving?" She gave him a little shove. "I pulled over quickly the other day so my tire wouldn't explode."

"I doubt a little nail would've made your whole tire blow up."

Her nose scrunched up as if she were trying to hide her amusement but not doing a good job at it. "It happens! Ask me how I know. I didn't want to repeat the experience."

"Well then, it's a good thing you had a big, strong man come to your rescue." He may have flexed his biceps a little for good measure, though he couldn't be sure.

"I already told you. I don't need to be rescued." She unlocked her car with the key fob in her hand.

On any other occasion, those words would've been delivered with a bucket full of ice. But the way she looked up at him through her lashes sent Brad an entirely different message.

Completely ignoring his earlier reminder to keep Cassie at a distance, he stepped closer to her. He slid his hand behind her back to grip the door handle, and his heart sped up, thumping against his ribcage. She startled when he leaned into her, and she backed up against the car quickly, sucking in a breath.

"And yet," he whispered, his voice low and husky, "I've rescued you twice now."

Slowly, her eyes traveled up to meet his, and something sparked in their hazel depths that he'd never seen before, especially directed at him. Not the annoyance she usually held for him. And not the flirtation he'd seen last night, but a softness. Dare he even think affection?

Nah. Definitely not that.

Whatever the cause though, it was doing something funky to his heart.

Distance. He needed distance.

Letting out a small cough, he stepped back, opening her door so she could slide in behind the wheel. He took his time circling to the passenger side. *Get a hold of yourself,* he silently reprimanded himself. *You are not falling for her.*

And yet, every nerve ending in his body seemed intent on contradicting that.

Chapter Seventeen

"Stop being so salty," Cassie said, elbowing Brad in the side as they walked along the pavilion of Buena Hills' outdoor mall. The sternness in her voice didn't mask the look of dry amusement on her face.

He begrudgingly followed her toward yet another shop, though he was strongly tempted to dig his feet in and say no more. "We've been at this for three hours already. I'm starving."

The apple he'd eaten for breakfast had worn off before they'd left shop number three, and now his stomach felt as though it was trying to eat through its outer lining. Shopping with Cassie was not for the faint of heart.

At least his grumpiness had the positive effect of overpowering the unsettling feeling that had punctured the air between them on the way to the mall. What had he been trying to prove, coming on to her like that? The way she'd reacted to his closeness, and the look she gave him had awakened a want inside him that he never allowed himself to pursue. Not after so many times of being played.

He moved his head from one shoulder to the other, attempting to combat the stiffness that had settled in his neck over the last little while, a sure sign that a migraine was most likely in his future. Perfect timing. If there was anyone he didn't want to witness his weakened state, it was the woman walking next to him.

"I need to pick up the bridesmaids' gifts for Gemma and then we can eat," Cassie said. Two shopping bags dangled from her hand, swinging back and forth as she walked. A few black-and-white prints of iconic actresses like Ginger Roberts and Audrey Hepburn were wrapped in tissue paper in the larger one. According to Cassie, her friend was a big fan of the glitz and glamor of the golden Hollywood era.

In the smaller bag was a set of avocado salt and pepper shakers to appease Sylvie's love for cooking. Cassie had said she wanted to get something authentically California. As a born-and-raised Californian, Brad despised the fact that his state was associated with such a despicable vegetable. Or was it a fruit? Either way, gross. And yet, he'd eat several right now if it allowed him to fight off this migraine.

He crossed his arms over his chest. "First eat, then shop."

His defiance didn't intimidate Cassie in the slightest. "Are you always this grumpy when you're hungry?"

He scowled at her in response, then pointed at the pop-up kiosk in the middle of the walkway between two lines of shops. Next to the cart, a teenaged girl sat bent over her phone. Her dark hair, with thin purple strands streaked throughout, fell over the side of her face. "See that taco stand over there?"

"Yeah."

"I'm pretty sure I could eat everything on it, plus the stand." He was only partly joking.

Cassie rolled her eyes. "Are you part goat?"

A nasally bleating escaped his throat that sent her into such a state of hysterical laughter that she couldn't breathe.

Awesome.

First, he'd contemplated eating his least favorite food, and now he was impersonating a farm animal. He needed to get some food in him stat.

At least he'd made her laugh harder than he'd ever heard her laugh before. Somehow that felt like a victory.

"I promise it won't take long," she said after she'd composed herself. "I think the boutique is right over there." She leaned forward, squinting to read the names of the shops at the other end of the strip. "*La Robe Parfaite*. Yep, that's it."

"But there are tacos right here." Brad pointed to the kiosk again with one hand, while discreetly rubbing his temple with the other.

She huffed out a dramatic sigh. "Come on." She grabbed his hand and marched toward the shop.

And now, not only were his head and stomach putting up a fight, but his heart had joined in too. It pumped hard, as if doing the Running Man at a college rave.

The princess was holding his hand. He shook his head. No, *Cassie* was holding his hand. After their conversation last night, the nickname didn't quite suit her anymore. He fell into step beside her, ignoring the delightful way her soft skin caressed his palm.

They approached a shop with *La Robe Parfaite* scrawled in pale pink lettering above the door. A short easel sat on the ground out front, advertising their twice-yearly sale.

Cassie came to a stop right inside the entrance and looked around. "I already love this place," she sighed.

The store wasn't large, but rack upon rack of dresses, tops, skirts, and everything else a shopaholic could love filled the floor. More clothes in every color shade were folded neatly on shelves along the back wall. Accessories took up the entire left side of the boutique, and a wall of mirrors stood on the right side, where brown wooden doors hid dressing rooms behind it.

"Can I help you?" a woman asked, approaching them. She looked to be a few years older than Brad and Cassie. Her amber hair was pulled back into a bun, and her eyes smiled behind her oval glasses. A small rectangular tag on her blouse announced her name as Laurel.

Cassie finally let go of Brad's hand and stepped forward. "Yes, hi. My sister ordered some monogrammed robes for her wedding. I'm here to pick them up for her."

"Of course. What's the name?" Laurel asked.

"It should be under Gemma Schalk."

Laurel nodded. "We keep the pick-up orders in the back. Feel free to look around while I go grab them."

"Thank you very much."

As soon as the other woman walked away, Cassie took no time to dive into the racks of merchandise. Brad followed awkwardly behind her.

"Oh, this is gorgeous," she said, handing him the two shopping bags and her purse so she could use both hands to pull out a white dress with tiny pink flowers on the skirt. A coordinating pink cardigan made up the bodice. "I'd totally buy this. It would be perfect for the rehearsal dinner."

Brad didn't answer, unsure if she was speaking to him or not.

She flipped over the price tag and sucked air in through her teeth. "If I still had a job." Sighing, she returned the dress to the rack.

Why did he suddenly have the desire to buy it for her? If he could ever convince a woman to fall in love with him for real, he'd willingly lavish her with gifts to show her how much she meant to him. He'd never let anyone see that side of him though, not even his family. If Beej ever found out he had a soft spot after all, he'd never hear the end of it.

But if Cassie wanted that dress as desperately as she appeared to —and the way she still stroked the tips of her fingers across the delicate fabric showed that she *really* wanted it—what was the harm in getting it for her after all the bad stuff she'd been through lately?

The harm? How about the fact that what they had wasn't real? It would be ridiculous to fork over a bunch of money to buy her something simply because she wanted it. How much did a dress like that cost anyway? Fifty bucks? Sixty? He caught a glimpse of the price tag as she let the dress drop.

A hundred and eighty dollars? Yeah, definitely not happening.

"Excuse me?"

They both turned. A woman about their age faced them, wearing a sky-blue dress with a price tag hanging from the armpit. Behind her, a mirror reflected the zipper still halfway down her back.

"I'm really sorry to bother you," she said, offering a hesitant shrug. "Can I ask your opinion of this dress? I loved it on the hanger, but I'm not sure about it on me. Ever since I started showing, nothing fits right."

"You're pregnant?" Cassie asked, clapping her hands together. "That's amazing! Congratulations!"

"Thanks. It's my first. I've tried maternity clothes, but they all look weird on me. I don't think I'm far enough along." She twittered a laugh. "Sorry, I'm rambling now, aren't I?"

Cassie's warm smile had an immediate effect on the woman. "First of all, you look beautiful. That color is lovely on you. But everyone deserves to feel comfortable in what they wear. Would you like me to help you find another dress?"

The woman's shoulders dropped as she visibly relaxed. "That would be wonderful. My husband is coming back from deployment next week, and I really want to look good when I meet him at the base."

"You have lots of things to celebrate then," Cassie said, nudging the woman near the closest rack of dresses. "Let's find you the perfect thing to wear. I'm Cassie, by the way. And this is Brad." She gestured in his direction.

"I'm Scarlett." She offered a small wave to Brad, who returned it seconds before Cassie whisked her away, leaving him alone by the dressing rooms.

Unfortunately, food was looking less likely in the near future. Lights had begun to crowd around the edges of his vision and the stiffness in his neck had grown more pronounced the longer he stood there. But he ignored it all as he watched Cassie work through a clothing rack with Scarlett. She pulled out dresses in various shades of blues and yellows and pinks, and though he wasn't close enough to hear every word she said, he could imagine her explaining the fabrics of each, as though she already knew everything there was to know about the garments.

Through the hazy vision of his oncoming migraine, he watched her work her magic. An unexpected awe came over him. Cassie had a way with people. He could see it in the way her face lit up as she listened when Scarlett spoke. And he witnessed it in the obvious way she made the other woman feel comfortable.

She truly belonged in this role. Not in the uptight arrogance of the New York fashion scene. She had a certain radiance when helping people. And that radiance had the startling effect of softening Brad's heart toward her even more, of drawing him to her.

Cassie wasn't the woman he'd expected her to be. This moment proved that, and served as yet another reminder that he'd been unfair to her from the beginning.

"Here we are."

Brad startled at Laurel's voice directly behind him.

"Sorry it took so long," she said. "My manager moved a bunch of things around in the back and it took me a hot minute to find where she put the orders."

He mustered a smile he hoped appeared carefree, even though his heart pounded much faster than could be considered normal. "That's all right. I can take it. Cassie's a little ... busy." His eyes traveled to the two women on the other side of the shop, chatting like they were best friends.

Laurel chuckled and held out a white shopping bag with *La Robe Parfaite* written in pale pink cursive across the side. "You're not the first boyfriend I've seen in here holding his girlfriend's things while she shops."

He choked out a laugh that sounded much too enthusiastic than her comment warranted.

Laurel gave him a strange look before walking away. As Brad turned his eyes to Cassie once more, his brain wouldn't let go of that one word.

Boyfriend.

Would it be so terrible if it were real? he thought before his whole body went cold.

He couldn't think that way. The moment he let that idea catch fire, he'd be in big trouble.

Chapter Eighteen

Cassie didn't bother holding back a smile as she sat across the booth from Brad, silently watching him devour five onion rings before coming up for air. He hadn't been kidding about being hungry.

"Are you going to live now?" she asked, then picked up a french fry from her plate and bit off the end.

He paused, another onion ring halfway to his mouth, and glanced up at her. "I don't know yet. Ask me again in five minutes."

She laughed. "By the way you're inhaling your food, I'd think you'd never had a good meal in your life."

"You mock me, but I was pretty close to expiring right in front of your eyes," he said before popping the remainder of the onion ring into his mouth. He rubbed at his temple with two fingers, something she'd noticed him do a lot since they sat down. "Then what would you have done?"

"I would've thrown myself over your wilted body, weeping uncontrollably, and spent the rest of my life wearing black in your honor." Men could be such babies when it came to their stomachs. Drew had acted the same way whenever hunger struck.

Brad stopped unscrewing a small bottle of Tabasco sauce he'd plucked from the condiment stand near the window to fix her with a dry look. "How thoughtful of you."

In truth, she did feel a little bad for how long they'd spent in *La Robe Parfaite*. By the time she and Scarlett had found the perfect dress for her husband's homecoming, Brad's stomach was growling so loudly it wouldn't be a shock if everyone in the whole mall could hear it. Possibly the entire state of California, too.

But the way Scarlett's face had positively glowed as soon as she saw herself in the mirror in the yellow high-waisted dress had made enduring Brad's hangry attitude totally worth it.

Besides, Brad was a big boy. He'd survive. And Cassie had been true to her word. As soon as they'd left the boutique, they'd gone straight to the nearest restaurant around the corner, even though she'd been tempted to stop at no less than three other stores on their way.

"What are you doing?" she asked, watching him lift the top bun of his burger and dump a generous amount of hot sauce straight onto the onion-and-tomato-covered patty. "That's a lot of Tabasco."

"I like things spicy." His attention strayed from his food only long enough to send her a flirty wink.

Cassie wasn't sure whether to laugh out loud or blush at the double entendre. Instead, she shook her head as he replaced the bun on top of the burger and brought the whole thing to his mouth.

"Mmmm, tasty." He swallowed. "Here, try it." He held the burger out so the uneaten side faced her.

She waved it away. "No thanks. I prefer to be able to taste my food."

"Suit yourself," he said before chomping down again. Then he winced, squeezing his eyes shut.

Cassie watched him curiously. "Are you okay?"

He squinted at her, and for a second, his eyes went slightly glassy. Blinking hard, he said, "Yeah, I'm fine."

Silence fell between them, and she picked up her chicken sandwich, still wondering about his behavior as she took a bite. Something seemed off with him. But if he didn't want to talk about it, she wouldn't press the issue. They were sharing a somewhat pleasurable lunch date. The idea of that would have made her shudder with disgust a few days ago. Yet, here he was, sitting across from her in a diner, and she hadn't once felt the urge to strangle him. She'd rather not rock the boat by prying into things he didn't feel like discussing.

"You were great back there with Scarlett," he said, taking her by surprise with the unexpected compliment.

"Thank you?"

Brad pushed his plate to the side and rested his elbow on the table to rub at his temple again. Besides the single bite he'd taken from his burger, he hadn't eaten any of it.

"What? You don't believe me?"

"No, it's not that," she hurried to explain but her brain focused more on his strange behavior than formulating a response. "You saying that ... it's so ... nice."

He chuckled, then sucked a breath in through his teeth as though laughing had caused him physical pain. Cassie's concern grew even more.

"I can be nice when I want to be," he said. "I mean it, though. I didn't realize you had such a way with people. If you can't find a job with another designer, you could always consider doing something like that. A personal stylist? Is that what they call it?"

Cassie set down her sandwich and shrugged her shoulders up to her ears. "It's definitely something to think about when I get back to New York." A heaviness settled over her at the mention of returning to her normal life.

Brad studied her with squinty eyes, and she felt a blush creep up her neck at the way his gaze seemed to pierce right through her. "Do you even want to go back to New York?"

She broke eye contact, shifting her focus to a group of teens passing the window, overloaded with shopping bags. The way he'd zeroed in on the very doubt she'd been having since arriving in Buena Hills unsettled her. Did she want to go back to New York? Being here had given her a nice break from her fast-paced city life.

He was still watching her when she pulled her attention away from the window. "I've wanted to live in New York City since I was twelve." She looked down at her fingers tangled together on the table. "I had this vision for my life. Go to fashion school, get my foot in the industry, and work my way up, eventually starting my own design label. I'd marry a successful businessman, and we'd become this power couple, maybe with a few kids in tow. It hasn't turned out like that at all." She shook her head, embarrassed at the tears stinging her eyes. "I know, saying it all out loud sounds juvenile."

She risked a glance at Brad. He still hadn't eaten any more of his burger, and the rest of the onion rings remained untouched. He sat with his elbows on the table, staring at her with an unreadable expression. His chin rested on the palms of his hands while he discreetly massaged his temples with his fingers.

"Seriously, are you okay?" she asked, unable to hide her growing worry.

Again, he deflected her concern by giving the slightest of nods. "I'm fine. It's just a little headache." He reached over to lay his hand on top of hers, surprising her with the gentle gesture. "Your dreams aren't juvenile."

She studied their ball of hands for a moment, then raised her eyes to meet his. His baby blues sparkled with a kindness that wrapped her up in a warmth she wanted to stay in for as long as she could. This wasn't the Brad Lucas she'd met two years ago. Nor the one she saw earlier in the week. The brash exterior he so often wore had fled to who knew where, leaving a man that made her feel safe and secure expressing how she truly felt.

With a heavy sigh, she slid her hands from under his and placed them in her lap. "Seven years." Bitterness crept into her tone. "Seven years I've wasted in that city, and I have nothing to show for it."

"Maybe." Brad sat back against the plastic covering of the booth and crossed both arms over his stomach. "Or how about this. You've spent seven years figuring out what you don't want."

Cassie scrunched her brows in thought. "What do you mean?"

"Think about it. You've been working your tail off for a boss who doesn't appreciate you. And you've devoted, what, five years?" She nodded, and he continued, "Five years to a man who minimizes you and brushes you aside until the moment he needs you. Is that really the dream you had for your life?"

"No," she whispered weakly. "The problem is that I have no idea what to do next."

"Is that really a bad thing? Now you have the freedom to open yourself up to unexpected experiences."

That was very insightful for a man she used to pass off as not particularly deep. "I didn't think about it like that. I guess now I get to figure out what it is I *do* want."

"Exactly." He squinted at her across the table as though shielding himself from a bright light. "And if there's anything I know about you, it's that you're not afraid to go after what you want. I bet you'll figure it out before too long."

Cassie thought about that for a minute. For years, she'd tried to fit her heart into this life she thought she'd wanted. But maybe what she wanted couldn't be found in New York. Hmm... She'd have to consider that more once she'd processed all the negative emotions of last week.

"So," she said, forcing her voice into a more cheerful tone, "what about you?"

He blinked at her, and she noticed for the first time that the coloring in his face had paled considerably in the last few minutes. "What about me?"

"What's your story?"

"I don't have a story."

She didn't believe that for a second. "Everybody has a story."

"Not me." He shrugged. "I'm just ... Brad."

Cassie saw right through the casualness he'd obviously intended. Annoyance flashed through her. "Why do you do that?"

"Do what?"

Eyeing him for a few seconds, she contemplated dropping the subject. But she'd already spilled her secrets. In the name of fairness, shouldn't he be expected to reciprocate? "You act like you don't care about anything, but it's obvious you do. Why is it so hard for you to be vulnerable?"

Brad matched her stare, and she could see the war going on inside his head. Then he frowned, dropping his eyes to the spot on the table directly to her left. "Because every time I am, I'm the one who ends up hurt."

His simple statement spoke volumes. Cassie's frustration immediately softened. He might put a lot of effort into acting macho, but it was all a shield to protect himself. Gemma's statement from earlier about his good heart began to make sense.

His sigh stopped her internal evaluation. "Sometimes I wonder if there's even anyone out there for me, you know? Every time I allow myself to fall for a girl, it's never real. She's only biding her time until the guy she's meant to be with inevitably realizes what he's missing."

"Oh." *Wow, Cassie. That's the best response you can come up with?* Then the meaning behind his words caught up with her. *"Oh."*

He'd been in this situation before; pretending to date someone to fool an ex. Guilt swirled around in her stomach. When she'd asked Brad for help, she'd only considered how to get herself out of an uncomfortable situation. She'd thought it would be a mere inconvenience for him. A few days of tolerating Cassie's presence before going back to his normal life.

But it was so much more than that. She'd single-handedly played into the narrative he'd already experienced.

At least he didn't have feelings for her this time. Knowing that didn't make her feel any better though.

"I'm sorry, Brad," she said, hoping it would be enough.

He shrugged but didn't meet her eye. "Whatever. It's not like you're trying to make your ex jealous, right? You only want to get rid of him. So, it isn't really the same thing."

Cassie didn't believe anything about that statement. And judging by the palpable discomfort radiating from him, neither did he.

"Want to know something crazy?" she asked, hoping a subject change would shift the mood.

Brad raised both eyebrows, waiting for her to continue.

"We've been together for the last four hours and haven't jumped down each other's throats once."

One side of his mouth lifted in a tiny smile, but he didn't say anything. The last of the coloring had drained from his face.

Alarm bells went off in Cassie's head, and she could no longer ignore the worry that something was seriously wrong. "Brad, please be honest with me. Are you really okay? You don't look well."

He dropped his face into his hands, pressing his fingers to his eyes. "Um, no. Will you take me home? I have a migraine."

Chapter Nineteen

A migraine?

No wonder he's been acting so weird, Cassie thought jumping into action. She hastily slid from the booth while dragging her purse along the bench. "Hang on. I'll go pay for our food and then we can go."

"I'll pay," he mumbled, removing one hand from his head to reach into his back pocket.

She waved away his offer. "Don't worry, I got this. You stay here."

"Cassie, you don't have a job." Every word he spoke sounded labored, as though it hurt his head even more to speak. Yet even in his misery, he still showed concern for her. She never would've expected that of him a few days ago.

She gave his shoulder a little squeeze, and he squinted up at her. "I can manage this." She'd already bought those gifts for Sylvie. What was one more purchase in the grand scheme of things?

No one occupied the cash register by the door when she approached, and Cassie stole another look at Brad in the booth. His hands covered his face again. Poor guy. She'd only suffered through one migraine in her entire life, and that was enough for her to know how awful they were.

She tapped her foot impatiently as she waited for someone to help her. Maybe she should flag down a server. Looking around, she saw no one. Of course.

After what seemed like forever, someone noticed her waiting and came to help her. She'd probably only waited a minute or two, but in her heightened state of urgency, it seemed like a lot longer. The server behind the counter took her sweet time processing Cassie's credit card, but she was finally able to pay the bill.

"We're all set," she said after returning to their table. Brad didn't respond at first, so she tapped him on the shoulder. "Brad, come on. Let's go."

He looked at her with bleary eyes for a minute before scooting from the booth, swaying a little as he stood.

Hesitantly, Cassie watched him grab the table to steady himself, and she debated whether she should step in to help. Drew used to hate it when she fussed over him. He claimed it made him less of a man.

But this was no little headache, and Brad was obviously in a lot of pain. She couldn't stand by and do nothing. After grabbing the shopping bags from her side of the booth, she went to him and snaked her arm around his waist. "Come on, buddy, let's get you home."

The small smile he gave her showed his embarrassment, though it also held a note of appreciation. He draped his arm over her shoulders as they made their way to the door.

The late July heat, oppressive and suffocating, bombarded them as soon as they stepped outside. With Brad's weight on her, Cassie started sweating only a few feet from the air-conditioned café. At this rate, her entire top would be drenched by the time they reached the car.

They made it past three shops before Brad stopped and leaned forward. He moaned, clutching his stomach with his free arm.

"What is it?" Cassie asked, leaning around him to look into his face. "There's a bench over there. Do you need to sit down for a minute?"

He shook his head. "I ... uh ... need to find a bathroom."

Oh no. She had a pretty good idea why. *Please not here.* Her gut twisted at the slight greenish tinge tainting his skin. "Okay ... um ..." She scanned the mall's corridor looking for any sign pointing in the direction of the bathroom. Seeing nothing, she wrapped her arms around his chest, urging him forward. "I think it might be this way."

Brad nodded mutely and straightened, breathing in deeply

through his nose, then out through his mouth like he was summoning up the energy to keep going.

They took one step. Then another.

On the third, he broke away from her with a groan. Rushing to a large gray garbage can outside a children's clothing store, he proceeded to empty his stomach.

"Never mind," he said through a pant, before leaning back over the trash.

She looked away, dialing in all her willpower not to lose her own lunch. That chicken sandwich was looking like a bad idea right about now. Bodily fluids always grossed her out.

As a child, her parents had often referred to her as a sympathy puker. Any time someone near her threw up, she'd follow without fail, even if she hadn't been sick. She still remembered the time Gemma got food poisoning when they were nine. Their parents insisted on keeping the girls apart so they wouldn't have to clean up vomit from two kids.

Cassie shuddered, busying herself with looking through her purse for a tissue. If only she could turn off the sounds coming from in front of her.

"How much do I have to pay you to keep this little incident to yourself?" Brad asked through a groan. He spat into the garbage one last time, then straightened to his full height.

"I promise I won't tell anyone." She took a few steps toward him. But not too close. The smell rising from the garbage had sent her stomach into a full churn. If she got any nearer, she'd surely be joining him at the trash can. She handed him the tissue. "Here."

Brad thanked her weakly and wiped his mouth then tossed the tissue into the trash.

"Do you think you can make it to the car?" Cassie asked. *Please say yes.* She had no idea how she'd get them both to her sedan if he gave a different answer.

He nodded, so she slid her arm back around his waist, if only to offer her support. She wouldn't be able to hold them up if he went down. But she didn't know what else to do.

"This is some migraine," she said as they struggled along the cement walkway past shops and kiosks selling anything from phone cases to little stuffed animals to glittery nail polish.

"They haven't been this bad for a while," he panted.

They? This had happened before?

She didn't have a chance to voice that question out loud. As they rounded the corner, she was so focused on getting Brad to the car that she failed to notice the tall figure coming at them until they almost bumped into it.

"Cassandra?"

The sound of her name brought her back to her surroundings. Stone cold dread dropped into her core as the familiar voice registered in her brain. Raising her eyes slowly, she took in Drew's perfect appearance, right down to the small white bag hanging from one hand.

"What's going on here?" he asked, his scrutiny starting with Cassie. When it switched to Brad, his lip curled in disgust.

She nearly groaned. Why couldn't the universe give her a break? This situation was already bad enough. Adding Drew to the mix sent it into catastrophic territory.

"Nothing. We were just finishing lunch." Her arms tightened around Brad's waist, helping him straighten.

To his credit, he made a good show of pretending everything was fine, like they were simply a happy couple taking a stroll through the mall. Glancing up at him though, she could tell he felt miserable. Cassie needed to get them out of here fast.

"Well, it was nice bumping into you Drew," she said, mentally crossing her fingers behind Brad's back since shopping bags filled her free hand. "But we really need to go."

Nudging Brad to keep walking, she sent up a desperate prayer that just this once, her ex would respect her need for space.

Today was not her lucky day, which fit the narrative of this entire week.

"I called you this morning," Drew said, snagging her arm as she passed, his grip hard and unyielding.

Cassie yanked her arm out of his grasp, almost dropping the bags. "I've been busy." She left it at that and kept walking.

"Didn't you get my voicemail?" he asked, falling into step beside her and Brad's awkward processional. "I have something important to discuss with you."

Cassie glared at him. What part of *we need to go* didn't he understand. "Now is really not a good time. I'll get to it soon." Another lie. She *had* received his message. And she'd deleted it without listening to it. But she'd say anything to get rid of him.

"Are you going to call me?" he asked impatiently.

That would be a hard no. She stopped for a moment and fixed him with a fierce look. "Drew, I said this wasn't a good time to discuss it. Brad isn't feeling well, and I need to get him home. Either help me get him to the car, or step aside so I can do it myself."

His momentary shock gave her enough time to create some distance. Luckily, this time, he stayed put instead of following after them. Yet she didn't dare hope he'd gotten the message that she wasn't interested in a reconciliation.

By the time she and Brad finally made it to the covered parking garage, she practically gasped for air. She hadn't had this much physical exertion in ... probably never. While she enjoyed going to yoga a few times a week, weightlifting didn't appeal to her at all. Dragging Brad through a parking structure was all the strength training she cared to do for a long *long* time.

Although he tried his best to keep most of his weight off her, she still struggled as they stumbled the last few yards to the sedan. When they finally made it, he slumped against the passenger side, rubbing at his eyes.

Cassie thumped the bags onto the hood to dig for her keys. They'd sunk to their favorite spot in the very bottom of her bag. She really needed to think about reorganizing it. Or at least getting rid of some things. She did find the face mask she'd used to sleep on the plane, which might be helpful to him on the ride home.

Once she'd located her errant keys, she unlocked the car. Brad didn't move, so she walked over to his side.

"Hey," she said, shaking his bicep, appreciating the solid muscle underneath her fingertips. *Now is not the time.* "It's open." To prove it, she tugged on the handle, pulling the door open.

As he folded himself into the seat, she put the shopping bags in the trunk and her purse in the backseat. By the time she slid behind the steering wheel, he was sitting with his head back against the seat, his eyes squeezed shut, and his mouth pursed into a thin line.

"Here." She nudged his chest with the sleeping mask. "Put this on. It'll block the light."

Cracking one eye open, he glanced down at the fur-lined, pink-and-white polka-dotted piece of fabric. Cassie giggled under her breath at the side eye he shot in her direction.

"Just put it on," she said, turning the key in the ignition.

The picture of strong, masculine Brad Lucas in a frilly face mask gave her something she didn't realize she needed but wanted to remember forever. The sight completely contradicted the tough guy persona he insisted on wearing.

Unable to resist the temptation, she picked up her phone from the cupholder in the center console and opened the camera app. Snickering quietly, she snapped a picture, a quick clicking sound piercing through the lull of the car's motor.

"Did you just take a picture?" Brad asked incredulously, whipping his head in her direction. The sudden movement made him wince, and he hissed a quiet curse. "I swear, Cassie, if you post that—"

"I'm not going to post it," she said, not bothering to wipe away her grin. He hadn't removed the face mask, and he looked so ridiculous that she had a hard time stifling the laugh attempting to force its way out. "It's for my own personal enjoyment."

He shook his head, mumbling something she didn't comprehend.

The drive to his sister's house passed mostly in silence, broken by the occasional groan from Brad. Once they arrived, Cassie parked at the curb and helped him up the steps and into the house. Muffled sounds from somewhere upstairs met her ears as she walked with him into the living room. Good, someone was home.

"Do you need anything?" she asked once she'd seen him onto the couch. "Aspirin or something?"

Brad slung one arm over his eyes. "There should be some Tylenol in the kitchen. If there's any caffeine in the fridge, will you bring that too?"

Cassie nodded, though it was more a formality since he couldn't see it. Picking up the blanket draped across the arm of the couch closest to his feet, she shook it open and spread it across his body. On her way out, she walked to the window and closed the curtains. Shadows fell over the living room. It wasn't completely dark, but hopefully the dimmer light would help him sleep.

Once he was as comfortable as he could be given his state, she turned her focus to finding something to help his head. She entered the kitchen through the swinging door at the same time that Brad's cousin came in through the garage, carrying several paint-filled brushes.

"Hey." Elise went straight to the sink and turned on the tap. "How long have you been here?"

"Only a few minutes," Cassie said, grateful she wouldn't have to search through all the cabinets and drawers to find what she needed. "Do you have any pain killers? Brad needs some."

"Migraine?" Elise asked, plunging her brushes into the stream of water falling from the faucet. Paint in several different colors mingled together as it washed down the drain. A red smear lined one of her cheeks, like she'd used her hand to brush her face while it was covered in paint. She looked at Cassie with concern, though she didn't seem all that surprised at her cousin's condition.

"It seems pretty bad." Cassie's stomach churned with worry. She hadn't allowed herself to dwell on Brad's health while struggling to get him home. But now that they'd made it through the hard part, her concern returned tenfold. What if he wasn't okay?

Elise gestured to the cabinet next to the fridge. "There's some Tylenol in there."

While Cassie located the medicine, Elise set her half-cleaned brushes down on a paper towel and opened the fridge to pull out a can of Dr. Pepper. A quick hiss punctured the quiet of the room as she opened it. "Here you go."

"Thanks." Cassie hesitated. She had no business gossiping about Brad's condition, but she couldn't help asking the question on her mind anyway. "Does this happen a lot?"

Elise returned to the task of cleaning her brushes, massaging the bristles in the water as she spoke. "Not as often anymore, at least not that I know. Unless he's relapsed since moving away and just hasn't told anyone. I don't know. Right after his concussion they were so bad that he'd have to stay in bed for days. They still creep up every so often, but for the most part, he seems to have a handle on them."

What a miserable way to live. Never in her life had Cassie expected to feel any sympathy for Brad Lucas, but in this moment, that's exactly what she felt. How could she not?

She gave Elise a thankful smile. "I better get these to him. Thank you."

Elise nodded and turned back to her brushes.

Cassie carried the medicine and soda back into the living room. Brad hadn't moved at all since she'd left him. With the crook of his elbow still covering his eyes, she thought he might even have fallen asleep. She entered silently and knelt in front of him. "Brad," she whispered.

A deep grunt emerged from his throat.

So he wasn't asleep after all. "I brought you some Tylenol."

Silently, he removed his arm, lifting his head enough for her to place two white pills in his mouth. She helped him take enough of a sip of the Dr. Pepper to swallow them. Once they were gone, he lay back down and replaced his arm over his eyes.

"I'll leave this here," she said, setting the can down on the coffee table.

He didn't answer, so she rose to her feet and adjusted the blanket around his body, resisting the urge to fuss over his well-being. Instead, she watched him for a moment, her heart softening toward him even more with each rise and fall of his chest. Every moment she spent with him seemed to open her eyes to the man he really was. The man behind the mask he insisted on wearing. And for perhaps the first time in two years, she found herself wanting to know more about him. Not just because of the current state of his health and how he came to be this way, but everything else too.

Another time though. He needed rest. And though the temptation to stay, to be the one to care for him, crossed her mind, there was nothing more to do. With one last lingering look, she tiptoed toward the entryway.

"Cassie?"

She stopped in the doorway and turned. Brad raised his arm onto his forehead so she could see his eyes in the semi darkness.

"Yeah?"

His mouth twitched upward a tiny bit. "Thank you."

The simple, yet genuine, expression touched her heart more than she expected it to. The stress of the last hour melted away.

"Any time," she said softly. She only hoped there wouldn't be another time. For his sake. "Get some rest."

He rolled over to face the back of the couch, his head disappearing underneath the blanket. Taking that as her cue, she silently slipped out of the house.

Chapter Twenty

The next afternoon, Cassie sat at the kitchen table at her grandmother's house, threading a slate blue ribbon through a hole at the top of a small tube of bubbles. Gram had retreated upstairs to rest once the lunch dishes were cleared away, and Dad had left to help Brad's father and Mr. Abernathy with some repairs that needed to be done at the girls' house.

"Cassie, I'm so glad you suggested bubbles," Gemma said, tying her ribbon into a bow and tossing the tube onto a growing pile at the center of the table. "I mean, who decided that tossing rice at people when they leave the ceremony was a good idea anyway? It's like 'yay! You just got married. Let's pelt you with a handful of hard rice. Hopefully, it doesn't get in your eyes.'"

Mom and Cassie shared an amused smile at the imagined scene.

"Actually, rice is a symbol of good fortune and prosperity," Cassie explained picking up another strip of ribbon.

"Again, with the wedding blogs," Gemma said through a laugh.

Cassie didn't comment on her sister's teasing but continued with her explanation. "And you're not supposed to throw it directly at the couple. You toss it up. If people are chucking rice at you, that's a pretty good indication of how they feel about you." Chuckling, she pulled into herself as her sister lightly smacked her arm with the back of her hand.

The doorbell chimed, interrupting their conversation. A knock followed a second later.

Cassie tossed the tube she'd finished onto the stack of bubbles and pushed back from the table. "I'll get it."

Mom and Gemma continued working as Cassie walked into the living room. She loved the open floor plan. She'd spent many carefree days in this room as a kid, learning how to play poker for candy with Grandpa Will, watching movies with Gemma, or flipping through fashion magazines.

Gram had upgraded her furniture since then though. The bright yellow couch that provided a base for so many of Cassie's core childhood memories no longer claimed space in the middle of the room. Instead, an elegant sectional stood in its place. The rest of the décor remained exactly the same as she'd remembered.

A set of two steps made up the entryway leading to the front door. As she approached, her stomach did a little nervous flip as she wondered if maybe Brad had decided to stop by.

Correction: she hoped that he'd be the one standing behind the door.

She hadn't heard from him since leaving his sister's house yesterday. Not that he had any obligation to call her, but that didn't stop her diving toward her phone anytime it chirped with a notification. Was he okay? Had he been able to rest? How did he feel today? All these questions ran through Cassie's mind on a constant loop.

Part of her couldn't believe that Brad Lucas had dominated so much of her thoughts in the last twenty-four hours. But if she stopped to think about it too long, she'd realize that he hadn't been far from her mind since she'd first seen him last Saturday, and certainly not since the bonfire.

Disappointment bubbled in her stomach when she opened the door. It wasn't Brad standing on the porch in front of her, but a guy who looked no older than about sixteen. A giant vase of red roses and baby's breath filled his arms. He flipped his head back to shake the wavy brown hair out of his eyes.

"I have flowers for a Cassandra Schalk?" His voice held that crackly sound that indicated a boy who hadn't quite left the throes of puberty behind.

Cassie held her arms out for the vase. "That's me. Thank you."

"Have a good day," he said, turning to go.

She returned the pleasantry then shut the door, a giddy thrill zipping through her as she carried the roses to the coffee table and set them down. Brad sent her flowers? He didn't seem like the type to lavish a girl with gifts, but she'd been wrong about so many things when it came to him. She wouldn't be surprised if he'd proved her wrong again.

Plucking the card from the three-pronged holder, she opened it, and her eyes immediately drifted to the signature at the bottom of the short note. She frowned.

> Cassandra,
> Please accept this gift as an apology for my actions on Friday. You mean the world to me, and I can't bear the thought of my life without you. Please call me.
> Love,
> Drew
> P.S. Look inside the flowers.

A stifled groan vibrated in her throat. Of course these flowers were from Drew. He didn't do anything small. Every bouquet, every gift was expensive and big. The way the delivery boy addressed her should've tipped her off that these were not from Brad. He never called her Cassandra. The only people who knew her by her full name were from New York.

Cassie read the note again, glaring at the postscript. *Look inside the flowers?* What did that mean?

Unable to help her curiosity, she set down the note and faced the bouquet. Careful to stay clear of the thorns, she dug through the roses until she found the little black box nestled between the silky red blooms. She freed it from the bouquet and flicked it open.

Gorgeous emerald earrings glittered back at her. *Expensive* earrings. She had a pretty good idea where he'd bought them. That explained his appearance at the mall yesterday. She huffed out a breath. This was the Andrew Covington she knew. The man who insisted on wooing himself back into her good graces with elaborate gifts.

She picked up the card again, glancing at the message for a long minute. Nope, his efforts wouldn't work this time. She refused to go back to him ever again. Resolutely, she ripped the note in half. After tearing it in half again for good measure, she tossed the pieces onto the coffee table.

Sinking onto the couch, she dropped her face into her hands. How was she going to get out of this mess? Why couldn't it ever be easy for her? She just wanted to move on with her life and figure out the next step. How could she possibly do that when Drew insisted on dragging her back into the muddy waters of their relationship every time she tried to escape?

Before she could dive too deep into her self-pity, the doorbell rang again. With a sigh, Cassie pushed herself off the couch, even though she had the sudden desire to lay down and take a nap.

Her red flag siren spun wildly out of control as she approached the door with hesitant steps. What if she opened it to find Drew on the porch?

There was only one way to find out.

Chapter Twenty-One

Brad couldn't remember the last time he'd felt this nervous waiting for a woman to answer the door. It had taken him more time than he cared to admit to work up the courage to come over to Cassie's at all.

As he stood on the porch, he shoved his hands deep into his pockets and rocked back and forth on the balls of his feet, listening for sounds inside the house. The events of yesterday afternoon were still a little fuzzy in his post-migraine haze, but one detail burned in the forefront of his mind.

She'd seen him throw up.

He squeezed his eyes shut, the humiliation of those moments returning in spades. As if he needed any more reason for her to be completely disgusted by him. She probably couldn't wait to get back to New York and never see him again.

The door opened and there she stood, gorgeous as always, her hair framing her face like perfection personified. But out of all the qualities that made her so beautiful, it was the way she looked at him that stood out to him the most. He didn't detect any disgust in her gaze. In fact, she seemed relieved to see him, maybe even happy, judging by the smile she gave him.

He'd take it. He loved that smile.

She eyed him from head to toe, her blonde eyebrows forming a deep V. "Hey."

"Hey," he echoed, rubbing at the nape of his neck and trying to hide the nerves welling up inside him. With his other hand, he pulled the hot pink face mask she'd let him borrow from his back pocket. "I just stopped by to give this back to you."

As she took the mask from him, her hand brushed his, sending goosebumps rippling up his arm. *Play it cool, man.* He'd already made a fool of himself at the mall. He couldn't let himself get all mushy over an accidental hand touch.

"Thanks. Do you want to come in?"

"Sure."

She stepped back so he could enter. As soon as he crossed the threshold, he caught sight of the elaborate bouquet of roses sitting on the coffee table. A small black jewelry box sat open next to the vase, and Brad glared at the emerald earrings twinkling in the black velvet. He clenched his teeth. Those had to be from Drew.

"I guess I should've brought you a better gift." Wow, did that sound as bitter to her as it did to him?

Cassie gave the flowers a mean side eye before responding. "Don't be silly, you gave me the best gift by wearing this mask," she said through a giggle. She tossed it toward the coffee table and the strap got caught on one of the flower stems. It dangled off it haphazardly. "I'll remember that little nugget forever."

"I can't believe you took a picture." He shook his head in disbelief, though he couldn't disguise his amusement. "I was already in so much pain I couldn't see straight, and you decided that was the perfect photo opportunity. Heartless woman."

Her grin grew wider. "I was only trying to keep your ego in check."

"Oh, is that what you were doing? I think seeing me with my head in the trash can should've done the trick." He grimaced. *Nope, it's still too soon to talk about it.*

All trace of her laughter fled in an instant, replaced with concern. "How are you? Really?"

He shrugged, playing off how much he still felt the aftereffects of the migraine. "The headache's gone, thankfully. My neck is really stiff and sore, but that should go away in a few days."

She studied him with an expression that he felt all the way in his core. No words were said. She just watched him as though pondering something she didn't feel like sharing.

"Come here," she said finally, grabbing his hand and dragging him further into the living room.

"Where are you taking me?" he asked, allowing her to lead him to the couch. The question was more of a formality though. With every opportunity he had to hold her hand, the more he decided he *really* liked it. She could take him anywhere right now and it would make no difference to him as long as she continued the connection.

She pointed to the cushion nearest the arm of the couch. "Sit right there."

"Yes, ma'am. You're cute when you're bossy." He jiggled his eyebrows seductively, satisfied at the light flush of her cheeks. So she wasn't immune to a little flirting after all.

Dropping onto the couch with his back facing the end, he straightened one leg across the cushions while planting the foot of the other on the plush carpet. She slipped behind him to sit on the arm.

"What are you doing?" he asked, unable to stop his brows from shooting upward.

With her body higher than his, her feet nestled on either side of him. "Just lean back against the pillow."

He complied, and soon her fingers found his neck, massaging the soft spots behind his ears in small circles. The gentle pressure relieved the lingering pain from his migraine and a moan of pleasure escaped his throat.

"I think you missed your calling as a masseuse," he muttered, relaxing deeper into the pillow at his back. His eyes drifted closed.

"I don't think I would like that. Giving a handsome man a massage is a lot different than some stranger with a skin condition."

Wait, did Cassie Schalk call him handsome?

Dropping his head back enough to look up at her, he noticed the surprise in her expression. Yeah, she definitely hadn't meant to admit that out loud. "So... You think I'm hot, huh?"

"Don't let it go to your head."

His sharp crack of laughter brought another one of her gorgeous smiles to the surface.

"Admit it," he said, puffing out his chest in feigned smugness. "You think I'm pretty awesome."

"Meh, you're all right." Her coy look said otherwise.

"Meh?" He popped up, turning all the way around to gape at her. "You gave me a meh? That's only slightly better than ew. I mean, I'm not fluent in teenage girl talk but that's what Brook says."

Cassie turned him back around and pulled him against the throw pillow as she laughed. The sound was like a symphony to his ears. Or a packed football stadium cheering just for him. For perhaps the first time, it really hit him how much he loved hearing it. Making her laugh was becoming his new favorite hobby.

He relaxed more deeply into her touch so she could continue her massage. They sat in companionable silence, though *companionable* might not have been the right word for the way his body reacted to her hands as they worked their way to his shoulders. It didn't seem possible for his heart to beat as rapidly as it did while also settling into complete contentment. Yet that was exactly what happened as her capable fingers not only loosened the knots holding his muscles captive but eased the lingering embarrassment of yesterday's events.

Nothing in her actions spoke of a woman disgusted by witnessing him throwing up in a trash can. She seemed genuinely concerned about him and wanted to relieve his suffering. Once again, her compassionate nature awed him.

"Can I ask you something?" she asked a few moments later.

"Hmm?"

She hesitated a few seconds as though debating whether she should proceed. "Never mind. It's probably none of my business."

Brad shifted enough to look up at her again. "No, go ahead. Ask me anything."

She bit down on her lip, dropping Brad's gaze to her bow-like mouth, and something stirred inside him. An awareness that had been there all along, though he'd refused to admit it before now.

"Elise told me you get migraines a lot," she said, her hands cradling his shoulders even though her fingers had stopped massaging. "And you said at the mall yesterday that they haven't been as bad for a while. But ... how often do they happen?"

He turned back around, pondering her question for a moment. Talking about his health usually made him uneasy, like people would attribute his medical condition as weakness. But she'd already called him out yesterday for not being vulnerable, and after the way she'd helped him, he owed her an answer.

"I've always been susceptible to them. Even as a kid, I remember having them occasionally. But they started getting worse after my last concussion. I used to suffer from several a month, ranging from mild to what you had the privilege of witnessing yesterday." He leaned his head back to look up at her again, shooting her a self-deprecating smile.

"Several a month?" Her mouth dropped open in horror. "That sounds awful. But they've gotten better?"

"For the most part. I still have them, but I take medicine for it, and as long as I'm diligent in managing my triggers, I've been able to keep them in check." The sound he made fell somewhere between a humorless laugh and a snort. "Apparently, I didn't do a very good job at that yesterday."

"What are your triggers?"

This was usually about the time when Brad began searching for a way out of the conversation. For some reason though, he didn't mind talking about it with her. "Extreme heat, mostly. And hunger."

"Hunger?" Her voice rose in an unnatural pitch as she no doubt relived the events of yesterday in her mind. "Brad, I'm so—"

He reached up and placed his hand on hers where it rested on his shoulder. "I didn't mean to imply it was your fault. It's not. You didn't know. This one's on me. I should've eaten more for breakfast than that piddly apple."

"Well, I definitely didn't help, dragging you around to all those stores before finally letting you eat." The guilt on her face hadn't eased. "Do you ever worry about how those concussions will affect your future health?"

He'd been worrying over that question constantly since his condition first started, though he refused to share those fears with anyone. He couldn't allow himself to succumb to the potentially crippling anxiety about the possibility of a long-term disability. Yet once again, Cassie didn't shy away from getting to the heart of his fear.

"All the time." His voice cracked with the admission.

He wasn't sure how long he lingered in the rising sadness, waiting for her to respond. She didn't. At least not in words. Instead, her arms came fully around him, cradling him from behind. He rested his cheek against the side of her knee and closed his eyes, soaking in the unexpected comfort that came from their odd sitting arrangement.

"I'm sorry you have to live with this," she whispered finally, resting her chin on the top of his head. "I can't imagine what it's like."

Brad reached up to hold onto her forearms crossed over his chest. "It's part of why I quit playing football. My last concussion was a really bad one, so my doctor recommended I stop. I listened, but I've always wondered if I made the right decision."

"Of course you did." Her voice rose with urgency. "You were prioritizing your health and your future. There's no shame in that."

He shrugged, releasing another heavy sigh. "I want to believe that, but my entire life, all I've wanted to do was play professional football. It's a tough pill to swallow being forced to give that up because of circumstances beyond my control."

"I understand that completely," she muttered.

Yes, she did. Maybe that was why he'd agreed to help her get rid of Drew. They were living a similar disappointment.

He swung his body around to face forward on the couch and motioned for her to slide down next to him. When she did, he held his hand palm up on his thigh. She covered it with her own, weaving their fingers together.

"We make quite the pair, don't we?" he asked, bumping her shoulder.

She chuckled, and the sound lifted the melancholy mood that had taken over the space between them. "I guess we do."

"Oh, and now Carlos is trying to talk me into applying for an assistant coaching job at the high school here in town." He wasn't sure what had prompted him to tell her that, but the way she'd responded to his earlier worries, perhaps she'd be able to help him sort out his thoughts about this newest complication. "He thinks I'll be a good role model for the boys."

"And you don't?"

How was he supposed to answer that question? Dad had tried to talk to him again this morning about applying for the job, but like last time, Brad sidestepped the conversation. Maybe it was the sensation of her hand in his, providing both comfort and encouragement, that made him an open book right now.

He ran his thumb along her soft skin, getting caught up in their unlikely camaraderie. Only a few days ago they couldn't get along. Now, she'd dominated his thoughts more often than not.

And he wasn't mad about it.

"It's not that I don't," he started. "I just hated my high school coach. He took the sport I'd loved playing my entire life and turned it into a chore. I almost quit because of him. The only reason I didn't was the hope that college would be better."

"Why did you hate him so much?"

"He knew how to win games, that's for sure. But he was ruthless during practice. His idea of conditioning was making us run wind sprints until we puked. It was supposed to toughen us up, take the wuss out of us, as he said." He screwed his voice to sound like his former coach. "'Pain is weakness. Show no fear.' Any time we messed up on a play during a game, we knew he'd punish us during the next practice."

Cassie's beautiful mouth pulled into a frown. "Isn't that abuse? I can't believe no one did anything about it."

Brad shrugged. "We wanted to win. And he knew how to do that. We wouldn't have made it to state without him."

"It's still wrong." She sank back against the couch cushion in a pout.

A smile crept onto his face at her reaction. "I know that now. But as a teenager, I'd do just about anything to play football. Now that I realize the lasting effects Coach Sanders had on me, I'd rather not have that kind of influence on other kids. Even if Carlos insists I'd be good at it."

"I think you're looking at it the wrong way."

"What do you mean?"

Cassie covered their connected hands with her other hand, deepening the physical support she was already giving. "You're so concerned about being a bad influence, but what if you thought of it as an opportunity to be the kind of coach you didn't get when you were in high school?"

He let that counsel stir around in his brain for a bit before responding. "I hadn't thought about it that way."

"Maybe you should," she said, her gaze meeting his. "Someone once told me that when one dream dies, you open yourself up to unexpected experiences."

Brad remembered giving her that same speech at lunch yesterday. "You're saying I should take my own advice?"

"It's up to you."

She pulled her legs onto the couch, then surprised him by leaning into his side. His pulse picked up speed, just as it had when they were snuggling at the bonfire. Letting go of her hand, he slid his arm out from under her and wrapped it around her shoulders.

"I'm not even sure I'd be able to make it work." He shifted enough to tuck her more comfortably against him. "The job is only part time, but I'll be traveling a lot to cover games for my career, plus the radio show. It might be tough to fit in coaching on top of all that."

"Maybe you're right," she agreed. "You could try though. If it ends up being too much, it's always okay to change your mind."

They lapsed into silence again while he considered her suggestion. Muffled voices carried to them through the kitchen door. With Cassie's parents, Gemma, and Grandma June all staying in the house this week, it had been a stroke of luck that no one had walked into the living room before now.

"I think I owe you another apology," Cassie said after a few minutes.

Another apology? For what?

"That night at the bowling alley?" Nerves sounded in her words. She bit her bottom lip again.

She seriously needed to stop doing that. If she kept drawing his attention to her mouth, he very well may discover how soft those picture-perfect lips really were. With *his* lips. Hmm ... he could get on board with that.

"I shouldn't have dumped your drink all over you," she continued, seemingly unaware of the direction his thoughts had taken. "It was inappropriate, and as soon as I did it, I immediately wished I could take it back."

"Why'd you do it?" he asked, though the memory of that night no longer made him angry.

"It was the trash talking." She sat up quickly, her head whipping in his direction. "You wouldn't stop, and it finally got to me. I know, it doesn't excuse what I did. The only thing I can say is that I wasn't in a good emotional state at the time. I was going through a lot with Drew, and I attributed my bad feelings toward him onto you. And then you called me princess and I just ... snapped."

"Princess?"

"I've always hated that nickname. You're not the first person who's called me that. But I'm not one." Her tone turned a touch desperate. "I'm not perfect, and I've done a lot of things I'm not proud of—especially in high school—but I've tried to be a good person. And it hurts that so many people seem to think I'm this stuck-up priss."

"Wow." That was all he could say at first as he took in the pleading in her glassy eyes. Seeing her sudden emotion planted a seed of guilt in his heart. He'd never meant to offend her. He'd only been running his mouth like he always did. "First of all, I fully admit that my trash talking can be a bit much. My family's used to it, and they dish it right back at me anyway. I forget that it rubs other people the wrong way sometimes. So ... I'm sorry."

Her face morphed into a relieved smile, and she blinked back the tears.

"And I didn't know that being called princess bothered you that much." He nudged her back into position at his side with the arm that still circled her shoulders. "I won't do it anymore. Now that I know you better, I know you're not like that."

"Thank you." She relaxed into him again, and they sat that way for a long beat before she spoke. "Brad?"

"Yeah?"

She lifted her chin to rest on his shoulder. "I don't want to be your enemy anymore. Do you think we could put the past behind us and just be friends?"

Turning his head, he found his face mere inches from hers. His pulse, which hadn't returned to normal since she'd sat down next to him, raced even faster. It would be so easy to kiss her right now. But was that what she wanted?

"I think we already are," he murmured, unable to look away from her eyes. The tears were gone, leaving a question there he couldn't quite interpret. He suspected they were even more than friends now. At least as far as he was concerned.

Closing the small gap between them, he pressed his mouth to her forehead, his kiss lingering for a long breath. Her sweet scent invaded his senses, wrapping him up in all of her. For a moment, he allowed himself to picture a world where she was actually his.

But she wasn't his. And she never would be. Not with her returning to New York in a few days.

The reminder had the effect of dousing him in cold water and he pulled away slightly. He couldn't allow himself to get caught up in real emotions over their pretend relationship. They might be friends now, but they weren't a couple. He had to remember that before he got carried away.

Because this time, he was determined not to get his heart broken.

He needed a distraction. Right now. Something to give him a reason to create some distance from her intoxicating scent. Especially since his willpower refused to do its job at the moment.

That distraction came in the form of uneven footsteps and a lot of grunting on the staircase behind them. Cassie turned toward the sound, allowing him enough space to catch his breath.

"Gram!" she cried, jumping up from the couch. "What are you doing? You're not supposed to come down the stairs by yourself. You could fall."

Her grandmother huffed, giving a very good impression of a child being denied her after-lunch treat. "I won't fall if I'm holding onto the handrail." She waved Cassie's worry away with the book she held in her free hand. "I refuse to wait around for people to come get me when I have places to be."

Now Brad knew where Cassie got her feistiness. As she hurried toward the stairs, he followed, then grabbed her hand to pull her back, giving her a look that he hoped communicated that he'd handle it. He didn't doubt her ability to help her grandmother, he just felt the need to relieve this task from her. To help *her*.

He took the stairs two at a time until he reached the older woman, who hadn't even made it halfway down. "Here, take my arm."

"Though from a strong, good-looking man, I'd be much obliged," she said with a wink before raising one of her white brows high at her granddaughter.

Cassie rolled her eyes.

Placing Grandma June's wrinkled hand in the crook of his elbow, he helped her take each step until they reached the ground floor. She nudged her granddaughter as they passed. "I like this one, dear," she said, her voice shaking. "He's a real keeper."

"Thank you, Gram," Cassie deadpanned. "I'll keep that in mind."

Brad leaned toward Cassie, not bothering to hold back his grin. "Did you hear that? She says I'm a keeper."

"Again, don't let it go to your head."

Once they saw Grandma June settled comfortably on the couch with a blanket over her legs, she opened her book and looked at the page, though her expression was too pointed to convince him she was actually reading.

"Just pretend I'm not here," she said into the book. "Go back to what you're doing. I promise I won't peek, even if it involves a little smooching."

"*Grandma!*" Cassie shrieked at the same time a laugh burst from deep in Brad's chest. "There will be none of that."

Grandma June shrugged innocently. "I'm just saying. Don't let me interrupt."

Cassie groaned, her cheeks turning as red as the roses decorating the coffee table.

Still chuckling, Brad backed away from the couch and shoved his hands into his pockets. "I should get going anyway. Beej let me borrow her car to go look at an apartment in the city. I need to do that before I have to be back to pick her up. We're heading over to Carlos' later for dinner and game night." Though he'd much rather stay here with Cassie.

No offense, Carlos.

He shook away that temptation. It was for the best that he had to go. Thoughts like the ones he'd entertained while being here had the potential of leading to real feelings. These desires that came over him every time he saw her lately—to hug her, to kiss her, to hold her hand—had to stop.

Cassie obviously had other ideas though. As she walked him to the door she asked, "Do you want some company?"

"You want to go apartment hunting with me?"

She kept her head down but looked up at him through her lashes. "You might need a second opinion."

He should say no. That would be the smart thing. Then why was he grinning like he'd just won the Super Bowl? "Let's go then."

They stood there smiling at each other for a long moment. Too long to be considered normal. But he didn't feel weird about it.

"You kids have fun now," Grandma June called, breaking the spell. "Don't come back too early if you know what I mean?"

Brad snorted as Cassie took his arm and dragged him from the house.

"Sorry about that," she said on the way to the sedan parked on the street. "My grandma can be a bit much sometimes."

He flashed her a wide grin. "Are you kidding? Your grandma is my new favorite person."

And despite how wishy washy it made him sound, he wouldn't mind following the old woman's suggestions.

Especially if it involved kissing her granddaughter.

Chapter Twenty-Two

Apartment hunting with Brad had been more fun than Cassie expected, so when he'd invited her to come with him to the Rivera's for dinner, she didn't hesitate before saying yes. Their romantic relationship might be fake, but she'd been serious about wanting to be his friend. And it was natural for friends to hang out together. The way her heart started racing every time he looked at her was also natural, right?

Once the dinner dishes had been cleared away, Carlos' wife, Sofia —a lovely woman who'd welcomed Cassie with a kiss on both cheeks—had suggested a rousing game of Pictionary, of all things, while their stomachs settled before dessert. Apparently, the Riveras, and their two kids, had a long-standing history of being ruthless with paper and permanent marker, in a hilarious way. Cassie hadn't laughed as hard as she had tonight in a long time.

Sitting in the cozy living room, she watched Brad scribble furiously on a white pad of paper perched on an easel in front of the fireplace. Commotion erupted all around her as their team shouted out guesses.

"A cyclops on crutches!" she called out over the noise, giggling when he shot a strange look in her direction.

"What? That's what it looks like!" Truthfully, she had no idea what to make of the black lines on the page. Brad was no artist.

"That's time," the Rivera's twenty-year-old daughter, Angelina, called over the ruckus.

Brad groaned, flipping the marker into the air in defeat. It landed on the woven rug at his feet. "Come on guys, it's a pirate. Don't you see the eye patch?"

Brooklyn tilted her head to the side and squinted one eye shut. "Ooooh, is that what that is? I thought his eye was swollen."

Incredulously, he looked back at his indecipherable drawing. "Okay, maybe his face is a little messed up, but how could you have missed his peg leg? It's completely obvious."

"What's on his shoulder?" Beej asked, leaning forward and furrowing her brows.

"It's a parrot."

"That summer of art camp really paid off, didn't it, son?" Mr. Lucas asked with a chuckle, rising from his chair and picking up the marker his son had tossed onto the floor. He clapped Brad on the shoulder as they passed each other.

Cassie scooted over on the couch to make room for Brad to sit next to her. She leaned close to him to whisper in his ear. "Art camp?"

One side of his mouth rose in a crooked smile that hatched a few butterflies in her stomach. "I made it two weeks before begging my parents to let me quit. Art is not my forte."

"Underachiever ..." She leaned toward him and bumped his side.

His full smile broke free at her teasing. "I know, I know."

Once the commotion of guessing started again, conversing grew more difficult, so she contented herself to sit next to him, laughing at the outrageous suggestions being tossed out at increasing volumes.

The longer the game wore on, the more hyperaware she became of every one of Brad's movements. No shift of his leg or twitch of his fingers went unnoticed. Cassie tried her best to remain present in the game even though a part of her wanted nothing more than to go back to this afternoon when she and Brad were alone in Gram's living room.

Finally, while Beej stood at the easel scribbling furiously on the pad of paper, Cassie gave in to the temptation to glance over at him. He stared intently forward, his face scrunched, and his lips pursed in a straight line.

Maybe already witnessing him suffer through one migraine first-hand was pricking her concern. Or maybe she'd just realized how much she'd come to care for him. Whatever the reason, she couldn't help the unease swirling inside her due to his discomfort.

Had he downplayed his recovery earlier? Was he suffering more than he'd admitted?

Touching his arm, she shifted closer to him enough to speak quietly but still be heard over the voices shouting out their guesses. "Are you okay?"

He turned a questioning gaze her way.

"Is it another migraine?" she pressed.

"I'm fine," he said with a simple head shake.

"Then what is it?" Something clearly bothered him. Did he often have two migraines so close together?

He shrugged a shoulder and spoke out of the side of his mouth. "You pointed out one of my flaws today, so I'm trying to work on it. Even though I'd like to tell Beej what I really think about her drawing abilities."

His simple statement sucked all the air from Cassie's lungs.

He'd listened to her.

It was more than that though. Not only had he heard what she'd said, he hadn't brushed off her frustration. He hadn't made her feel like she was being too sensitive. Instead, he'd taken her words to heart and was actively trying to change.

That touched her more than fancy gifts and extravagant bouquets of flowers. This was the kind of man she'd always wanted. The kind of man Drew used to be.

And yet, Drew hadn't measured up to her expectations after all. But the man she'd written off as not her type seemed to be checking all her boxes.

Who knew life had such a twisted sense of humor.

With their already close proximity on the couch, it would be so easy to thread her arms around Brad's elbow right now. Or place her hand on top of his where it rested on his thigh.

But that would be a very couply thing to do. And since Drew was nowhere nearby, and at least some of Brad's family knew about the ruse, Cassie had no business acting out her part.

Even though she suspected her feelings weren't acting at this point. They were crossing into real territory now.

After the game ended—Brad's team losing miserably—Sofia clapped her hands onto her thighs and declared it time for dessert. They all moved back into the dining room. Carlos offered to dish up the strawberry pie, insisting that his wife enjoy the Lucases' company.

Brad had wanted to pick the man's brain since his conversation with Cassie earlier, so he jumped at the opportunity to talk to him without the rest of his family listening.

"Need some help?" he asked, stepping into the kitchen.

Carlos stood at one counter, his back to the door. The kitchen was smaller than the one at Beej's house. Plates and silverware took up one side of the double sink, and the leftovers were lined up in their serving dishes along one counter. But other than that, the space was spotless.

Carlos barely glanced up from slicing the pie. "There's some ice cream in the freezer. Would you get it?"

"Sure." Brad walked over to the refrigerator and opened the bottom freezer, then pulled out a tub of vanilla. Thumping it on the counter next to the pie dish, he went in search of a serving spoon.

"There's an ice cream scoop in that drawer over there," Carlos said, pointing to one side of the stove.

Once he found the scoop, Brad went to work dishing the ice cream next to the slice of pie on each of the blue and white china plates.

"So, I've been thinking about what you said," Brad started, not looking up from his task. "About the coaching job."

"Oh, yeah?" Carlos's tone held a note of interest, and he set the knife into the pie tin to give Brad his full attention. "And?"

Brad snapped the lid on the top of the ice cream. "You might be right about being a role model for those kids. Maybe after everything I've been through, the lessons I've learned, I have something to teach them after all."

Leaning his hip against the counter, Carlos crossed his arms over his chest and studied him thoughtfully. "I know the last few years haven't been easy for you. You were put in a difficult position and forced to make a decision you didn't want. That would be a tough thing for anyone."

Brad swallowed the sudden lump in his throat, keeping his focus on the pattern of the wooden floor at his feet. How was this topic still so hard to talk about even five years after the fact?

"I know you're frustrated," Carlos went on. "And that frustration can lead to bitterness, which I've sensed from you for a while." He clapped Brad on the shoulder. "Being disappointed with the bad cards you've been dealt is human nature. But you can't let it take away from all the good things you have in your life."

Brad thought about that. He fully recognized that he had a lot of things going for him. He'd been raised by outstanding parents. He'd just landed a great job that could lead to more opportunities in the future. His family loved him despite his flaws. Even his relationship with Beej had become so much better lately, though he could still try a little harder on that front.

And Cassie...

What about Cassie? He could no longer deny that he'd grown to care for her. In only a few days, she'd worked her way into his heart —the same heart that threatened to beat out of his chest at this very moment. Because thinking back on the time he'd spent with her, he realized that he'd opened himself to the one thing he'd promised himself not to do.

He was falling in love with her.

How could that be? She was going back to New York in four days.

On top of that, all of Brad's previous relationships had ended in disaster. Even being fake, this one would likely follow the same destructive path. He had to protect his heart, though at this rate, he feared it was already too late for that.

What was he supposed to do now?

"Huh," Carlos said in a tone of contemplation. "Now that doesn't look like the face of a woman who hates you."

Brad recognized where that comment had come from. He'd said that same thing about Cassie at the auto shop the other day. But why would Carlos bring it up now?

Furrowing his brows, Brad turned to his mentor, then followed his gaze into the dining room. No door separated the kitchen from where the rest of the group sat at the table. Conversation buzzed through the room, but amid the chatter surrounding her, Cassie's eyes were focused solely on him. How long had she been watching them?

She didn't look away once she realized he'd caught her looking. Instead, a soft smile graced her face that eased some of the panic that had crept into his body with his realization. A sense of calm settled over him, even though his heart beat an irregular rhythm. What a weird phenomenon.

It had been doing that a lot around Cassie lately.

Carlos was right about one thing. She didn't hate him. Brad believed that now. And his more-than-friends radar pinged wildly out of control at the look she gave him. Yet he'd learned not to trust himself when it came to women. It only took a few failed relationships to make a person jaded when it came to dating.

But his jaded mind didn't prevent him from questioning everything right now. Could she be picking up on the more-than-friends vibe too? Dare he risk his heart one more time with the possibility of getting burned again?

"I'll finish up in here," Carlos said, snapping Brad out of his spiraling thoughts. He handed Brad one of the dessert plates. "I'm guessing your woman would like some pie."

Your woman. Brad shouldn't like the sound of that so much.
But he did.

Chapter Twenty-Three

The energy buzzing around Dodger Stadium during the game Friday evening was no match for the electricity pulsing through Brad's body. He'd spent most of the past twenty-four hours attempting to explain away the realization he'd had last night at the Rivera's. He couldn't have possibly fallen for Cassie so quickly. They'd been pretend-dating for three days. *Three.* Only six had passed since she'd arrived in town. This had to be a record for him.

No, he couldn't be in love with her. It was too soon. He had more self-respect than that.

And the fact that he'd not only confided in her about his pathetic dating life but also his deep-seated worry over the future of his health made him uneasy. He never shared those vulnerabilities with anyone. The more people that knew about these weaknesses, the more ammo they had to use against him.

But somehow, Cassie had seen right through him. She knew all the right questions to ask to get to the heart of everything.

And that terrified him.

Because although she'd shown herself to be different than he'd originally expected—in the best possible ways, he might add—she'd be leaving at the end of the week. He had to keep his head out of the clouds concerning her.

He tried to concentrate on the game, but with Cassie sitting next to him at the end of the row, his ability to focus on the action happening on the field became more impossible by the minute. Especially with the way she leaned closer to him every time she wanted to tell him something. She currently sat with her legs crossed toward him, her bare knee nudging against his thigh.

"Why doesn't the first baseman have to tag the runner to get him out?" she asked, resting her chin on his shoulder to speak into his ear, a necessity thanks to the raucous chanting of the bare-chested guys a few rows in front of them. They had to be on their third or fourth round of beers already, and though the last play didn't warrant such enthusiasm, their buzzed state gave them enough reason to celebrate.

Brad normally loved the pulsing energy during sporting events. But he found he didn't enjoy it nearly as much as the way Cassie's hand caressed his arm. *Focus, Brad.* She'd asked him a question. He searched his mind, trying to recall it.

"Because it's a force out," he said, then chuckled at her blank look. "That's when a runner has nowhere to go but forward. In those cases, the fielder only has to touch the base."

"Ooooooh. Makes sense." Cassie removed her chin from his shoulder, though she didn't sit back.

Her intoxicating scent invaded his senses, rising above the always present aromas of hot dogs and popcorn. He'd never smelled any other perfume like the one she wore—sweet but with a kick to it. Like her.

Uh, what?

Head out of the clouds, buddy.

"So, what happens if the batter makes it to first base and is heading toward second?"

"Then it becomes a tag out situation," Brad responded, and he tried to focus on her endless questions instead of how much he liked the way she smelled.

"I think I get it now." She moved away, resting her back against the seat. "Gemma tried to explain the rules once, but it's like a foreign language to me."

Now that they had some distance between them again, his breaths came easier. He rolled his shoulders a little, trying to relax. "The more you watch it, the easier it gets to understand. Tyler and Gemma know more about the rules than I do. Honestly, I prefer football. Baseball is a little too slow. Not enough action."

"Well, naturally you'd prefer the sport you used to play," she said, angling her body toward him again. With the tight space between their seats and the ones in front of them, she was forced to slide her foot behind his. Her leg brushed his calf in the process.

The sight of a man coming down the steps behind them caught his attention and ruined the cozy moment. He frowned as Drew's tall figure stopped at their row, sliding into the empty seat on Cassie's other side. He'd ditched the loafers and dress shirt, but that didn't do anything to make him appear any more inviting. Seriously, what had Cassie seen in him?

"What is it?" Cassie asked, confused at Brad's dark expression.

He gestured with his head past her shoulder.

She swiveled around in her seat, then groaned. "What are you doing here, Drew? You hate baseball."

"I need to talk to you," he said, cupping his hand around her elbow and gesturing for her to stand.

She yanked her arm away. "How did you even know where I was sitting?"

That same question had crossed Brad's mind too. Tyler hadn't invited him, had he? That didn't sound like something he'd do though. He knew about the whole reason behind Brad's relationship with Cassie. And Brad trusted him with his life. There was no way he'd go behind their back to invite her ex.

Cassie leaned forward to look down the row to the other end. Brad did as well. No one in the bridal party noticed the argument happening except Gemma. She was also leaning forward, her elbows resting on her thighs, staring back at her sister with wide eyes.

What's he doing here? she mouthed.

Well, that answered Brad's question about whether Drew had been invited.

"I have my methods," Drew said once Cassie had turned back to him.

Her posture tensed. and Brad grabbed her hand, giving it a

squeeze for support. "You're stalking me now?" she asked, an under-lying anger in her voice.

"I wouldn't have to if you'd answer your phone when I called." Drew didn't sound at all repentant about his actions. What a jerk.

"And you didn't think for one moment that maybe I didn't answer because I'm tired of allowing myself to be manipulated by you?" Cassie turned her back to him, scowling at Brad, though he knew her frustration wasn't directed toward him.

Straightening in his chair, Brad shot a steely glare over her head at Drew. "Hey man. She's already told you she doesn't want you around anymore."

And Drew had made it obvious he didn't intend to respect her wishes. First, by staying at the bonfire a few nights ago, and now by showing up here today. No wonder she'd begged Brad to help her get rid of him. The guy was a total misogynist.

"It's time for you to take the hint," Brad said, his tone allowing no arguments.

"I don't see how any of this involves you," Drew responded coldly. "Why don't you get back to the game, and Cassie and I will just go up there and talk. You can understand that man to man. Right ... Chad?"

Brad clenched his teeth so hard his jaw hurt. *How original,* he thought, absolutely certain Cassie's ex knew his name. It was a power move he'd seen many times before in situations like this. A way to intimidate him.

Too bad Brad didn't get intimidated easily. In fact, the attempt only heightened his protective instincts. He'd gladly follow Drew out to the concourse to give him a piece of his mind. Or maybe his fist. Brad didn't consider himself a violent person, but he could definitely take the guy out if it meant making sure he never mistreated Cassie again.

He almost said as much when Cassie suddenly whipped around to face her ex. "His name is Brad," she snapped.

Brad smiled at her quick defense of him. He didn't need her to protect him—he could take care of himself—but he appreciated it all the same. Slipping his arm around her shoulders, he pulled her closer to him and kissed her temple. With her pressed against his side, he could feel her shaking, though out of anger or some other emotion, he couldn't be sure. And it didn't matter. He wouldn't let her suffer through Drew's presence alone.

She relaxed into his embrace, seemingly appreciative of his support.

Drew scowled at them both.

"Cassandra," he practically growled through his unnaturally white teeth, his impatience growing with each word, "this is getting ridiculous. Will you please act like an adult and go up there with me for a few minutes?" He pointed toward the concourse several rows behind them. "I have something important to tell you."

Cassie shook her head. "No. I don't want to hear it. Just go back to New York. You're not welcome here, and I refuse to let you keep treating me like this."

Drew made some retort, but Brad didn't catch what he said over the elevated cheering of the crowd. He looked to the field, only then realizing the game was between innings. Yet people were cheering as if someone had hit a grand slam. And why did the goons a few rows below keep looking back at them with matching drunken smiles? One of them, his chest so hairy he almost resembled a gorilla, kept chanting something, though Brad couldn't make out the exact words.

Elise elbowed his arm from his other side. "Brad." She pulled her hand out of the box of Sour Patch Kids she held between her knees and pointed at the jumbotron above left field.

Brad's gaze followed her finger, and he groaned. A giant red heart took up most of the screen, outlining none other than Brad with his arm still around Cassie's shoulder while she argued with Drew.

"You've got to be kidding me," he complained to his cousin. "The kiss cam?"

Elise's eyes sparked with more amusement than she'd exhibited the entire time he'd been in town. "Apparently, someone in the broadcast booth has a twisted sense of humor."

Brad gave her a side eye.

"Will you please do something?" she muttered before popping a blue Sour Patch Kid into her mouth. "This is embarrassing."

"Tell me about it." Fire engulfed his skin from his neck all the way up to his forehead. He didn't often get embarrassed. Not since the incident with Kendra back in high school. Which was also witnessed by thousands of people. Why did his humiliation always seem to wind up on camera?

The exes hadn't noticed they'd become the focus of the big screen, or the object of a stadium full of chanting. Who was the kiss cam even intended for? Brad and Cassie? Or Cassie and Drew?

He shook his head, waving away the attention with his free hand. That only managed to rile the crowd up even more. Shouldn't the cameraman have moved on to more willing participants by now? A kiss in this section of the stadium wasn't going to happen. Not in a million years.

On the other hand, kissing Cassie would be a good way to stick it to Drew. And perhaps make their relationship more convincing. He'd be lying if he said he hadn't thought about what it would be like. In between innings at a baseball game wasn't his preferred location for a first kiss, but maybe now was as good a time as any.

Before he talked himself out of it, he gently turned Cassie's face away from Drew. Ignoring the alarmed expression on her face, he leaned forward and captured her lips in his. The crowd exploded, the rumbling of an entire stadium of cheers shaking Brad's seat.

Cassie tensed, sending an anchor of dread into the bottom of his stomach. Maybe this hadn't been the greatest idea after all. He'd kissed her without her consent, proving him to be just as pigheaded as her ex.

His brain was already forming an apology as he started to pull away. But then her slender fingers slid behind his neck, and she pressed herself against his chest, deepening the kiss. Brad brought his other arm around her, encircling her in his embrace, barely registering the whoops and surprised laughter from the rest of the wedding party.

It was only supposed to be a small kiss. A little peck to appease the camera and annoy Drew enough to get him to go away. But as the seconds ticked on, Brad lost all sense of timing as his heart seemed to burst from his chest, its rapid thunder muting the commotion surrounding them.

This is how it should be, one side of his brain admitted while the other half screamed for him to protect his heart. There could be no happy ending in a fake romance. And theirs was definitely not real.

Then why did kissing Cassie feel so right?

When he finally managed to untangle his lips from hers, he couldn't pull his eyes away from her. She stared back at him, her tempting mouth dropped open in obvious shock as she fought to catch her breath.

Say something, he pleaded with himself. *You can't kiss a woman like that and not say anything.*

But no words came. He dragged his eyes away from her, hoping it would help restore function to his brain. The murderous scowl on Drew's face snapped Brad from his stupor. Raising a single eyebrow in challenge, he twisted his mouth into a triumphant smirk. Replacing his arm around Cassie's shoulder, he pulled her close to whisper in her ear.

"I think he bought it, how about you?"

Chapter Twenty-Four

All through Gemma's bridal shower the next day, Cassie's mind vacillated between confusion and this giddy kind of glee she hadn't felt in a long *long* time.

Brad had kissed her.

Brad had *kissed* her.

Brad had kissed *her*.

Why though? Where had it come from? One minute, she'd been pleading with Drew—again—to leave her alone, and the next thing she knew, Brad had rendered her completely speechless with his affections.

And oh, what a kiss ... It probably topped the list of the most toe-curling kisses she'd ever experienced in her life, even if it only lasted a minute or two.

But along with it came a whole boatload of emotions she'd been fighting off since she'd first suggested the plan to fake date. Emotions that were very near to bursting through the surface.

At the rehearsal dinner that evening, she sat next to Brad at one of the tables in the main garden of Sunset Cove Estate—the location of the wedding that would take place the next day. Lanterns lined the perimeter of the reception area, creating a cozy glow, increasing in brightness as twilight fell. Small bulbs strung on thin cables above the tables wove throughout the intimate space, bathing the area with a cozy ambiance straight out of a romantic movie.

And yet, she was on edge.

What are you doing to yourself? she thought, picking at the salmon on her plate. *You can't be falling for him. A week ago, you were engaged to someone else.* Not to mention that with no job and no plan, her life was in complete upheaval. Giving her heart to another man—one who, by his comment immediately after the kiss, was still clearly *pretending* to be in love with her—could only lead her spiraling off the cliff toward heartbreak.

But if he was only pretending, why hadn't he removed his hand from where it casually rested on her thigh during the entire main course? And how could he act as though that simple connection was the most natural thing in the world when *she* felt about ready to jump out of her skin?

Oh boy. This ruse had deviated way too far from the original plan. It should've only involved a few days of pretending before they'd both go back to barely tolerating each other. Maybe they'd laugh about it later. Real feelings were never supposed to get involved.

Channeling her best attempt to look unaffected by his touch, she dropped her hand on top of his, and turned her body toward him, so she could tune in to the conversation with one of Tyler's other groomsmen, a guy Brad had introduced as Christian.

Brad gave Cassie a warm look that made her heart flip flop in her chest before addressing his friend. "I'm glad you came tonight. I know it means a lot to Tyler that you agreed to be in the wedding."

Unlike the other members of the bridal party, Christian hadn't attended the rest of the week's activities. She'd overheard Tyler and Gemma talking about circumstances at home that made it difficult for him to participate in more than the rehearsal and ceremony. Whatever that meant.

Christian acknowledged Brad's comment with the barest of smiles that didn't reach his brown eyes. A noticeable sadness pooled in their depths that piqued Cassie's interest in the man.

"It's the least I can do after the way he's been there for me lately."

"Brad told me the three of you used to live together," Cassie said before taking a sip from her champagne glass.

He gave her a polite nod. "Tyler and I were roommates in the freshman dorms before the three of us moved into the house."

"That was a crazy six months, wasn't it?" Brad nudged his buddy's arm with the back of his hand. "Do you remember when we built that skateboard ramp in the backyard?"

Christian chuckled, reaching up to scratch the side of his sandy brown hair. "Epic. Hey, did you ever regain feeling in your thumb?"

Brad lifted his hand from off Cassie's thigh and wiggled his thumb. "Good as new."

"What happened to your thumb?" she asked, arching her eyebrows.

He grinned at her. "Nothing I care to disclose at the moment. My coach threw a fit when I showed up at pre-season training unable to move it though. That brought an end to skateboarding for me." He turned back to Christian and said, "Too bad you had to go and get married."

"You're married?" Cassie asked. Why didn't he bring his wife? The minister's wife had come, and one of the groomsmen had brought his fiancé. Even Beej had invited her waiter friend, whose name turned out to be Tim.

Christian's eyes dropped to his empty plate as he sucked in a breath. "Not anymore," he muttered so quietly that Cassie almost didn't hear him.

"Oh."

Awkward silence fell between them, broken only by the other conversations going on at their table. So that explained the somber way Christian carried himself. She glanced at Brad, only to discover a man who very obviously wished he could take back what he'd said.

Fortunately, the clinking of silverware against glass saved them all from the discomfort. Cassie looked toward the head table as Tyler's dad stood, holding his champagne glass.

"On behalf of Amy and myself," he said, smiling down at his wife seated beside him, "we're honored to welcome you tonight to celebrate Tyler and Gemma. I still remember the day we landed in Santiago fifteen years ago and moved in next door to the Schalks." He turned his attention to his future daughter-in-law. "Gemma, if it weren't for you, Tyler's transition would've been so much harder. I want to thank you for saving our entire family from the wrath of a tween boy intent on making our lives miserable."

Ripples of laughter moved through the garden, but Tyler laughed the hardest of all.

Mr. Abernathy continued speaking to Gemma. "From the moment you entered our lives, you became more than our son's best friend. You became part of our family. Sure, your friendship had to go through its rocky crevices as you both grew up and figured out life and yourselves. But the fact that we're here today to honor the promise you're about to make to each other is a strong testament of the power of forgiveness, friendship, and most of all, love."

Christian muttered something under his breath, though Cassie couldn't make out what he said over Mr. Abernathy's speech. Glancing over at Brad, she caught the worried look he cast at his friend. What could've happened in Christian's life to make him so serious?

No, serious wasn't the right word. Bitter, maybe?

She leaned toward Brad to voice her questions quietly when Mr. Abernathy raised a toast to the almost-married couple.

"To Tyler and Gemma," Cassie echoed the rest of the guests, then clinked her glass against Brad's. Was it just her, or had he shifted even closer to her during the speech? His hand had found her thigh again, eliciting more delicious tingles reverberating up and down her leg.

She tried unsuccessfully to quiet the confusion in her mind. Dare she hope that he'd developed the same feelings for her that she had for him? Was a relationship even possible between two people with an entire continent between them? Then again, now that her life in New York had imploded, did she even want to go back?

She pulled herself out of her constant questioning as Mr. Abernathy spoke again. "If anyone has some words of wisdom or congratulations for Tyler and Gemma, the floor is open for that now."

"I'd like to say something."

Cassie froze. *Oh no.* She knew that voice as well as her own. She turned in the direction of the mansion as Drew emerged from the shadows and into the cozy light of the garden.

Mr. Abernathy hadn't sat down, and now Dad rose to his feet a few seats from him at the head table. "This is a private event." Her father would never hurt a fly, but right now, his tone carried a protective edge.

Sydney, the wedding planner, jumped from her seat and hurried over to Drew, attempting to usher him from the garden. She was a tiny, wisp of a woman, and Drew brushed her off easily.

"I have something to say," he repeated emphatically, his words slurring slightly.

Brad slid his hand out from underneath Cassie's. He shook out his fingers, making her realize that maybe she'd been squeezing a little too hard. She pinched the bridge of her nose with her thumb and forefinger, summoning all the patience she had left. Which wasn't much after the week she'd had. Heat crawled up her neck.

"Drew, please don't make a scene," she said after raising her face again.

At her voice, his head whipped in her direction as if he'd just now realized she sat there. "Cassandra, you have to listen to me, baby." His posture shifted from cool and confident to tense and panicked. Breaking his arm from Sydney's attempts to steer him away from the spotlight, he stumbled toward his ex. "I can't lose you."

"It's a little late for that," Gram's shaky voice came from somewhere behind Cassie. Drew ignored her and steered toward Cassie's table, swaying a little in his path.

As he approached, Brad shot to his feet, stepping in front of her to block her ex from getting close. Despite the barrier, the alcohol on Drew's breath twisted her stomach. No wonder he was acting this way. Sober Drew would never become this unhinged.

Manipulative, yes. But he never allowed himself to look anything but polished.

"Look, man," Brad said, an underlying threat barely tainting his words. "You've harassed Cassie more than enough this week. The way I see it, you have two choices. Either you turn around and beat it on your own, or I'll escort you out myself. Take your pick."

"Back off," Drew sneered. "You think you're better for her than me? The other day proved that you're far from superior. Getting so drunk that you had to have a *woman* help you to the car. Yeah, I saw right through your act."

"That's enough, Drew." Cassie clenched her fists in her lap. He had no right to accuse Brad of inappropriate conduct when he'd completely misunderstood the situation.

But Brad didn't take the bait. Instead, he stood his ground, puffing his chest out a little and making himself more formidable against Drew's slight height advantage. "Come on, pal," he said, grabbing Drew's arm. The forced calm in his voice sent shivers up Cassie's spine.

"Don't touch me." Drew yanked his arm out of his grasp. "This is none of your business. You have no reason to get involved."

A small smirk appeared on Brad's face as he shook his head. "You're wrong about that. If it's about Cassie, it's absolutely my business."

She sucked in a breath as warmth spread through her body. What did he mean by that?

"Now, I believe I gave you a choice. You refused the first one, so I guess that leaves the second. It's time to go."

Drew struggled against his grip, not willing to leave without a fight. "Get your hands off me!"

Cassie was tempted to jump in to help, but she was no match for Drew. Instead, Brad gestured with his head toward Christian, who immediately stood, taking Drew's other arm.

"Cassandra!" Drew hollered as the men hauled him from the garden.

She dropped her face into her hand, willing her cheeks to stop burning as she felt everyone's eyes on her.

"Please listen to me! I can love you so much more than this guy, and I can prove it. Why else would I have convinced Adriana to give you another chance?"

Her head jerked up, and all the people, the tables, the grass, began to spin in a dizzying blur of colors. What? He'd talked to Adriana? No. That couldn't be right. The woman didn't concede once she made up her mind.

"You lost your job?" Gemma asked from the head table, reminding Cassie of the audience witnessing this mortifying scene.

She looked to her sister. Sympathy, and maybe a little hurt, were written on Gemma's face. Instead of answering, however, Cassie rose from her seat, tossed her cloth napkin onto her empty plate, and hurried after the men.

"Wait!" The word echoed through the spacious foyer as she entered the mansion. The jostling between the three of them stopped, and they all turned as she approached. "You win, Drew. I'll talk to you," she said in frustrated defeat. She met Brad's eye, and his brows pulled together in a deep V. "Will you guys give us a minute?"

Brad let go of Drew's arm and took a step toward her. Cassie closed the distance between them so they could converse in relative privacy.

"I don't think that's a good idea," he whispered. "He could be unpredictable. I'm not comfortable leaving you alone with him."

Was his protectiveness still for show? She could no longer tell. It felt like someone had taken a big pink eraser to the line between real and pretend, leaving smudges and indecipherable markings behind.

But she'd have to explore his intentions later. Right now, she needed to hear what Drew had to say and then get rid of him.

She placed a light hand on Brad's chest. "He's never hurt me before. I'll be okay."

He didn't seem at all placated by her assurances. "Are you sure?" he asked, brushing his knuckles lightly along her cheek.

Cassie turned her face into his touch and closed her eyes, savoring his gentle affection before nodding. "If I'm not back in ten minutes, I give you permission to come find me."

One side of his mouth ticked up in a humorless smile. "I'm setting a timer."

His loyalty momentarily softened the frustration in her heart, which burst with the realization of how much she'd come to care about him. And she trusted him. He'd come back for her should this interaction with Drew go south. That buoyed her resolve to get through this conversation she had no desire to have.

Stretching onto the balls of her feet, she pressed a light kiss to Brad's cheek. He held her gaze for a long moment, then gestured to Christian, who dropped Drew's arm and followed Brad out.

She watched them go until their footsteps faded into nothing. When they had disappeared out the doors of the mansion, all the warm feelings she'd experienced during her moment with Brad vanished in an instant, replaced with anger.

Drew stopped straightening his suit coat as she whipped around to face him. At least he had the decency of dressing for the occasion he was crashing.

"You're drunk," she said in disgust as she marched over to him.

"I'm significantly buzzed," he corrected, holding up a finger. "I don't get drunk."

She scoffed, shaking her head. "Hanging around the beach the night of the bonfire and stalking me at the baseball game were one thing. But how dare you show up here like this tonight! You've ruined my sister's rehearsal dinner. Why are you doing all this? To get back at me for breaking off our engagement?"

"No." He walked over to the winding staircase near the front entrance, lowering himself onto one of the lower steps. He dropped his head into his hands, massaging his temples like he was in pain.

"Then why?" she asked, standing in front of him. "And why didn't you just text me about talking to Adriana?"

"Would you have read it?"

He had her there.

Drew blew out a breath. Now that they were alone all the fight in him had deflated. And the lines on his face made him appear ... tired.

"You told me after your fight with Adriana that I wasn't being a good partner. I thought about that for a few days and realized you were right. So, this is me showing up for you."

Cassie narrowed her eyes at him. "You've put me in awkward positions this entire week. How is that showing up for me?"

He held up his hands in surrender. "I know, I know. Maybe my actions haven't been the best. Believe it or not, I came to California with good intentions. I wanted to tell you that I managed to convince Adriana to give you another chance with conditions—she's still mad at you for that stunt you pulled on Friday—"

"That stunt? You mean standing up for myself?"

He made a small grunt in response.

"What kind of conditions?" Cassie asked, momentarily side-tracked from her task of getting him to leave.

Drew sighed. "A bump in pay, decreased responsibilities, and you wouldn't have access to her designs until they were released to the public. Those are only the start."

So she'd really be just an errand runner. No perks allowed. That didn't sound appealing at all.

"I know it's not great," he continued. "But you'd be able to prove yourself again. Maybe even work back into her good graces. That's really why I came. And ..." He shifted in his seat a little.

"What?" Cassie asked, uneasiness falling over her. She had a pretty good idea about what he was going to say.

"I'd hoped that when you found out what I'd done for you, you'd give me another chance. But then I saw you with *him*—" his lip curled up at the mention of Brad "—and I snapped. How can you even think that he'd be able to give you the kind of life you've always wanted?"

"This has nothing to do with Brad," Cassie said, sitting down next to him. "It's not even about Adriana and the dress. This is about the fact that we haven't been okay for a long time. I tried to ignore that for a while, but I can't anymore."

"Then why did you accept my proposal?"

She threw her hands up in an *I don't know* gesture. "Maybe I was hoping we were only going through a rough patch, that eventually we'd find our footing again. Or maybe I thought getting married would help us recommit to each other."

And, she realized as shame twisted her stomach, she hadn't been ready to say goodbye to the life of privilege she'd have with him.

She placed a hand on his arm, wanting him to understand. "But I deserve better than maybe. And even though I'm angry at you for everything you did this week, I still think you do too."

Silence dropped between them as Cassie let Drew process everything she'd said.

"I guess it really is over, then." He stared ahead into the open doors of the ballroom. It was mostly set up for the wedding ceremony tomorrow afternoon. Only the flowers were missing, which wouldn't arrive until the morning.

"Yeah." She spoke just as quietly, unable to help revisiting some of the good times from early in their relationship. "Thank you for talking to Adriana. I really appreciate it."

"Should I tell her you don't want the job?"

Cassie didn't answer right away. What was she supposed to say? "I'm not sure yet. I need time to think about it."

"Okay." Drew rose from the step, swaying a little on his feet. "But don't take too long. You know how much Adriana hates to be kept waiting."

"I know. Call me tomorrow. I'll have an answer for you then."

He nodded sadly, then turned toward the decorative front doors of the mansion.

She watched him take a few steps before another concern jumped into her mind. "You're not driving anywhere, are you?" No matter how angry she was right now, no matter how much respect she'd lost for him, at least part of her would always care about him as a person. "Do you need me to drop you off somewhere?"

Turning around again, he pulled his phone from his pocket,

jiggling it in front of him. "I'll schedule an Uber." Then he left, the large doors echoing as they shut behind him.

Cassie dropped her face into her hands with a sigh, unsure whether to feel relieved that the drama was over or cry out of sadness. Despite the last week, despite the last couple of years really, their relationship had started out great, and she couldn't help mourning that time in their lives.

Soon, her thoughts shifted to her other predicament. What should she do about Adriana's offer? The idea of going back to work for her former boss didn't sit well with her, but it wasn't like she had a plan B to fall back on. She liked what Brad had suggested a few days ago about working with people. She'd had her heart set on fashion design for so long though. How could she give up that dream when she'd already worked so hard for it?

But was there even a place in New York for her still, or had she outgrown it?

For perhaps the first time in her life, she was beginning to wonder if she had.

Chapter Twenty-Five

"I can honestly say nothing crazy like this happened at my wedding," Christian said, swirling the contents of his champagne glass.

Brad pulled his focus away from his watch to raise his eyebrows at his buddy. They'd returned to the table seven minutes and twenty-six seconds ago, and he'd already checked it at least ten times. He hadn't been kidding about setting a timer.

"Considering you eloped, I don't think you have any room to judge someone else's crazy." He glanced at his watch again. Seven minutes and forty-five seconds.

Christian grunted, his glass halfway to his mouth. "Touché." He drained the rest of it, allowing the bitterness in his tone to ruminate in the silence.

Brad didn't press the conversation. A few years ago, a good-natured ribbing had been a daily occurrence between them. Then Sabrina entered the picture and everything changed, including Christian's once optimistic demeanor. Brad had never liked his buddy's ex, and his vocal objections to their marriage back in the day had taken an unfortunate toll on their friendship. At least they were back on relatively friendly terms, though they weren't as close as they used to be.

Glancing at his watch again, he sighed. Eight minutes, twenty-five seconds.

Why was time moving so slowly? Cassie may have shown confidence that Drew wouldn't lay a hand on her, but no part of Brad trusted the man. He'd obviously had a few too many drinks. Who knew how he'd respond if he didn't get his way while in this state of inebriation?

At nine minutes on the dot, Brad decided he'd waited long

enough. He pushed back from the table, catching Christian's attention.

"Need backup?" he asked, sliding his chair back.

Brad shook his head. "I got it, thanks." Leaving the garden behind, he retraced his steps from a few minutes earlier, listening for any sound of an argument once he stepped inside the mansion.

Nothing.

As he walked through the foyer toward the front entrance, the low lighting made it difficult to see, but it appeared to be empty. Unease pricked in his stomach. Cassie wouldn't have left with the guy, would she?

Turning from the doors, relief replaced his worry when he spotted her sitting on a step almost halfway up the winding staircase to his right. A vintage lamp shining from the second-floor landing behind her reflected off her hair like a halo.

"Hey," he said as he climbed the stairs and sat down next to her. "You okay?"

A desperate laugh escaped her. "I don't know." Propping her elbow on her thigh, she dropped her forehead onto her fingertips.

"Where's Drew?"

"He said what he needed to say and then left."

Just like that? "What did he want?"

Cassie sighed, then launched into a recap of her conversation with her ex. When she got to the part about going to work for her old boss again, she said, "I told him I'd think about it."

"Is that what you really want?" Brad held his breath, waiting for her answer. He knew she'd eventually have to return to New York but over the last couple of days, he'd started to hope that she'd decide to hang around a little longer. Once he started his new job in a few weeks, he'd be living here for good. The idea of being in LA without her was becoming a tough pill to swallow.

"The possibility doesn't thrill me," she admitted with a shrug. "But I'd be lying if I said the prospect of a steady paycheck isn't tempting right now." With a small whimper, she dropped her head into her lap. "How could I have possibly screwed up my entire life in only a few days?"

"You didn't screw it up that bad."

She gave him a disbelieving look. "I should've been honest with everyone about what was going on. I only wanted my sister's wedding to be flawless. I didn't want to take the focus off her by admitting that I wasn't living the perfect life I'd been trying to convince them of for years."

"No one's life is perfect." Brad placed a hand on her back. "I mean, you're talking to the guy who can't seem to date a woman without it turning into some kind of primetime drama. Thank you, by the way, for not capturing my humiliation on camera for the whole world to see."

"Someone did that?"

"I wish I could say no." Brad gave a self-deprecating laugh. "Do you want proof? I'm sure you can still find the video somewhere on the interwebs." He dug into his pocket for his phone. She stopped him with a hand on his arm.

"I believe you," she said, humoring him with a smile.

He removed his hand from his pocket, leaning forward to place his forearms on his thigh. "The point is that everyone has problems. And your family loves you. I don't think opening up to them about what happened would've taken the spotlight away from the wedding. They may even be able to help you figure out what to do next."

She studied him silently for a moment. "I know you're right. I just wish I'd realized that before I messed everything up."

"You didn't mess everything up." Brad bumped her shoulder with his. "The wedding's still on. Tyler and Gemma are still nauseatingly in love—" Cassie laughed at that. "—and you're still stuck with a dashingly handsome, yet sometimes grumpy, best man." He pulled at the cuffs of his dress shirt with exaggerated movements.

Her face fell. That wasn't the reaction he'd expected.

"I guess there's no point in pretending to date anymore. Drew is gone, and everything's out in the open now." She dropped her chin into her hands. "I'm sorry for dragging you into this."

Brad reached over and turned her face until she looked at him. "I'm not." He pressed a gentle kiss to her forehead. She didn't pull away. "It forced me to get to know you better. You're not who I thought you were, and it would be a shame if I hadn't gotten the chance to realize that."

Leaning her head on his shoulder, she slid her arm through his and wove their fingers together. "You're a good guy, Brad," she whispered. "You don't deserve to be hurt again."

Then why did her tone make that possibility sound inevitable?

Confusion swirled around in his gut. Was this a breakup?

Granted, this relationship hadn't ended the way they usually did —with him being humiliated and threatened by jealous egomaniacs —but he still felt like his heart was about to get flattened again.

What would happen if he opened up about his growing feelings for her? That he'd fallen in love with her? Did any part of her feel the same? Was a future together even a possibility for them?

He didn't know the answers, especially the one to the question stirring up above them all.

Was he willing to risk his heart one more time to find the answers?

Chapter Twenty-Six

Anticipation rippled through the mansion the next morning as the bride and her attendants bustled around the prep room in various stages of readiness. Cassie was already dressed in her slate blue, strapless gown. She'd styled her curls in an elegant twist before arriving at the estate. As the person tasked with doing Gemma's hair and makeup, she'd made sure to get ready long before everyone else.

She stood behind her sister's chair, putting the finishing touches on Gemma's braided low bun. The elegant updo sat loose on the left side of her neck in a way that perfectly displayed her abundance of curls. After placing one more tiny white flower in the dark tresses, Cassie stepped back, tilting her head from one shoulder to another to admire her handiwork.

"Perfect," she said, spinning the chair around so everyone else could see. As expected, a chorus of gasps followed.

"Gemma!" Beej practically squealed, clasping her hands together. Her hair and makeup were done, but she still wore her silk robe. "You're so gorgeous!"

"Breathtaking," Elise agreed. The blue of her gown brought out the blue in her eyes, which Cassie had noticed on more than one occasion sometimes looked greener depending on her outfit. She held a curling iron in one hand, and she separated a strand of Kendall's chestnut hair, twisting it around the barrel.

Hallie shared a mirror with them both as she smeared her lips with a shimmery lip gloss. Only eleven months younger than Elise, the two looked almost like they could be twins, though Hallie's blonde hair was a tiny bit darker. She smiled at her soon-to-be sister-in-law. "You look beautiful."

Gemma beamed in reply before turning back to the mirror to

look at herself for the first time. A soft *oh* escaped her lips, and she touched a thin curl that hung loose, framing her face. "I love it," she said wistfully. "Thank you."

Cassie knew she'd done her job when her tomboy of a twin was impressed, almost to the point of speechlessness, over her hair. She wrapped her arms around Gemma's waist from the side, careful not to mess up her hard work. "It's my pleasure. You know I can never pass up a makeover opportunity."

Gemma chuckled as she pulled away, breathing in deeply. She shook out her hands like she always did when the nerves were getting to her. "I can't believe this is really happening."

Cassie reached over to give her sister's fingers a squeeze. "It's only natural to feel some jitters. This is the day you've been dreaming about ever since you reconnected with Tyler. You get to marry your best friend. Your soulmate. How amazing is that?"

A whimsical smile formed on Gemma's mouth. "I couldn't have gotten through this week without you."

Guilt twisted in Cassie's stomach at her sister's appreciation. Truth be told, this week probably would've been a lot less stressful for her sister without her here. "I'm really sorry again for how everything played out with Drew. I should've been honest with you about what happened as soon as I got here. It could've prevented last night's disaster."

Gemma waved away Cassie's remorse. "Stop apologizing. I'm not mad. Yes, I wish you would've told me about losing your job from the beginning, but I understand why you didn't."

After returning to Gram's house following the rehearsal dinner, Gemma had crawled into bed with her sister, refusing to leave until she'd told her every last detail about what had led to the end of her engagement with Drew. Surprisingly, it hadn't been as difficult to open up as Cassie had expected. She'd already hashed and rehashed it all in her mind enough over the course of the week that the shock factor of losing everything in one day had finally diminished. Now she was simply tired of dealing with it all.

"Have you decided whether you're going back to New York?" Gemma asked.

Cassie shook her head. "I'm not sure what I'm going to do yet."

Now it was Gemma's turn to squeeze Cassie's hand. "You know you're always welcome to stay at Gram's while you figure things out."

"I'm sure Tyler would love that." Cassie rolled her eyes with a smile. "It's bad enough that he'll be newly married and living with his wife's grandma. Let's throw in his sister-in-law too. We just need to convince Mom and Dad to move down here, and we'd be one big happy family."

Gemma laughed at that. "Okay, I admit, it might not be the most ideal situation. But I'll settle for anything that would get you to live close by for a change. I miss you all the way in New York."

Her words provided the same effect as enjoying a cup of hot cocoa near a cozy fire. Cassie and her sister hadn't always had the best relationship, especially the first few years after Tyler's family had moved away from Chile. She hadn't discovered the hand she'd played in her sister's emotional distance until years later, but they'd worked hard to rekindle their relationship in the time since then. The possibility of living close to Gemma—and Gram for that matter—added another element to Cassie's pot of considerations.

A knock at the door interrupted any response she could've given. Sydney poked her head inside the room. She took one look at Gemma and gasped, bringing a hand to cover her mouth.

"Aren't you a vision?" she gushed. "Are you ready? Tyler is waiting in the back gardens for your first look, and Mark and his crew are standing by with all their cameras to capture the beautiful moment."

"I'm ready. Just give me a second." Gemma crossed the room, beckoning for Cassie to follow. Digging through her bag, she pulled out a small, black box and handed it to her sister. "Will you give this to Brad for the ceremony? It's Tyler's wedding band."

Cassie took the box. "I'll make sure he gets it."

At her assurance, Gemma took a step toward the door then stopped. "Oh, and don't let him try to talk his way out of showing up for the pictures in thirty minutes."

"I'll escort him out there myself," Cassie said, unable to help the grin sliding onto her face. More time with Brad. She liked the sound of that. With all the last-minute craziness of the morning, she hadn't seen him all day.

"I'm sure you will." Gemma gave her a knowing look before taking another cleansing breath. She placed a hand on her stomach, possibly to control the pre-wedding jitters. Once the ceremony was over, Cassie had no doubt the nerves her sister experienced now would be long gone.

Cassie followed the other women out the door, searching for Brad. The guys were getting ready in one of the rooms on the upper floor, so she headed for the same spiral staircase she'd found herself during the rehearsal dinner. She smiled at the memory of sitting with him last night. They hadn't said much after she'd told him about Adriana's offer, but a sense of peace had enveloped her as she sat with her head on his shoulder, their hands woven together. Her situation hadn't improved; in fact, with her old job back on the table, it may have become even more confusing. But there was a certain comfort in talking out her options with him. A comfort she hadn't felt for a long time.

Stepping onto the upstairs landing, she spotted Christian exiting a doorway halfway down the hall. With his phone pressed against his ear, he nodded a polite greeting as he passed.

Cassie continued down the hall, stopping at the door he'd come out of, and looked inside. Alone in the room, Brad stood before a tall, rectangular mirror. He wore a gray tux, minus the jacket, and he fiddled with a strip of fabric around his neck.

"Hey there, handsome," she said, leaning against the door frame. "You clean up nice."

His hands fell away from the fabric, and he turned to face her, holding out his arms so she could get a better look at him. "What do you think? Am I worthy of walking you down the aisle?"

Had it only been a few days since they'd had that ridiculous spat in the car on the way back from the auto shop? She'd been so wrong about him.

"You always were," she said, entering the room all the way. "I just didn't see it."

A playful smile tugged at the corners of his mouth, sending delightful prickles all through Cassie's body. He had no reason to keep pretending to like her, yet he continued to look at her as though he cherished her, even with no one watching. The very idea that he could have developed some of the same feelings she had for him filled her with warmth.

Shaking herself out of the hold of his captivating gaze, she held out Tyler's ring box. "Gemma asked me to give you this."

Brad opened the box, extracting the ring and sliding it into the tiny pocket in the front of his vest. "Thanks. I'll keep it safe."

"You better. The entire wedding rests on your shoulders. Lose the rings, and the whole day is ruined." She was only joking but teasing him felt a lot safer than trying to define their relationship.

"I think I'm up for the challenge," he said, his mouth twitching. He went back to fiddling with the fabric around his neck. "It has to be easier than conquering this battle. Seriously, a bow tie? Why couldn't Tyler choose a regular tie? I know what to do with those. I'd even settle for a bolo over this thing." He flicked one end of the fabric.

Cassie pursed her lips in mock consideration before shaking her head. "Mmmm, you don't have the right neck for a bolo." She laughed at the side eye he gave her. "Here, let me do it."

Stepping closer to him, she reached up for the fabric. He lifted his chin to expose his neck, and his masculine scent wrapped her up like a warm blanket. With her forearms near his torso, she could feel his chest rise and fall with his breath, sending her stomach flipping at the lack of distance between them.

Would it be terrible if she forgot about the tie altogether and wrapped her arms around him? Maybe they could try that kiss again. She hadn't been able to get it out of her mind since the game. But this time, they'd be alone. And she wouldn't be taken by surprise.

Focus, Cassie. Focus.

"Where did you learn to tie a bow tie?" Brad asked.

Cassie refocused her attention on the half-formed bow as she answered. "I designed an entire men's formal line for fun in high school. I taught myself how to do it and practiced on my dad until I mastered it."

Brad chuckled. "You and I have different definitions of fun."

Cassie spared him an amused look before going back to her work. She gently tugged the tie back and forth to straighten the bow. "There." Retrieving his jacket from the velvet wingback chair nearby, she helped him shrug into it. "Now you're ready."

Turning him to face her, she smoothed his jacket over both his shoulders, enjoying the feel of solid muscle underneath her fingertips. Her hands lingered on their task longer than necessary, just for the excuse to continue the physical connection.

Her heart stuttered as Brad's hands found her waist and he inched closer to her, his lips lightly grazing her temple.

"It's really not okay," he murmured, his voice husky. His breath rustled the curly tendrils of hair framing her face.

Tingles raced up her spine, then back down again. "What's not okay?" she asked in a breathless whisper. Her eyes fluttered closed as his lips brushed another kiss to her temple. *He's not pretending.* He couldn't be. In no world could his actions be anything but real.

He skimmed his nose along her cheek and all air escaped her lungs. "It's not okay to look more stunning than the bride."

"You shouldn't say things like that," she said on a sigh as he continued his affections.

"Even if they're true?"

Cassie's eyes traveled slowly up his chest, to his neck, those kissable lips, and finally met his mesmerizing stare. His blue eyes burned with an intensity that resonated deep in her soul. They flitted down to her lips and back to her eyes, removing all doubt about his intentions.

Stretching onto her toes, she lightly brushed her lips against his. One little kiss was nowhere near enough to satisfy the desire burning in her chest. She came back for more, willingly giving herself up to his affections as he pulled her closer, hands splayed across her back.

Her fingers brushed along his jaw, the faintest hint of blond stubble prickling her skin. Sliding her hand to circle the back of his neck, she pressed tighter against him, deepening the kiss as her heart beat wildly out of control.

But underneath the exhilaration and passion, another sensation emerged. A quieter sensation. A sense of calm she hadn't felt all week.

She wanted this.

Wanted him.

All the angst she'd put herself through the last few days—all the doubting about whether she still saw a place for herself in New York —all seemed pointless now.

Standing in Brad's arms, caught up in the intensity of the moment, she realized where she wanted to be.

Here. She belonged right here.

Not on the East Coast. Not working for Adriana.

Despite the uncertainty of her career prospects, this was her place. With her sister, with Gram. For new opportunities. And most exciting of all, to explore this budding relationship with Brad.

And she needed to start by coming clean with him.

"I need to tell you something," she whispered against his lips.

Brad pulled away, searching her face. "What is it?" Worry flashed across his features before he could stop it. Was he thinking of his past relationships?

She gave him another kiss, hoping to reassure him. "I—"

Quick, high-heeled footsteps broke their connection as Beej

rushed into the room. "Oh, Cassie! We've been searching everywhere for you."

Reluctantly, Cassie dragged her attention away from Brad. His shaky breath reached her ears even as he stepped back.

"What happened?" she asked, turning to his sister.

Beej's expression turned apologetic. How much had she seen? "Hallie got her dress caught on something, and now there's a big tear near the bottom. We're supposed to be outside for pictures in ten minutes."

This was a crisis Cassie could solve. She desperately needed to talk to Brad, but sadly, it would have to wait until after the wedding.

"I always keep a sewing kit with me," she said, ushering Beej toward the door. "It's in my bag. Come on, I'm sure I can fix it."

Before exiting the room, she turned to get one last glimpse of Brad. He stared after her, one hand shoved in his pants pocket, the other rubbing the back of his neck. Shock was written all over his face as though he couldn't quite wrap his head around the last few minutes.

That makes two of us.

Mouthing an apology, she silently vowed to confess her feelings as soon as possible, then hurried from the room.

Chapter Twenty-Seven

The wedding went off without a hitch, aside from a small hiccup when Brad almost didn't hear the minister asking for the rings. In his defense, Cassie had caught his eye from across the ceremony space only seconds before, sending him a smile that had blocked out everything else around him. He was pretty sure he sported a bruise where Christian had jabbed his side to get his attention.

With the reception in full swing, Brad found himself alone, sitting on the cement steps overlooking the back gardens, which were now dark except for a sliver of moonlight illuminating the walkways zigzagging through the grounds. It was a perfect night. The day had cooled off once the sun disappeared, leaving the air pleasant but not cold. His cousin was now married to his dream woman. And the memory of Cassie's kiss from earlier still dominated his mind.

He had every reason to be happy. But with Cassie on the phone with Drew somewhere in the estate, an edgy tension had taken over his body. The fact that she'd answered his call in the middle of her twin sister's reception only meant one thing.

She'd made a decision. And he couldn't shake the worry that it didn't include him.

He barely registered the cheers and whistles drifting through the night air from the reception. There were too many questions running through his mind, the most pressing centering around Cassie returning to New York. He hated the possibility of her going back to work for her old boss. After everything she'd told him about her job, she deserved so much better.

And then there was the matter of their so-called relationship. Did she even want to pursue something with him? He hoped so, but he also knew how uncomfortable she was with not knowing her next step. Maybe he could help her find a job in California. Maybe ...

"Hey. What are you doing out here all by yourself?"

Brooklyn's voice startled him from his thoughts. He turned on the step enough to face both his sisters standing over him, the younger holding a dessert plate in her hand.

"I needed some air," he said.

Beej lifted her eyebrows. "Yeah, because the air out here is so much fresher than the air back there." She gestured toward the path leading back to the reception. Muted sounds, and a steady bass carried to them through the darkness.

"Don't ask." He turned back around. Leaning forward, he braced his forearms on his thighs.

Gingerly, Beej sat down next to him, arranging her dress with her free hand so it touched as little of the cement as possible. Brooklyn plopped down on his other side, unconcerned about the state of her attire. Not for the first time, it struck him how different the two of them were, and still, *they* had no trouble getting along. Maybe he needed to try harder with Beej.

"You missed the cake cutting," Brooklyn said, handing the plate to him. "We wanted to bring you some."

"And we thought you needed help dragging yourself out of your head," Beej added.

Hmm ... was that their only motive? Or were they fishing for information? Brooklyn didn't usually get involved in his relationship stuff, but with Beej instigating this intervention, he could totally see his youngest sister following along.

"Thanks for the cake." He held up the plate as though offering a toast to his pathetic life. To Beej, he asked, "Where's Tim?" They hadn't left each other's side all evening.

"He's back at the table. Dad cornered him to talk about golf." Brad heard the eye roll in her comment, and it brought a small smile to his face. Dad could get chatty with just about anyone, no matter the age or how long he'd known the person. "It got really annoying, so Brook and I decided to come cheer up our mopey brother."

"I'm not moping."

"Sure."

"Okay," Brooklyn said at the same time.

"Is this about Cassie?" Beej asked.

Man, she didn't ease into this conversation at all. He kept his mouth shut. She never needed his response to continue her train of thought.

"I told you that you'd fall for her in the end, didn't I?" she asked. "Your situation was too perfect to prevent it."

Brad grunted. He sensed both his sisters' gazes on him. The night sounds took center stage as silence trickled between them.

"You really do like her, don't you?" Brooklyn asked finally, her tone full of sympathy.

He angled his body enough to turn to her. "Yeah, I do." Fighting it was useless at this point. Puffing up his cheeks, he blew out a forceful breath.

Brooklyn leaned her head on his shoulder like she used to as a little girl when she needed the support of her big brother. "I like her too."

"Me too," Beej agreed. "I think she'd really fit into our family, especially with Brookie and me."

Brad gave her a sideways look. "Oh yeah, because I really need my girlfriend becoming besties with my little sisters. I'm already outnumbered in this family."

She huffed an exasperated breath. "I like her with you too. She has a good effect on you. It's been nice seeing you so happy the last few days."

"Aw, I didn't think you cared."

"I don't." She crossed her arms over her chest. But her tone couldn't hide her amusement. "When you're happy, you're less likely to pick on me."

Brad leaned toward her, bumping her with his shoulder hard

enough to knock her to the side. "Yeah right. You're always the insti-gator. I'm just the one who gets in trouble for everything because you scream louder."

She pushed him back. "That's so not true." She shrieked when Brad wrapped an arm around her shoulders in a hug disguised as a headlock.

"See?"

Fighting to get away, she hollered, "Watch the hair. It took a long time to tame these curls."

Brad tightened his arm around her neck. "Can't a big brother show his little sister some love?" He laughed when she jabbed him in the ribs, even though the force of it knocked some of the wind out of his sails.

"Is that what this is?" she asked through a grunt. "It feels more like torture."

A throat clearing from behind them put a halt to their wrestling. Cassie stood over them, tilting her head to the side with a smile. He let his arm drop from his sister's shoulders.

"Can I talk to Brad for a minute?"

Rising as gracefully as she could, Beej ran her hands down her thighs, smoothing out the wrinkles in her dress. "Come on, Brook. Let's leave these two love birds alone." Beej leaned toward Cassie and talked in a loud whisper. "Don't mind him, he's a little grumpy."

Cassie responded by shooting a flirty look in his direction. "I think I can handle him."

An answering grin spread across Brad's face.

Beej shrugged, glancing between them both before walking away. Brooklyn elbowed him in the arm twice and wiggled her eyebrows before getting up and following after her.

"I've been looking for you," Cassie said, lifting the long, flowy fabric of her gown to sit down next to him. "When I got back to the reception, you weren't there."

"How'd it go?" he asked, diving right into her conversation with Drew. He almost put an arm around her shoulders but held back.

Cassie clasped her hands together, sliding them between her knees. "Drew was boarding a plane back to New York. That's why I couldn't wait until after the reception. I wanted to get it over with, you know?"

Brad nodded. "And?"

"I told him thanks but no thanks." She turned to face Brad, her eyes finding his, her gaze imploring him to understand. "I'm not going back to work for Adriana. I put up with that for years, and you're right. I do deserve better."

"I'm proud of you." He meant that completely. "You're good at what you do. Something amazing has to turn up for you."

She gave him one of her gorgeous smiles. "Thank you for saying that."

"So, what's next then?"

"Well," she started, drawing out the word. "Gemma and I haven't lived close to each other since we left home for college. I thought it might be nice to change that. And I don't know how much longer Gram will be with us. I want to spend as much time with her as I can while she's still here."

Brad's heart pounded in his chest. "It sounds like you're planning to stick around for a while."

"I have to return to New York to pack up my apartment, but I'll be back soon. Even though I still don't have my job situation figured out, I know it's the right decision. I feel peace about it."

"Good." She deserved that.

She looked up at him through her lashes, the flirty expression adding more speed to his already racing pulse. "Besides, there's this guy I'm really into, and it kind of seems like he's into me too."

"Oh, he's totally into you." He leaned toward her, pressing his lips to her forehead. "I think I've been falling for you this whole week."

Slipping her hand into his, she slowly wove their fingers together. "You've been the best surprise I could've asked for after everything that's happened recently. I really want to see where this goes."

He continued to hold her gaze as he raised their clasped hands to his lips and kissed the side of her thumb. His mouth lingered on her skin as he murmured, "So do I."

Cassie leaned against his shoulder and his head came down to rest on top of hers. They sat in peaceful silence as the crickets sang their nighttime melody around them.

A contentment Brad had never experienced settled over him. She planned to stay in California, giving them time to explore their growing connection. He didn't know where it would take them, but for the first time in his love life, the possibilities excited him.

After basking in the sweet stillness of the moment, he broke the silence. "So, I guess you no longer think I'm a problem then, huh?" he asked, referring to the argument they had on the way back from Carlos' auto shop.

"You're going to be one if you refuse to share that cake with me."

A surprised laugh burst from Brad's gut. He glanced at the untouched plate on the cement next to him. He'd forgotten it was there. Lifting it onto his lap, he said, "Oh, this cake? Do you really want it?"

"I kind of do," she said sheepishly. "There was a huge crowd swarming the dessert table after the cake cutting. I wasn't able to grab one before I slipped out of the garden to find you."

"That's too bad because I'm afraid I can't give this to you." He cut off a sizable bite and shoved it into his mouth. The chocolate cake melted in his mouth. Hallie had done a good job on it.

Cassie's bottom lip turned down in an exaggerated pout that made him chuckle. "Why not?"

"Germs." Brad tried to put on his most serious expression, a feat made more difficult because of the incredulous look she gave him. He swallowed a snort.

"Since when are you paranoid about germs?" she asked with a

laugh, pressing her chest against his side. She grabbed for the fork that he held out of her reach.

"I'm very concerned about spreading disease."

"You are not." She shoved him to the side a little. "And sharing a slice of cake isn't going to make you sick, considering you've already kissed me twice."

He flashed a devilish grin at her. "Mmmm, and I'm about to do it again." He leaned toward her, but she turned her face, so he only got her cheek.

She stuck her pert nose in the air with feigned superiority. "Cake for kiss."

"Difficult woman," he murmured affectionately, cutting off another piece. He held the fork out to her.

She gave him a satisfied smile and went to take the bite, but he pulled the fork away before it reached her lips. He turned his back on her and ate the cake himself.

Cassie gasped, reaching her arms around his middle to pinch his stomach. "You're horrible, Brad Lucas."

A gargled, close-mouthed laugh bubbled out of him, and he wriggled from side to side, trying to evade her hands.

"Sorry, that one had my name written all over it," he said after he'd swallowed. He sawed off another bite. "Here."

Narrowing her eyes at him, she grabbed his wrist with both hands and guided the fork into her mouth.

There was a beat of silence as she swallowed, then he angled his body toward her, leaning closer. "Now, about that kiss ..."

Cassie closed the rest of the distance, placing her hand on his cheek. Their lips met in a kiss full of possibility and hope, and none of the uncertainty of the ones they'd shared before. This week had been nothing short of surprising, and he couldn't help but wonder what surprises lay in store for them ahead. But no matter what happened, she'd definitely keep him on his toes.

And he couldn't wait.

Epilogue

Fourteen Months Later

Cassie was absolutely, one hundred percent certain the day couldn't get any better.

Juggling the five various-sized shopping bags she held to one hand, she let herself into her cute apartment in downtown LA. It had been some time since she'd allowed herself to indulge in a frivolous shopping trip, but today was a special occasion.

Sylvie lounged on the couch in the living room, her design book in her hand. "Hey there, birthday girl," she said as Cassie set the bags down on the floor by the door, flexing and unflexing her fists to restore circulation to her fingers. "How was lunch?"

Earlier that day, Gram had treated her granddaughters to lunch to celebrate them turning twenty-seven. Over Indian food at Curry & Spice, Gram and Gemma had tried to convince Cassie to embrace the quieter lifestyle by moving to Buena Hills. It hadn't been the first time since she'd moved to California a year ago. In fact, it was becoming more common each time they all got together a couple times a week. Again, she'd refused. She wasn't ready to give up the big city vibe after experiencing the electric atmosphere of the Big Apple for so long.

Maybe someday, but not yet.

"Amazing," Cassie said, answering Sylvie's question. "I'm pretty sure I had the best tikka masala I've ever tasted in my life."

Sylvie added a few strokes to her book before looking up again. "Even better than that one place we used to go to in New York?"

"That place was good, but this one..." Cassie brought her hand up to her mouth and mimicked a chef's kiss. "The next time I visit Gram, you should come. You seriously need to try it."

She joined her bestie on the couch, pulling her legs up underneath her. The beautiful bouquet of pink and white azaleas decorating the coffee table caught her eye, and she smiled. They were a pleasant surprise to wake up to this morning. She suspected Sylvie had something to do with how Brad had managed to sneak them into the apartment without her noticing. The two of them had been in cahoots about something for weeks. And when the best friend conspired with the boyfriend, something big had to be in the works.

Behind the couch, the old black-and-white photos of Hollywood actresses that Cassie had given Sylvie over a year ago hung on the cream-colored walls. The apartment they shared wasn't large—the front area consisted of only a living room and connected kitchen—but it rivaled her little studio apartment in New York in cuteness. Except for the view. But hey, nothing beat waking up to Central Park out her window every morning.

"What are you working on?" Cassie asked, nodding at the sketch in her roommate's lap.

"Something for the shop." Sylvie made one more stroke on the paper, then held out the book. "What do you think of this?"

Taking it in her lap, Cassie studied the drawing of a sleeveless blouse that wrapped around the middle and tied at the side with a ribbon. "I love it! This would go great with the skirt we added last week."

After waffling over the idea for several months, she'd finally decided to open her own online clothing boutique last September. And there was no other person she'd wanted to go into business with than her best friend.

Luckily, Sylvie had accepted her proposal without hesitation. It helped that she'd already grown so desperate for a change that she gladly quit her job as Adriana's thankless errand runner. She was also just crazy enough to pack up everything and move across the country not knowing whether the shop would be a success.

Thank goodness it *was* a success. Sure, it had taken a few months for the first sales to start trickling in. Cassie had to get a side job as a personal stylist at a high-end department store to pay the bills at first. But with hard work and a lot of hustling, the shop caught on, and she'd quit her extra employment after only six months of working there. And now, they were getting ready to launch their own personal styling option, an idea that Brad had suggested.

"Don't you have to get ready for your date?" Sylvie asked taking back her design book.

Cassie felt around for her phone before remembering she'd left her purse by the door. Leaning forward, she squinted at the clock on the oven in the kitchen. "Shoot, I don't have a lot of time, and I need a shower before Brad gets here." The mid-September day had been warm, and she needed the opportunity to freshen up.

She rose from the couch, grabbing the shopping bags and her purse by the door before heading to her room, the closest of the two to the living room. Upon entering, her eyes immediately fell to her neatly made bed.

An elegant halter top dress in sapphire blue satin lay across the duvet. That hadn't been there this morning. Setting her bags on top of her vanity, she approached the garment.

"Sylvie?" she called through the open bedroom door as she ran her fingers along the material. It was smooth against her skin, and she could only imagine how good it would feel to wear it.

"Yes?" Sylvie asked in response, an unmistakable eagerness in her tone.

Cassie picked up the dress carefully, holding it in front of her as she walked back into the living room. "What's this?"

"Do you love it?"

Holding the dress out to the side, she gave it a once over. "Well, yeah, it's gorgeous. But what is it doing on my bed?"

"It's for tonight," Sylvie said with a simple shrug of her shoulders. "Happy birthday."

"You made it for me?" Cassie squealed. Rushing over, she wrapped one arm around her friend from behind, careful not to wrinkle the fabric. "Thank you, thank you, thank you! How did you even manage to keep it a surprise?"

"Now you know why I gave up my social life for weeks," Sylvie responded with a smirk. "The only time I could work on it was when you were out with Brad. I thought for sure you'd figure it out, especially that time you two changed your plans and came home early to watch a movie."

"You're the best, Sylv," Cassie said, giving her friend one last hug and walking back to her room to lay the dress on her bed while she showered.

"And don't you forget it," Sylvie called back to her.

A little more than an hour later, Cassie stood in front of the mirror, admiring the perfect fit of the dress. It hung in all the right places, and paired with her favorite diamond earrings, she loved the elegant way she looked. Brad had kept a tight lip about his plans for her birthday, but he'd texted her a few hours earlier, instructing her to dress in a way that made her feel the most beautiful. This dress definitely fit the bill.

A knock came at the front door.

"Can you get that?" she called, crossing to her vanity and picking up her perfume. "Tell him I'll be right there."

"I'm on it," came Sylvie's voice from the front room.

Cassie heard Sylvie moving toward the door, and a second later it opened. Flutters danced around in her stomach as she tossed her phone, some lip gloss, breath mints, and a few other things into a small clutch. After checking herself once more in the mirror on the vanity, she left her room.

Her best friend and boyfriend were in the middle of a whispered conversation when she entered the front room. They stopped as soon as they saw her standing in the doorway. Yep, they were scheming about something.

Brad's face lit up the moment he saw her, spreading warmth through Cassie's whole body. "Wow." He opened his arms for a hug as Sylvie backed away to give them space. "I have no words."

"That would be a first." Cassie stepped into his embrace before placing a quick kiss on his lips. "You're never speechless. And look, we're twinsies." She stroked the silk tie underneath his gray suit coat. It was the same shade as her dress.

"Uh oh, you know you've become an old married couple when you start to dress alike," Sylvie said from the kitchen.

A married couple? Not yet, but Cassie liked the sound of it.

Laughing, she and Brad said goodbye to her and left the apartment, heading for the covered parking spaces behind the building.

"How was the game today?" Cassie asked, slipping her hand into his as they walked. He'd been unable to celebrate with her earlier in the day because of the USC soccer game he'd had to commentate.

He shrugged. "It was cool. I would've rather spent the day with you though."

"Aww, you're sweet." She stretched onto her toes to plant a light kiss onto his stubbled jaw. He tilted his cheek down toward her to make it easier. "But I understand. There's always next year. Besides, you wouldn't have wanted to come shopping with me anyway. Dragging one reluctant human around the mall is bad enough. And I'd think it would stir up bad feelings for you after what happened last time we were there."

"Thank you for saving me from reliving my worst memory. I take it Gemma wasn't a willing participant in your little excursion?"

They arrived at his Pathfinder, and he held the door open for her as she hitched up the ankle length skirt enough to climb into the seat. She waited for him to jog over to the driver's side and get in before answering his question. "She wasn't too bad. She said her gift to me was a shopping trip with no complaining. We picked out these adorable onesies that'll work for both a boy and a girl, depending on what they're having." She clapped her hands together quickly in her excitement.

Tyler and Gemma had broken the news to them about the baby last month, and now Cassie was tempted to buy all the cute newborn things. She'd already indulged in several purchases for her new niece or nephew, even though Gemma had insisted multiple times that she save her money. Little did her sister know, their little one would be the best dressed kid in all of Southern California.

"Have you ever thought about designing clothes for babies?" Brad asked, a wide smile forming on his face at her enthusiasm. "You could add a section to your shop so the moms you sell to can dress like their kids."

Cassie gasped. "I love that idea! Wait until I tell Sylvie." She forced out a small squeak of excitement that made him chuckle.

"I'm just full of good ideas," he said, not exaggerating in the slightest. He'd been one hundred percent invested in her shop since its opening, providing honest feedback on her ideas and even suggesting some of his own. "Are you going to be one of those moms who force your kids to dress the same and schedule family pictures every other month?"

"Every other month? What about the ones in between?"

He rolled his eyes.

"Kids change so fast," she said in her defense. "I want to capture them at every stage. And they're so cute when they're matching."

"Lucky for them, I'll be there to tone down your enthusiasm."

Cassie attempted a glare, but his cheeky grin was too cute for her to be offended at his comment. And the way he talked about a family and kids, as if it was obvious they'd be raising them together sent goosebumps sliding up her arm. Conversations about their future had become more commonplace over the last several months, and each time she marveled at how right it felt to think about spending forever with him.

"Where are we going for dinner?" she asked, reaching across the gear shift to gently squeeze his thigh.

Brad dropped a hand over hers, then brought it to his lips before glancing briefly at her. "That's a surprise. We have to make a stop anyway."

"Will you give me a hint about what that stop is?" She batted her lashes as she met his eye again.

One corner of his mouth twitched upward, and he turned his attention back to the road. "Oooh no. Uh-uh. Don't look at me like that. Your seduction might have worked on me before, but this is one secret you're not going to crack until it's time."

Cassie sat back against her seat. "You can't blame a girl for trying."

Her curiosity grew as they continued driving, heading west out of the heart of the city, but she didn't ask any more questions about where they were going. They filled the time with a variety of topics, including the upcoming Fashion Week she'd bought tickets for earlier that week.

"I can't believe you're willing to go with me," she said, admiring his strong profile as he kept his eyes on the road. "I didn't think you'd want to."

He lifted both shoulders then let them drop. "I figure after all the football games I've forced on you in the last year, it's the least I could do."

"I don't mind them," she said, a flirtatious undertone in her voice. "Football games make good snuggle times."

Brad shot another quick look in her direction and winked. "Amen to that."

When they finally reached their destination, he parallel parked the car along the side of the road and shut off the engine. Outside Cassie's window, the secluded beach and its surrounding bluffs stirred up memories she'd recalled many times in the last year. The sun had already begun its descent toward the horizon, its rays reaching out across the dancing waves like confetti.

"Wait a minute."

Brad was looking at her expectantly when she turned to him. "Do you recognize this place?"

"This is where we had the bonfire." She was sure of it, though she hadn't been back since the night she'd begged Brad to act as her boyfriend. There were closer beaches to drive to from their neighborhood.

He leaned over and kissed her cheek. "The exact place," he murmured, sending shivers up her spine.

Cassie waited as Brad got out of the car then swung around to the passenger side to open her door. She slipped her hand through the crook of his elbow, and they made their way down the steps.

Once they reached the sand, she kicked off her heels, dangling them from her fingertips as they meandered toward the water. There were a few people milling about the beach or lounging in the sand, basking in the golden glow of the evening sun, but the bluffs offered some secrecy that other beaches didn't get.

Cassie snuggled underneath Brad's arm, soaking in the additional warmth he provided. The air had cooled off significantly out here next to the water, and she appreciated the way he somehow knew she'd need his body heat. Her dress was too gorgeous to cover up with a sweater.

"Why did you bring me here?" she asked as they walked along the water line, far enough from the waves that they wouldn't get wet. "Are you hoping to live out your dream of running into the ocean fully clothed?"

"What?" he asked, his voice laced with humor. A mixture of playfulness and exasperation crossed his handsome features. "Sylvie would murder me if I let you ruin that dress. Besides, it would be a shame if you could never wear it again. You look incredible."

Heat touched Cassie's cheeks as he bent to capture her lips in his. When he started to move back again, she wrapped her arms around his neck, pulling him down to her level. For several moments, she forgot her curiosity over why they were here as she lost herself in his affections. Being here with him, she couldn't imagine this moment getting any better than this.

Finally, Brad pulled back enough to speak, though maybe an inch separated his tempting mouth from hers. "I brought you here," he murmured, then planted one last lingering kiss on her lips before continuing, "because this is the place where it all began. If it weren't for that night, we wouldn't be together right now."

"That would've been a shame."

He kissed her forehead. Shrugging one shoulder, he stepped back a little, finding her hand in his then shifting his body to face the water. "It's not Mexico, but it's a pretty nice beach. And the sun *is* going down."

"All of this is true," Cassie said through a little laugh. Where was he going with this?

"You've got the dress ..."

Wait ... The beach. At sunset. Stunning dress.

Her mind recalled a conversation they'd had a few months ago during another beach walk similar to this. That night, she'd blushed her way through telling him about her younger self's idea of the perfect proposal. He'd remembered that silly fantasy?

Of course he did. Or maybe he'd had another motive for getting it out of her than mere curiosity. Because he was literally checking every box of that dream now. Had he been planning this night even back then?

Don't get ahead of yourself, Cassie reminded herself. *He hasn't asked you yet.*

Cassie was bursting with anticipation as she turned toward the final component of that dreamed scenario: the perfect guy.

A mischievous smile slid onto Brad's face as he pulled a little black box out of his suit pants. Time slowed to a crawl as he dropped to one knee and opened the box to reveal a gorgeous sapphire ring, the circular blue gem surrounded by little diamonds.

Her shaking hands rose to cover her face as moisture welled in her eyes.

"Cassandra June Schalk," he began, but his voice sounded so far away over the roaring in her ears. "Life with you has been ... an adventure. You drive me crazy in the very best ways. You keep me on my toes, and you're not afraid to call me out when I need it."

Cassie made a sound that was half laughter, half sobbing.

"But most of all, you've loved me in ways I never knew I could be loved. You've stood by my side and supported me through all of my issues. And you've taught me what it looks like to love with every-thing you have. You are the queen of my heart, and I can't imagine doing life without you. I want to spend forever cherishing you the way you deserve to be cherished. Will you marry me?"

Lowering herself into a crouch—the move made difficult in her dress—she threw her arms around him, burying her face into his neck as the tears flowed down her cheeks. She held on tight, using him to anchor her in the moment as the overwhelming emotion came crashing around her like the waves rolling onto the sand. This man, this imperfectly perfect man had come to her when she'd least expected it but when she'd needed him most. And in this instant, she became the luckiest woman in the world to get to spend forever building a life with him.

The ruse she'd dragged him into hadn't gone the way it was supposed to. But sometimes, failed plans had a funny way of working out so much better than she could've planned herself.

Thank goodness for that.

"Is that a yes?" he mumbled into her hair.

Cassie laughed and pressed her forehead against his. Cradling his face with both her hands, she said, "Yes. My answer is an absolute yes."

I hope you enjoyed Brad and Cassie's story! If you'd like to get a peek into their happily ever after, sign up for my newsletter to receive a free bonus epilogue.

https://BookHip.com/QQGMXZG

Have you read Tyler and Gemma's story already? It's a good one! Turn the page for a chapter one preview of Discovering Her Heart.

Discovering HER Heart

A BUENA HILLS ROMANCE

April

Nothing on earth could make a guy feel dumber than spending a Friday evening attempting to comprehend the inner workings of a calculus textbook. And Tyler Abernathy wasn't a dummy, no matter how much his grades sometimes said otherwise. Math just wasn't his subject. It never had been. If he didn't need the credits to fulfill his general education requirement in quantitative reasoning, he would've skipped retaking it altogether after failing his first semester.

He sat at the kitchen island in the home he shared with his cousin, Brad, grateful again that his journalism major didn't require any more math. His textbook lay open on the counter, though his attention was diverted to the Dodgers game streaming on the laptop right behind it. The Miami Marlins, his favorite team, were in town for a three-game series. What he'd give to be sitting in the stands rather than studying for his test next week.

But he'd already put off the torture by going to the game last night, promising he'd stay on task today. That promise was proving difficult to keep.

He glanced at his notes from his latest tutoring session sprawled out around the textbook like an explosion of leaflet paper. More like white flags of surrender. He picked up the nearest one and squinted at his tutor's chicken scratch, trying to decipher what it said. Giving up, he set it down and picked up another. This one was in his own writing, which wasn't much neater, but simpler to read. Too bad it wasn't any easier to understand.

Buzzing his lips, he scanned the kitchen, rubbing his temple with two fingers, trying to alleviate the oncoming stress headache. His eyes landed on the microwave. There was a large burn mark on the inside from the time Brad had tried to heat up a can of baked beans a few months after they'd moved in. He'd almost burned the house down with that mistake, making his dad question the wisdom of allowing his barely nineteen-year-old son and nephew to live in the house he'd inherited after his parents' deaths.

The five-bedroom bungalow had belonged in Brad's family for generations, since the founding of Buena Hills—a Los Angeles suburb not too far from USC's University Park campus. It had been a good home for the last four years. But with graduation looming in a little over a month, Tyler and Brad were heading off in different directions—a sports broadcasting internship in San Francisco for Brad and grad school at Berkeley for Tyler. Assuming he passed calculus.

He glared at his notes. *I better pass.*

And once his sisters and cousin moved in, things would look pretty different around the house. Uncle Brent was most likely happy about that.

"Pizza's here," Brad announced, barging through the swinging kitchen door. "I found these street rats outside. They looked hungry, so I invited them in for some food." He gestured to the four women filing in behind him.

Brad's sister, Bridget, known as Beej to everyone in the family except Grandma Abernathy, shoved her older brother as she passed him.

"Shut up, Brad. You're not as funny as you think you are. Besides, I paid for the pizzas. You all owe me seven bucks by the way." She wagged a finger at everyone else. Mumbles of agreement echoed through the room.

Tyler's sister, Elise, peered over his shoulder at the mess of notes on the counter. "Whatcha studying, big brother?"

He slid a piece of paper out of the way so she could see the book underneath. "I'll give you twenty bucks to disguise yourself as me and take my calculus test next week. You'd probably do better than me. Didn't you get an A when you took it in high school?"

"Heck no. I barely managed a B-minus. That dumb class killed my GPA." She scrunched her nose as she sat down next to him. "You could beg Hallie. She *did* get an A."

His sisters had always been much better students than he was. Somehow, the intelligence gene seemed to skip over him. He liked to think he was smart; he just hated school. Correction: he hated math. The rest of his classes weren't so bad.

He turned exaggerated puppy dog eyes on his youngest sister, who dropped onto the stool on his other side. Hallie laughed.

"You know you'd be able to internalize more of what you're learning if you turned off all the other distractions." She pointed to the laptop where the game was on commercial break.

Tyler rolled his eyes. His sister ... always the practical one. "I'm trying to minimize the agony."

"Well, someone's being dramatic." Beej's mouth curved up in amusement as she joined them at the island.

Before he could respond, Brad thumped the two pizzas down in front of them all, scattering the papers. He flipped open the top box and steam rose from the mountain of mozzarella, pepperoni, and olives. "Eat up while they're hot."

"Did you get Hawaiian?" Hallie asked.

Brad turned up his nose. "It's underneath. How you can eat that monstrosity is beyond me though. Pineapple on pizza is a crime to humanity."

"Says the guy who puts so much hot sauce on everything it overpowers whatever you're eating," Tyler said, gathering up the last of the papers and placing them in the center of the island. "I'm surprised you have any taste buds left."

Brad was too busy digging through the fridge for the hot sauce to respond, so Tyler turned his attention to the fourth woman in the room. Kendall was searching through the cabinets to the right of the stove, all three of them open.

"Plates are one door over," he said to her before pulling out a slice of Hawaiian from the box. A long string of cheese hung onto the rest of the pizza. Just the way he liked it. There could never be too much cheese.

She paused her search and faced the room. "How much time do I spend in this house? I know where the plates are."

"Than what are you doing?" With his pizza still in his hand, he walked over to her. Reaching into one of the open cabinets, he pulled out several plates and handed one to her.

Kendall accepted it with a shrug. "I'm getting a feel for the place. Trying to figure out what kind of kitchen supplies we'll have to work with once we move in."

"Hey, don't get ahead of yourself," Brad mumbled through a mouth full of pizza. He swallowed hard. "This place is still ours until July."

"It's never too soon to start planning. Three months will go by like that." She snapped her fingers.

"Speaking of the house," Beej said, filling a glass of water from the tap. "You two are the only ones living here since what's his name moved out."

What's his name's actual name was Christian. He hadn't lived in the house for over two years, longer than any of the girls had been living in Buena Hills, so it was weird that she was bringing him up now. He'd been one of Tyler's best friends since freshman year, so Brad had invited him to live with them when the'd moved into the house. They didn't see much of him anymore though. What was it about getting married that made a guy drop off the face of the planet?

Brad shot a suspicious look at his sister. "What're you getting at?"

"Well…" Beej drew out the word longer than necessary. A sure sign she was up to something. She gestured to the other women. "We were talking the other day about those three extra bedrooms."

"What about them?" His eyes narrowed even more.

"What do you think about us moving in early?" she asked. "There are four of us, but any of us would be willing to share rooms."

"Absolutely not." Brad shook his head so hard that Tyler worried he'd give himself whiplash.

"Why not?" Hallie asked. "It could be one big family party. There's a reason we all go to this school, right?" Their family had a long-standing tradition of being proud Trojans, starting with Tyler's grandparents. "Well, I mean, I don't go here yet, but I will soon."

As an aspiring baker, she'd opted to take a year of culinary classes before starting her business degree at USC.

"Just because it's tradition, doesn't mean we all have to live in the same house." Brad's mouth twitched. "Besides, I'd hate for word to spread that I'm living with my little sister."

Beej stuck her tongue out at him. "You just don't want us to get in the way of your bachelor pad."

"It's not like you can throw parties here anyway," Kendall said, continuing the conversation. She joined them at the island, seemingly satisfied with her snooping. "You'd have the cops called on you in no time. The neighbors are already suspicious of two college-aged guys living in the neighborhood. Having us responsible family members here keeping you in line should help."

Kendall wasn't actually related to any of them, but she'd come to live with Tyler's family right before his senior year of high school, so she may as well be another one of his sisters. Though it had taken much of that year for her to finally acknowledge his existence. He didn't know what had spurred her trust issues with men. Elise knew, and he suspected his parents and Hallie did also, though none of them had ever elaborated on Kendall's past. And though he was curious, he valued his life too much to ask about it.

"Ty, would you help me out here?"

Brad's desperation brought Tyler back to the conversation. What were they talking about? Oh yeah, the house. "Actually, it might be nice to have more people splitting the utilities."

Brad threw his hands into the air. "Really, bruh? You're supposed to be on my side."

Truthfully, Tyler wasn't thrilled with the idea of sharing the house with the girls either. Not that he had any objection to them per se. His sisters were some of his favorite people in the world. But it was kind of nice not having to fight for time in the bathroom in the morning like he used to when he lived at home.

However, he did see the benefit to their plan. And it would only be for a few months. It might even allow him to cut down on his hours working at the university bookstore. That would free up more time for calculus. He glanced at his textbook and shuddered.

On second thought...

"Anyway, we can talk about this later," Elise said with a wave of her hand, probably realizing, like Tyler, the pointless nature of the conversation. Having Brad and Beej living under the same roof wasn't the best idea. Their vastly different personalities made it difficult to get along, even if they did love each other. "Guess who I ran into on campus today?"

Tyler paused, the slice of pizza halfway to his mouth. "Who?"

"Does Gemma Schalk ring a bell?"

"No way!" he shouted, much louder than he'd intended.

Hallie jumped a little, her slice of pizza dropping from her hand.

After sending an apologetic smile her way, he turned to Elise. "What's she doing in SoCal? She always insisted she'd go to college in Oregon."

Elise tore off a paper towel from the roll in the center of the island and wiped her hands. "She did, but she graduated last spring. She's starting her master's program down here in the fall and came early to help her grandma for the summer. Apparently, her grandpa died right before Christmas."

Tyler's stomach dropped. "He did? Poor Gem."

"Who's Gemma Schalk?" Beej asked, plucking an olive from Brad's pizza and popping it in her mouth.

Tyler helped himself to another slice of Hawaiian as he

explained. "She was my best friend when we lived in Santiago. Her mom taught at the same university as our dad." He'd thought about her a lot in the years since his family had moved away.

"Best friend, huh?" Brad nudged him with his elbow. "Or sweetheart?"

Tyler shook his head, a small laugh bubbling in his throat. "Nah, it wasn't like that. She was just one of the guys."

"She must not be hot, then." Brad winced when Kendall came up behind him and smacked the back of his scalp. "Oww! What was that for?"

"Why is it always about looks for you, Brad?" She reached over his shoulder and grabbed a slice of pepperoni from the box. Before taking a bite, she added, "It's no wonder you can't keep a girlfriend."

Brad slumped on his stool with a huff. "I'm doing perfectly fine in the lady department, thank you very much."

Tyler shared a doubtful look with his sisters. He couldn't even remember the last time Brad had been in a semi-serious relationship with anyone, let alone a serious one. Most of the women he'd dated didn't stick around for more than a few dates.

"Well, is she?" Brad asked, returning to his original statement.

Tyler didn't know how to answer that. The last time he'd seen Gemma, they were both awkward teenagers, covered in acne and braces and still growing into their bodies. He'd never really thought of her as pretty or not. She was just Gemma. His best friend. "I guess she was pretty."

"I invited her to go to the movie with us tonight," Elise said. "I hope that's okay."

"Are you kidding me?" He'd never heard a more pointless question than that. "Of course it's okay. I'd love to see her again. It's been way too long."

Seven years too long. She hadn't even come outside to say goodbye the morning his family left Santiago for good. And she wouldn't accept his calls in the weeks after either. Why was that? It couldn't have been because of what happened the night before.

Or could it?

Nah. He shook the thought away. There had to be something else that had caused her to ignore him.

"Great," Elise said. "I told her to meet us here at seven, so she should be here soon." Right on cue, a quiet knock came from the front door. She started to get up. "That's probably her."

Tyler stopped her with a hand on her arm. "I'll get it." He tried to keep the anticipation off his face so no one would catch how eager he was to see his childhood best friend.

But he *was* eager. Excited even. Speaking of her again had reminded him of how much he'd missed her.

He reached the entryway and all but threw the front door open. Then he froze. Standing in front of him was not the sixteen-year-old girl he'd left behind in Chile. Gone were the braces and frizzy pony-tail. Gone were the basketball shorts and baseball glove.

The woman in front of him was all feminine curves and loose, dark curls. Her smile, though uncertain, was no less familiar than he remembered. The light freckles still dotting her face gave her a more youthful look than her twenty-three years.

But even her freckles couldn't disguise what was staring him right in the face: Gemma Schalk was all grown up.

Thank you for reading this sneak peek of Discovering Her Heart. The full novel is available in ebook, Kindle Unlimited, and paperback.

Buena Hills Series

Discovering Her Heart

Book 1

Chasing Her Heart

Book 2

Champion of Her Heart

Book 3

Surrendering His Heart

Book 4

Risking His Heart

Standalone Bonus Book

Stay up-to-date on all my new releases by following me on Amazon.

Acknowledgments

Thank you for reading Brad and Cassie's story! I know your time is valuable, especially your reading time, so it means the world to me that you'd spend it with my book.

So much has gone into bringing this story into the world. I lovingly refer to it as the book that wasn't supposed to be written. The idea took me by surprise and grabbed a hold of my brain, and refused to let go until I wrote it—and I'm so glad I did.

I have to recognize the amazing authors of my critique group—Sarah, Danyelle, and Judy—who have read through multiple drafts of this book to help me get it just right. I admire these women so much, and I feel incredibly blessed to have them in my corner.

My saint of an editor, Raneé, has been with me from the very beginning. She went above and beyond, helping me enhance the ideas I already had while also offering new ones to make this story really shine.

To my proofreader, Roxana, thank you for catching all the pesky little mistakes that slipped through the cracks during multiple rounds of editing and critiques.

And last, but never least, my family is my absolute rock in everything I do. In some ways, this book has been the hardest I've written so far, simply because of all the heavy stuff going on in my life right now. Writing a book is challenging enough when everything is perfect, but finding time to write during the summer while my husband is deployed added an extra layer of difficulties. Thank you to my children, who have been so patient when I was up against a deadline and needed to work. And thank you to my husband, who has always been my biggest cheerleader no matter where in the world he is. I love you all!

About the Author

Allison Gygi wrote her first official story in third grade from an old word processor in the computer lab of her elementary school. Since then she has crafted countless tales both on paper and in her head. As a mom, her days are spent trying to find a few minutes to write in between the never ending dishes, meal prep, and helping kids with homework. She loves fairy tales and gravitates towards books with happy endings and swoony kisses. Allison enjoys reading, hiking, and traveling the world. She lives with her husband and three children in a cute suburb of Chicago.

Learn more at https://allisongygi.com

instagram.com/authorallisongygi

amazon.com/stores/author/B0B27C16JN

bookbub.com/authors/allison-gygi